PRAISE FOR **FUTURE FEELING**

"Smartly set in a strange, yet familiar American offscape, Lake weaves a tantric tale that measures the timelessness of trans identities not in well-intentioned DSM diagnoses, civil rights movements, or social media pedantries, but by cherishing the fissures in the rock wall of intersectionality. For as *Future Feeling* proves, it's in these misalignments, misunderstandings, and inappropriate joking where we have space to be ourselves."   —Paul Beatty, author of *The Sellout*

"Who is this Joss Lake who seems to have peered into my mind? I loved this weird, fun book, and now I want to bite Joss Lake's hypnotic style or maybe live in this book for a time. Or maybe we already do? If you want to feel better or worse about the time you spend on the internet, take my advice and buy this very book and then go post about it on Instagram. Joss Lake's *Future Feeling* is turning everything upside down. I think I might still be buzzed from reading it."
                    —Andrea Lawlor, author of
                    Paul Takes the Form of a Mortal Girl

"The uneasy future conjured by Joss Lake is really a naked readout on our crumbling present moment. Like every ambitious literary visionary, Lake uses his delirious imagination and potent narrative gifts to sharpen the mirror on how we live and feel now."   —Ben Marcus, author of
                    The Flame Alphabet and *Notes from the Fog*

"*Future Feeling* marks a delightful contribution to the ultra contemporary sci-fi canon. Like (and unlike) the best of cyberpunk, Lake transforms the alienation and flatness of technoculture into a fully dimensional and absorbing alternate reality complete with sprawling queer resistance movements, t4t flirting/obsessions, and sexy magic plant life. And like the best humor writing, *Future Feeling* is ridiculously fun and smart, and accomplishes that rare and difficult goal: the conversion of anxiety into laughter. I loved this book. It is about the internet, but it is more fun than the internet!"

—Jordy Rosenberg, author of *Confessions of the Fox*

"I devoured this funny, charming book of trans friendships and sly cultural commentary; a story about what truly matters for those of us lost in the maelstrom of identity and media. Here's how unable I was to put it down: I accidentally dropped it in the toilet, fished it out, and kept right on reading."   —Torrey Peters, author of *Detransition, Baby*

"A wildly imaginative, subversively futuristic romp through the depths of the trans psyche, *Future Feeling*'s rendering of the forces that converge upon queer lives not only provokes while it entertains, but ultimately leaves us so much more hopeful for the world to come."

—Meredith Talusan, author of *Fairest: A Memoir*

"In this brilliant and breathtakingly inventive debut, Lake captures the nuances, pain, and absurdity of obsession and idolization as we follow this refreshingly original narrator navigating the all-too-relatable process of feeling comfortable in one's own skin and becoming a self. I couldn't put this book down."

—Zaina Arafat, author of *You Exist Too Much*

"Weird and wondrous, Lake's eye-popping debut recalls the transgressive gender- and genre-bending of Jeanette Winterson and Samuel R. Delany but fashions something entirely original." Michelle Hart, *O, The Oprah Magazine*

"*Future Feeling* will fit on your shelf right next to *Paul Takes the Form of a Mortal Girl* . . . Lake has constructed a wonderful world where trans identity is celebrated and centered, where trans characters are allowed to be messy and complicated and human. It's, quite honestly, the kind of book I've been waiting for for a really long time. I'm so glad it's finally here." Christina Orlando, *Tor*

FUTURE FEELING

A Novel

JOSS LAKE

SOFT SKULL

NEW YORK

This is a work of fiction. All of the characters, organizations, and events portrayed in this novel are either products of the author's imagination or are used fictitiously.

First Soft Skull edition: 2021
ISBN: 978-1-59376-688-7

Library of Congress Cataloging-in-Publication Data
Names: Lake, Joss, author.
Title: Future feeling : a novel / Joss Lake.
Description: First Soft Skull edition. | New York :
Soft Skull, 2021.
Identifiers: LCCN 2020043040 | ISBN 9781593766887
(trade paperback) | ISBN 9781593766894 (ebook)
Subjects: LCSH: Transgender people—Fiction. |
Social media—Fiction. | Blessing and cursing—Fiction.
Classification: LCC PS3612.A5195 F88 2021 |
DDC 813/.6—dc23
LC record available at https://lccn.loc.gov/2020043040

Cover design & Soft Skull art direction by
www.houseofthought.io
Book design by Wah-Ming Chang

Published by Soft Skull Press
1140 Broadway, Suite 704
New York, NY 10001
www.softskull.com

Printed in the United States of America
1 3 5 7 9 10 8 6 4 2

A.B.L.

FUTURE
FEELING

The summons arrived the day after the wedding. Through honeyed dreams, I heard the knock.

Pulling on a stiff cotton robe, I shuffled to the door, stepped into the dark hallway.

There it was on the navy carpet, the magenta wax seal on a normative manila envelope.

I picked it up and pressed it to my muscular chest.

It was a literal miracle that I had gotten this far, that I, once-lowly Pen—always prying into other peoples' lives, loosening the line around myself and diving headlong into others' dramas, tastes, phrasings, ways of wearing a dick—was now being called to the Rhiz-Port for the next level of initiation.

I snuck back into the stuffy room with the summons and threw myself down on a sofa to prepare myself to open the envelope. My love rolled over in bed.

I wanted the Rhiz to know how I felt. *Read me with your Bio-meter! See the golden power that lights me up!* I wanted to shout, but the messenger was gone, and my love still slept.

1

In order to explain how I was called to the Rhiz-Port the day after the wedding of Aiden Chase and Rachel Remedios, we have to start back in my less-enlightened days on the other, more miserable coast.

A few years ago, I became a man in the city while working as a dog walker, creeping into other peoples' houses to retrieve their pets, obsessing over their interiors, their quilts, and their adv-tech aromatherapy spritzers. I'd been a hopeful child—even after my parents were killed—but as I transitioned, injecting myself with shaky hands every week, I crossed into the Shadowlands, where inconvenient oozes get dumped and scorpions scuttle.

In the mornings I'd wake up in my shitty apartment, open my phone, and go to the Gram, where Aiden, also a trans guy, spent his days lounging in pools of California sunlight, drinking maple water beneath a palm tree, wearing not-yet-released SpaceShoes, musing about how to be your "true self." I admit, if I hadn't been incredibly insecure back then, none of this would have mattered to me. If I'd possessed a solid sense of self, he could have molded each pube-like hair of his beard into a style that was milder than full-on gay bear and more kempt than the average cis, and it would not have destroyed my entire day.

I would have accepted my own patchy mess of facial hair—and dark urges—with a wry and full heart.

Alas.

I didn't know it at first, but I needed to track down Aiden's shadow as much as I needed to generate my own light.

Every damn weekday, Aiden unveiled a new portrait and the world (his 99,000 followers) watched his creepy mustache change from fuzz to a blond block, his biceps grow into pastel muscle tees, his lips receive anointments of juice and juniper water, his facial structure harden out of abject female fleshiness, and his limbs extend on all manner of mid-century modern furniture inside his minimalist, plant-filled enclave, and each morning, I thought about killing him in a metaphorical way, the trans-father whose shadow I wanted to step out of, even tho dude was younger than I was.

His first post. Picture it.

Him, reading, shirtless, on a wicker sofa out on his patio, framed by hanging candle sconces. He stared languidly at the camera, as if the mirror had always been his bruh. He held a book tilted toward himself at stomach level so you couldn't see the cover, only his directive, BE TRUE, tattooed above the fading surgery scars. Out in the darkness beyond, his partner was surely waiting to be fucked, if only Aiden would stop fucking himself over and over again with his phone.

It would be a minute.

The only caption was a repetition of his tattoo, BE TRUE, and when I saw it, I thought, *Ugh, here's this beautiful trans guy in his lush backyard and I can't even video-beam with my former guardian without wanting to apologize for transitioning and bringing drama into what could be her staid retirement!*

Doubtless you are wondering, *What kind of fool would take a Gram seriously, anyway?*

Yes, that is where Aiden and I both erred. In our defense, Grams are one of the few places to see trans folks; blame it on the peculiar manifestations of late capitalism—*Saintly Secretions of Non-Solace!*—but only newer media contain any evidence at all that trans people are doing more than being murdered and getting kicked out of the familial abode. One could say my Aiden-rage reached hurricane-level swells because here was a trans dude—on the public internet, with hologram status—and all he could offer my impoverished imagination was a life as sleek and empty as all architecture since 1991.

Back then, I was casually hooking up with a celebrity, and on an intellectual level, I knew how much production went into façades: the makeup, the lighting, the PA who handled credit card statements and seltzer runs. And yet, with Aiden's Gram, I still got seduced into believing his perfection was real, and then I was left gutted, like a teen who has binged a TV series on a long weekend and was disappointed at reentering a world that is never cut into episodic bites.

I sometimes fancied myself an evolved person, but would an evolved person spend at least fifteen minutes every morning comparing my long scroll of curlicued flaws to this person, as flat as a screen?

The list included flabby abs, trauma responses to loss and sudden noises, a tendency toward fantasies of spanking someone in a field full of gently swaying flowers, midwestern sensibilities including "niceness," a future that appeared clouded in smog.

Each morning, I awoke, went to the backyard, and immediately scanned Aiden's bod on the Gram, asking, *Why can't I attain such delicious perfection?* A holey apple staring at a waxed, genetically modified one. I had no other trans role models, so who could really blame me for moving toward this trans-parent like a toddler swimming to open, tanned, and muscular arms?

We all need parents, and mine had been dead since the avalanche.

Disgust and love are self-perpetuating states. With Aiden, I swung back and forth between loathing and longing, and the universe always offered evidence for either pole.

My friend Sid generally tried not to inflame my Aiden-obsession, but one day he couldn't resist and told me about Aiden's pet goose.

Sid, my first friend in the city. We'd met in a bodega. I must have been looking particularly forlorn, staring at a row of flavored water, trying to decide whether I wanted the upscale cloudberry in a glass bottle or the everyperson's lemon in a plastic, Earth-killing one. He walked straight up to me and asked if I wanted to dog-walk with him.

He read me.

I had my carabiner attached to my shorts, and at the time I was walking dogs in the fancier neighborhoods where you were required to fill out the following after each fifteen-minute stroll:

Walk Assessment
Mood (100 words):
Negatively influencing experiences (100 words, if
*   applicable):*
Activity for intellectual stimulation:
Doggie friends or enemies made (100 words):
Size, color, shape, and approx. weight of feces:
Duration and quality of urine:

I immediately agreed. Sid had known I was trans from my height, my beautiful face, and my irregular beard. I knew he was trans because he properly identified me. Even though he got on my case for not taking the job seriously enough, we were each happy to have a trans buddy in the dog-care world.

We spent a blissful year together, and then Sid asked his business partners to buy him out and he moved to L.A., like every trans person who found themselves wanting resurrection in a less gritty place. Who doesn't dream of waking up from gender-affirming surgery to palm trees?

Still, there weren't any good top or bottom surgeons in L.A., and the fantasy, like all fantasies, remained even more potent in its insubstantiality.

After he'd settled into a studio apartment with pea-soup-and-bacon-shaded carpeting, Sid texted me: I was at a party at Aiden's place and the putz (he liked to interject a little Yiddish now and again) has a goose named Agatha.

That was all I needed to know to make a complete character assessment of Aiden Chase.

The laws of common internet decency rest on the understanding that if you have a goose named Agatha, you are obligated to overrepresent her. The fact that he chose to micro-document the reddish hair growing at the tip of his chin when he had Agatha running around, eating bananas, told me that his value system was all askew, and yet there he was, instructing an entire generation of young white queers on how to cock your snapback just enough to denote rakish young non-str8 without crossing into either "urban" or skater poseur territory.

Now that you know how disgustingly seductive Aiden was, I can proceed to the day when the balance shifted and the gawking voyeur and the flat subject were thrown into an industrial blender and wholly reconstituted, like that new meal-replacement line, Whizzerd.

Let me set the stage. The Black Rains had not yet begun, tho forest fires, flooding, and next-level storms had been reshaping the terrain for many years. I was still a lowly dog walker, creeping in and out of other folks' homes. In my own apartment, I'd become a worn-down receptacle of my roomies' substances. Walls did very little to stop the passage of the Witch's beetle-shell extracts, asparagus decoctions, burning angelica leaves, moss, and myrrh, and the Stoner-Hacker's weed, Mexican food, laughter at his video games, angst at his video games, and loud thumps every time he picked up *Infinite Jest* and then threw it back down on the floor.

I was no longer in the deepest part of the Shadowlands, nor was I in the light; I had found a ledge between the ooze below and the crisp air above.

That fateful morning I put down my plant, Alice the Aloe, and my coffee. I knocked three times, waited for the Witch's booming "Enter," picked up my things, and crossed into the heather-moss-and-dried-insect smell of my roomie's bedroom. She knelt on the floor, her head under a violet shawl, reciting "The Hymn to Promote the Fecundity of the Fields." The door to the backyard was open, the feeder swinging with birds. They loved the Witch's honeyed insects, and she loved their shit.

The Witch paused and the unclean smoke of her room spooled around me.

Without moving her head, she said, "Note if there is any disturbance in the air today. We crossed under the light of the Worm Moon last night, a potent time when those wriggling creatures begin to wend their way through the cold earth.

"Blessed Bringers of Beatitude," she howled scathingly, and I nodded as if I knew what she was talking about.

I passed through her room and stomped down the steps.

An empty packet of cigarettes had blown onto the grass-patched ground. The Witch kept crumbs, hairs, plastic strips that protect bottle seals, business-class envelopes, specialty bird shit, and other detritus for her spells. I was always trying to be a "good" roommate, and I forced myself to leave the white packet there. It would remain part of the tableau, along with the rose bushes, the apocalypse-gray condo across the way, an indifferent sky between tree branches, and the chain-link fence that someone had woven strips of plastic through, crude textile art that would soon be removed to go into some biennale.

I brushed construction Styrofoam off the stairs and made sure Alice was soaking up the early March sunlight. When I'd moved in, someone had left her (IDK why I gender her this way) in the dirt, not even buried, her roots exposed. Before I could take into account that I would be living in a windowless room in a Ridgewood apartment with two strangers, I'd gone to the hardware store to buy her a pot and some better soil and then walked her to the bathroom to get cleaned up. I started carrying her outside with me every morning to get some air. She soothed me if I got sunburned at the gay beach.

I sat down on a lawn chair, opened the app, picked up my coffee mug with FUTURE BUSINESS SCHOOL written in faded gold dust, and prepared for some Cali bullshit that would sink my bioaffective levels half a bar closer to depression.

The internet is just a low-grade representation of human consciousness, I reminded myself, *and all those coding dendrites and coiled fiber-optic cables and locked web server catacombs are shittier versions of how trees talk to each other.*

Why was I about to look at him if it made me miserable?

"Human beings are funny," my therapist Sophie always said, which I took as a lighthearted way of accepting that we often run in the opposite direction of our desires, and that even knowing that we're running in the opposite direction doesn't necessarily change anything.

In his Gram, Aiden stood on the roof of a hotel, looking out into the distance. Of course, he was shirtless. He'd set up the tripod and his tattoo could be seen, a shadowy banner across surgically sculpted pecs. He was not in his usual biome. Instead of woven furniture and fruit trees, there were skyscrapers sitting vacant and unfinished.

Heaping Hillocks of Hellfire! I cursed in the style of the Witch.

He was here.

The caption: So gr8ful to be in the city for a special project. I am always replenished when I get to bathe in the hum of New York. Sending muscular love + light.

My phone's screen started to turn white, and the matchbook-sized hologram projector lifted out of its side. His perfect body hovered in my backyard, just below the cherry blossom tree. Aiden had enough of an audience to activate hologram-tech.

Welp, I thought, *maybe it's time to see this character IRL because when moments are strung together like language, in a breathing place, it is harder to hide behind a pose, a tired line, a landscape overswept.*

When the hologram faded, I waved my hands through the space where his body had been.

Buzzing with anxiety, I texted R, my celebrity booty call. We had met the summer before on Cape Cod, due to forces so providential that they proved the tired-ass world was still enchanted. We continued to fuck each other, she a B-list movie star still playing teenagers and I a melancholic dog-walking trans guy from the non-coast, which made a kernel of inexplicable sense.

Hey, (I always had to sound aloof) u know Aiden Chase from the Gram? Could u get me a meeting with him while he's here?

She did not respond.

Even tho we (men) are supposed to be rugged individuals who embark on heroic journeys alone, needing nothing but our Siren-barren solitude, the truth was, I couldn't stalk Aiden by myself.

My other roommate, the Stoner-Hacker, was winding down his midnight-to-nine shift of *Galaxy Hunt*. Soon he would light a bowl and sleep until three, order some food, smoke another bowl, do some high-level hacking, reject his pinky-ring-wearing father's calls about getting a real job, smoke again, and settle in for another nighttime battle as an intergalactic druid warlord.

As long as he opened the window, turned on a fan, used Bluetooth headphones to mute the constant bombing of Viking spaceships, and wiped up his late-night microwave explosions, I didn't much care what he did. The fact that we had opposite schedules cut down on the awkward encounters when he walked around in his underwear yelling at his dad or trying to press his bean-sauce-and-cheese-splattered Styrofoam box on top of the trash instead of taking it out, and I had to pretend that I didn't see his medium-sized dick through the opening of his penguin-printed boxers.

The S-H had assailed me with his immaturity for so long (the molding potato-pipes left in the sink, the waking me up at three in the morning to tell me about the colors of his existential dread, the immersing into VR soccer games until he became a dehydrated puddle on the floor and his father called me looking for him) that it was hard to conceive of him as useful.

Even so, I found myself walking back through the Witch's bedroom. I passed her immobile on the floor, crossed the kitchen, and tapped on his door. No answer. Knocked harder.

"Hey, man," I said casually, giving no immediate signal that I was stepping out of my role as compliant trans roommate who transferred the S-H's untouched delivery food in the sink to the trash can after three days and had a supply of *That's okay*s to all his friends who, before I had robust facial hair, used to stumble, "She . . . he . . . I mean, shit, sorry, I mean, he, does he want a hit?" The S-H would go, "Sorry, dude, do you want some?" and I'd say, "That's okay, I have stuff to do."

I cracked open the door and inhaled a smell-lasagna of takeout containers, weed, Febreze over the weed and takeout containers, and some brand of manly cinnamon aftershave. The S-H swiveled around in his desk chair to look at me. He was shirtless in his Grinch boxers, showing his pale little-boy chest, which never fattened no matter what he fed it.

"Can you geo-tag someone for me?"

It was less a question of knowledge (I knew he siphoned imperceptible amounts of money from the many bank accounts of his father's clients) than a question of his willingness to help. I hadn't sent him exasperated texts about the marshes of hair-in-toothpaste left in the sink in a while; I figured our relationship was in a good place.

"I don't know, bruh."

"What if I drop off and pick up your dry cleaning?" I asked.

The pile was probably composting in his closet. The S-H's father bought him clothes for the job he *wanted* him to have, a junior investment analyst, and the S-H wore each button-down shirt once, over his underwear, and then threw it into a pile and closed the door.

"Can I get that in writing?" he asked, his refrain for everything that was too complex for him to parse in a very high moment, and that he would return to during a brief spell of coming down. I wrote out the terms and Aiden's Gram info on a stained napkin while he guided his spaceship into the Circle of Toth.

Before I left the apartment, I grabbed my trunks and a tiny spray bottle of vinegar and tea tree oil to protect my feet from the fungus of the men's locker room. I kissed my pointer finger and placed it on the postcard of a hamburger above my desk, part of my sprawling mood board. Last year, before he left for L.A., Sid had invited all the dog walkers over for drinks in my backyard to try to humanize the disgruntled mass he saw coming in and out of the office with their carabiners and toned calf muscles. Dog walker Jewel "got lost" on the way to the bathroom, and I'd found her sitting on my bed with the postcard in her lap.

She couldn't stop herself from asking, "Don't you know that the beef industry is worse for the environment than cars?" as if we were still in college, just learning about the atrocities of the world and trying to earn activist cred as a way to get laid.

At the time I said, "Um, yes?" and walked away.

If we could redo that, I would say, "Well, Jewel. Somewhere out beyond the tidal pools of correctness where everyone is supposed to keep track of rules about all these annoying marginalized folks you used to be able to make fun of, people have pleasures, and our pleasures are complex, contradictory, and sometimes involve eating a hamburger next to an aloe plant in a squat room after fucking a partner who happens to be a celebrity while she wears blindfolds to stay inside her own head, and when she texts to ask you how you're doing, you give her a shrugging emoticon that means, *I could bring you a catalog of my feelings, glossy and sportive like L.L. Bean, with shades more exotic than Sea Glass and Reed Green, if we weren't just fuck buddies.*

You know, if it were possible to annotate the future and the past, my one true wish.

Once Sid left for L.A., his business partners fired Jewel due to numerous complaints about her throwing away dog parents' meat-based food products. I missed her sometimes.

Ready to enter the aquatic realm, I waited for the train and got on a car with a raspberry-pink interior. After seven stops, I exited and walked up the subway steps in Williamsburg and waltzed past jewelry stands, where antique pocket watches ticked away. Visitors from far away were safe inside gauzy expectations. They did not notice the towers of empty mirrored condos watching over us.

I turned toward the shock of color on a bus shelter. For once, all the wires of the universe were connecting. I'd known that R was a model for Vines, the sorta-sustainable store that sold "basics." However, I had never encountered her likeness on the street before.

There she was, taking up the entire side of the bus stop, creamier (whiter?) than she looked spread over her bed, blindfolded, pussy smelling of damp sawdust. In the ad, she was a pure object wearing a plain dandelion-yellow dress in a field of unnatural flowers with curling stems and squiggly leaves. They'd *naturalized* her strange moods, the times when she went vacant or exuberant. I felt protective, not in a patriarchal way, *I hope*, but as someone who had seen her unkempt, stung by a bee, yelling at her mother on the phone, trying to paint her own nails, picking up a book and then throwing it down a moment later because it reminded her of something more interesting.

A regular dude in a Brooklyn hoodie waited for the bus at the edge of the bus shelter. I wondered if he thought I was checking him out. Since I was a short, well-dressed, soft-spoken man, no one could help but assume I was gay. I wanted him to know the inside scoop, that I was actually checking out my babely sex partner on the wall, but the tech had not come out yet that would allow me to present the truth to him in hologram form.

And I was still working on the whole verbalizing-my-thoughts thing.

Dude entered the clay-brick-red bus without a glance back at me. It was about time for senior swim to change into adult swim, and I kept walking down Bedford Avenue.

The Metropolitan Pool was built in 1922, the same year its architect, Henry Bacon, designed the Lincoln Memorial, an epoch when cities cared more about the public and less about foreign investors buying up property. In the lobby, I placed my finger on the scanner and got beeped into the natatorium. I no longer worried about someone noticing my lack of thick schlong. Men were so at home in this habitat that they didn't scrutinize. On this first day after the full Worm Moon, a few middle-aged men with no bellies lounged on the benches. I took off pants, shirt, and underwear, let my dick have a second out in the air.

I came for the light and for the water.

Surely everyone could see my chest scars, through goggles, with swim-cap-squeezed heads, but underwater I was no longer trans because trans presupposed a before and an after, one concrete form and then another. There I was a municipal citizen using a public amenity, following the rules about removing your lock every night or it will be cut off, and there I was, water meeting chemically treated water, and there I was in the medium-speed lane, trying not to get mad when some dude with a back full of muscle passed me, and there I found a little capsule of freedom, letting the managed and scrunched-up body unravel into its nature. I moved without all the noise. Light hit the water and moved across the pool floor, and I knew nothing, I had no commentary, all my effort and plotting and holding-up of chest had earned me one moment of gliding.

You were not technically supposed to use your phone in the locker room, but when I was aching and showered, I took it out and positioned my face against the gray lockers. I was breaking the rules, on top of breaking the social rules about who is allowed to roam safely inside a pack of men.

Set timer. Ran back to bench. Snapped. Posted to my Gram. Sans caption. Hot.

Men were lying on benches nearby, their dicks slumped and peaceful on their legs. They were in their bliss; they didn't even open their eyes to the shutter-sound of my phone. Happy odalisques, here in this male harem.

I sprayed tea tree oil on my toes and lay back on a bench in the corner, approaching a warm thought about how I'd rather be here, in this damp, moldy locker room, than anywhere else.

Except, maybe, the sauna. I hadn't ventured there yet because the etiquette was total nudity. And I didn't think the motley assortment of aging gay dudes, guys who were unreadable in their vulnerable Speedos with slight bellies, and old str8 men who wore their necklaces in the water—sending sparkling reflections across the pool floor—could handle the sight of naked Pen.

Could I?

That was always the question.

Crystalizing crumpets of Cassiopeia! I decided to go for it.

I reasoned: *If I get hate-crimed, I'll either detransition or I'll become a queer extremist, beating up gaybashers with a bike U-lock like one of my exes.*

I slipped on my shirt, left my trunks in the locker,

wrapped a towel around my waist, and walked on the slimy floor toward the door marked SAUNA in yellow painted letters, like a sign at camp.

The door led to a damp anteroom. I couldn't help but remember all the books from childhood where a lost cabinet, a forgotten wardrobe, a branch-covered door always led the (white, cis) character to some enchanted realm.

A beefy guy stared at me. He was shirtless and wore red Adidas track pants. They shimmered in the fluorescent lights, like the night ocean.

"What will you bring to our sanctum?"

As he said that, I thought, *Rectum*.

The more I was permitted to enter male spaces, the freer I was to observe how men were totally obsessed with each other!

"Huh?" I was too busy thinking of how much anal sex had taken place in the locker room to focus.

He grabbed my shirt and dragged me back out to the shower area, where two men showered under the same head, their hairy butts almost touching. He pressed my back against the wall, and I felt one of his rings against my breastplate, where there used to be more adipose tissue. No one in the locker room paid any attention. They did not want their languor broken.

"You think you're a tough guy, huh?" this ringed man asked, even as shower spray misted him.

"No, I really don't. That's not a hang-up for me." I tried to stay calm inside my knowledge that masculinity was a farce, a pyramid scheme.

"The sauna is the apex of the male locker-room experience. To gain admission, you must pass a test of wills and prove to the assembled body that you are offering some piece of yourself worth hours of pore-opening, branch-beating, and eucalyptus-fresh male bonding."

I made rough calculations. I always knew that joining groups meant horrendous and unforetold compromises.

"Have you ever met a trans before?"

He reddened. "I mean."

I could see his internet search history: "shemale fucking muscular basketball coaches," "shemale striptease," "tranny fucks naughty buttholes."

"Okay, well, what if I offered something that would glorify the hormonal structure of testosterone and the male archetype?"

"Yeah?"

"I could do my testosterone shot in the sauna, naked, and we could all celebrate the yellow, oily substance and the late blooming of my dick."

The white-gray curls of his chest hair were damp. "All right."

"On one condition."

"Yes?"

"That I am allowed to distribute scientific research proving there is no inherent link between testosterone and aggression."

"I'll have to check with the Grandmeister."

"Like from that old TV show?"

"Yeah." The gatekeeper looked sheepish. "I'll return in a

moment." He opened the door to the sauna. Closed it, sending a wave of fragrant air toward me.

The grout on the floor had been expertly cleaned and shone white.

I waited and waited, counting squares, straining to hear what the Grandmeister might say. Nothing.

Finally, I left the anteroom. I had to get to my first client.

As I was walking out of the lobby, the guy at the front desk called out, "Penfield Ruth Henderson."

The *Ruth* outfitted me in shame: I hadn't changed my name yet.

"Yes?"

"The Grandmeister will see you next Thursday at nine a.m. No research."

I bowed my head in deference to the pool's wacked-out cultural norms and didn't mention that I might have a scheduling conflict.

I walked Oggie, Starburst, and Palm Tree together without incident. As Buford took a shit on someone's lawn, a guy in a tank top came flying out the front door and screamed from the top of the stairs. I waved my poop bag at him like a flag, but he was still yelling in Polish, saying something along the lines of "Make that dog shit in the street," which was impossible.

I smiled and gave him a thumbs-up.

My first summer dog-walking, as Lola the Havanese was kicking up dirt to bury the poop that I had already picked up, a small stone hit a dude's Mercedes. He had been washing the other side, and poked his head up to give an unbelievable monologue about how he had worked his way up from nothing to buy this car, how it was his *baby*, having no other family or close relations, and how denting it was analogous to stoning an infant.

Lola's parents ended up paying him five hundred dollars to stop harassing me, and I realized just how little I could control in the world. Assholes (human and canine) aside, walking dogs helped me to re-create the suburban village I had grown up in. During restless midwestern summers, as my friend Jillian and I would walk past people on the street or, later, drive past their homes or the site of their DUIs, we would create a little map of our town, the divorces and the family secrets and the infamous soup party that went awry, the density of our stories vacillating between gossip and tales of biblical proportions. We never tired of embellishing the story about the high school science teachers who hooked up together in the chemistry closet and developed lung problems. When we were thirsty for the epic, we'd say, "Remember when Mr. Redderick and Mrs. Locke had sex in the chemistry storage closet?"

"And Mrs. Locke's kid Talon walked in?"

"And then he went to rehab and her husband blamed her?"

"And then she was sent to a sanatorium?"

"And then she fell in love with the janitor, who made mince pies for all the patients?"

"And then Mr. Redderick moved away to Alaska to study

salmon hatcheries, but not before carving her name into the big oak tree by the football field, as if they had role-reversed with their students?"

From walking my dogs, I could tell which humans had gotten a raise, or had broken up, or had a detoxing relative on their couch, or had decided to move back from whence they came.

I took Buford home, envying the fact that he had no clue about the screamer's insults and the general pettiness of human emotion. I walked Harris. Back at his apartment, an airy Bushwick loft with huge vacuumed rugs covering the paint-splattered wood, I sprawled out on the ground and Harris lay down next to me. I checked my phone.

The S-H had come through!

He'd sent me a link to a basic HTML page with photos of Aiden—some selfies and some taken by the plethora of cameras in every modern city—along with time stamps and map coordinates. The latest, from 6:02 p.m., was at 40°44'28.4"N 74°00'29.3"W, blurry Aiden in an elevator. I fumbled around trying to figure out how to read the coordinates and there it was, his hotel.

Once I possessed the key, I had to go through the door.

I patted Harris goodbye, and he looked up at me over his long Italian greyhound nose, bemused.

I was dressed in my dog-walking joggers and T-shirt, conveying casual elegance. Two lions guarded the front of the Juniper Ash Hotel. I rubbed their heads for luck and stamina.

The lobby was strange because I'd been living in city subsistence mode, without extravagance or leisure. I did have a trust fund from the hoarding of my grandparents, but I never liked to use it with my prospects still unknown. They passed on money, and they also passed on a belief in scarcity. In the city of hideous wealth, I was not rich at all. I simply had a cushion against despair; I could afford to take sick days from dog walking and pay Sophie, who did not accept insurance.

Art-collector moms in athleisure, tech bros wearing silver visors to easily identify one another, women in their flowing prairie-goth gowns, a famous pianist with his fingertips encased in silver regenerating pods: they all moved across the room in varying states of disregard for my gaze.

I ordered sparkling water with shrub and sipped slowly.

After an hour of trying to classify all the types of people who had the time and money to be trailing through a hotel lobby at six on a Wednesday evening, I saw the body I knew so well coming out of the elevator.

My plan was to observe any flaws from a safe distance, but once I saw him, a trans–magnetic field pulled me closer. I went over.

I stepped in front of him before he could cross through the lobby.

"Hey, not to be stalkerish, but can I talk to you?"

There it was, the face I'd loved and hated from afar. He blushed in an Abercrombie-model kind of way. Wow, I was pretty into queer women, but I was crushing on him hard. Damn the fluidity of queer desire.

"I"—his voice came out with a preadolescent crack—"don't do interviews."

Was that wariness on his face?

"Well, I'm not a journalist, I walk dogs. How about if we just talk trans to trans?"

"Aight," he said, a little nervous, which made me grow enormous and potent.

"Great. I'm Penfield, but don't infer from that that I'm a WASP. My parents were Jewish," I said as I led him back to my seat.

Somehow I'd started asserting the upper hand. Damn, was I topping him in this convo? For once, it was my city.

"Aiden, obvs," he said.

I was getting a bioaffective spike as we settled into the velvet chairs; inside my giddiness, the lobby colors sharpened and bloomed.

"I'm going to be direct here, which is not my usual tactic. This will sound naïve for someone such as myself, but you must know how we trans are often furiously spinning through various life stages at once, so pretend it's coming from a fifteen-year-old trying to talk to a cool, older sixteen-year-old."

"K."

"Are you really perfect?"

"Wha?"

His blankness was a door slammed.

"Never mind."

He looked down at his phone.

I wanted to pour my shrub on him. And his gadget.

What had I expected from this advertisement of a human? A dense encounter?

TBH, I wanted to absorb his otherworldly perfection, which was still intact across the low lobby table. And punch him.

For so many mornings, I had given his bod my rapt and self-disgusted attention, and now all he could return was generic, glazed-over, limp distraction that any cis adolescent teen could have offered.

"I must know what is up with your goose," I said, my voice getting louder and higher. "You just leave her behind on the other coast?" My distrust of California was evident.

"Say again?" He was still looking down at his phone.

"I . . . I asked you about your goose."

"That's personal," he said shortly. "I should be going."

He stood up and I caught his scent. Laundry with April Fresh–scented dryer sheets, the heady BO of trans anxiety, and pine-based cologne.

"Cya," I said, hoping to sound aloof.

For a moment, I was a crushed child. Then the swell of rage returned, though arguably it had never receded.

I called an apartment meeting. This was highly unusual, and the roomies must have thought we were getting evicted.

We sat in our tiny living room, a few feet between the entrance to the Witch's room, my room, and the start of the kitchen. The S-H was cross-legged on the floor, and the Witch and I sat too close together on two sectional pieces that had once belonged to a longer, nicer couch.

"I need to curse someone, in both the old ways and the new."

The Witch gave me the same look she'd given when I suggested a chore wheel. "This is not child's play," she said.

"Exactly. That's why I need a professional witch and a professional . . . hacker."

"You remember what I told you about this man?" she asked.

"Yes, that our conflict is purely astrological. His Jupiter-blessed Leo sun conflicts with my strident, truth-seeking Sagittarius sun, vindictive Scorpio rising, and watery Pisces moon. But he has slighted me! He has lied. He has tried to attain perfection, and someone needs to punish him!"

She did not look convinced. I had to use her language.

"This person resides inside his devices, devices made from leaching the earth's minerals. He watches neither sun nor moon nor California wildflower blooms. His message is facile, though his body is hard."

The Witch hated technology that did not involve an intention, ancient rites, and smelly ingredients.

"What sort of hex are you considering?"

"He needs to visit the Shadowlands."

"You do know that when one is sent to the Shadowlands, one is cellularly rearranged, beset by mind-spiders, and on occasion destroyed?"

"I know this quite well. Remember when I moved in and you said you smelled the 'brine of the Shadowlands' on me? I'm just now emerging from the darkness and this *guy* is frolicking in the sunlight, offering harmful advice to young people."

"You did not travel to the Shadowlands due to a hex. Your entry was natural, brought about by the state of your own evolution."

Still, she tilted her head, which meant she was considering it.

"What do you want me to do? I already found him for you," the S-H whined.

"I want you to hack into his Gram, where I shall place a photo of Alice that will at least temporarily disrupt his flow." Sure, I thought about posting a photo of the inside of my butthole, with some caption about the abyss and the abject, but it was really Alice—that tender extension of my being— that could counter his bullshit.

"Hm, maybe I could use the aloe as well," the Witch said. She refused to call her by her name.

To get him to help me, I had to promise the S-H that I would write his online dating profile (leaving out many key details), help him track his dread on a crisis chart to determine his baseline, and call the landlord about the leak in the bathroom. The Witch required that I bring her a demiard of fired comfrey oil.

I ordered a pizza to celebrate our fragile teamwork and Aiden's impending doom.

That night, in bed, wrapped in the smell of burnt yarrow bundles, I made my gratitude list:

1. For the Witch's powers
2. For the S-H's powers
3. For my own trans powers

4. For mushrooms on pizza
5. For the insane hope that I can take back some of what I'd lost

Two days later, the Witch, the S-H, and I gathered on the back steps before the sun rose. The Witch had decreed that the first spring sunrise would be the most potent. The S-H was in his pajamas, ready for bed. I cradled Alice in my arms. I promised her that the sacrifice would be worth it.

The Witch lit two person-tall incense sticks stuck into the dirt. I inhaled, imagining us hooded, out on some heath, performing ancient and twisted rites. The Witch took Alice from me and placed her on a piece of velvet. She removed a blade from a leather holster—my paring knife, which had gone missing months prior! I looked away as she sliced off one of Alice's tendrils, then pressed down the arm in her mortar, forcing out the aloe. She sprinkled crushed insect shells on top of the gel and chanted under her breath. The S-H was more attentive than I'd ever seen him, perhaps because he thought we had entered a VR pagan biome and were about to fight off marauding bandits.

As the Witch chanted, the S-H hacked into Aiden's Gram. This was less dramatic. I had given him the photo and the caption already, and all he had to do was post it to @AidenChasesTruth. We sealed the hex, in both new and old forms, circling Alice thrice on the scraggly lawn.

The hex: *The first to behold the aloe will sink into the Shadowlands.*

Each morning, I awoke, made coffee, took Alice outside for air, and watched Aiden prancing around the city. I was too scared to scroll back and see if Alice was still there, with the caption: I want to splay like her, throw my limbs, full of juice, over ceramic sides of pots, and persist no matter how dark, dry, hot, barren. She is a medicine. She knows that trans is more than suicide or iced coffee on someone's Oakland patio with mid-century modern teak furniture and a story that goes, First I was a miserable girl, then I was a happy man. That's a special kind of bullshit, with this aloe plant as my witness. Penfield here. At least until Aiden deletes this in about five seconds. @fieldsofpen.

No one could blame me for wanting to be internet-famous. The entire fractured country agreed on one premise: only fame carried anything like substance across socioeco-nomic/racial/gendered boundaries.

I got a few new followers from my short-lived coup, walked dogs, tolerated the roomies, and wondered what exactly was missing in my life.

One afternoon, I walked Gwenivière, the obese bulldog. She moved slowly, shaking her little butt, smelling every clover. Instead of pulling her, I grazed on my phone. When my timer buzzed, I scooped her up in my arms and carried her back to the apartment. I'd have to report that she did not go #2, which often prompted dog parents to send humiliating follow-up texts, insinuating that I had not tried hard enough.

I set Gwen down and unlocked the apartment. She

waddled in and threw herself onto the bright orange ortho-pedic dog bed.

I tried to catalog the smell of each habitat that I visited. This one had notes of vetiver, gentle cleaning products, and scented trash bags. I opened the fridge to pour a glass of well water that Gwen's parents had brought back from their upstate cabin. When I closed it, a throat cleared. I peered around the corner into the long living room.

Lounging on the slatted modernist bench was a tall being in a long silk dressing gown. Short hair. White. Piercings. A hybrid ghost of Kathy Acker and a 1920s "new" femme.

I hadn't met all my clients in person, but I knew this was not one of them.

"Penfield R. Henderson?"

This person knew my corrected my name before I'd le-gally changed it.

"Yes."

"I'm the Operatrix."

"You've been summoned." The Operatrix put down a mug on a stone coaster.

"Am I in trouble?" My voice cracked.

"We received a signal from a young trans man whose bio-affective levels rapidly deteriorated after he looked at a photo of your aloe plant. He was the first viewer."

"I—"

"Let me finish. Aside from noting that you have sent a vulnerable trans man into the Shadowlands, we have mea-sured your bioaffective aggro levels toward Aiden Chase. We think that having you and Aiden help pull this person back toward his baseline would be a healing process for all involved."

"Wait. The person in the Shadowlands isn't Aiden?"

An almost imperceptible smile line crossed the Operatrix's face. "No."

Sparkling sacks of shungite!

We'd fucked up.

"We need you and Aiden to fly to California and retrieve Blithe from Joshua Tree National Park, which is where he entered total darkness."

"I didn't have a whole extraction team when *I* was in the Shadowlands," I pouted.

"We sent you to Sophie, didn't we?"

"True. So what happens after we pick Blithe up?"

"You'll decide on a stable place to bring him back to health. You must ask the Witch how long her hex will last. And, Pen?"

"Yes?"

"You must find something to do with all your rage."

"What if Aiden doesn't want to come with me?"

"He must."

I stared as the Operatrix rose, trying to connect the person before me to my idea of a shape-shifting autonomous being who roved around the world connecting queer people through a subaltern, mycorrhiza-modeled network. In the recent past, the queer child of a billionaire had started funding the Rhiz, and so the network could jet Operatrixes around and pay for surgeries and offer health insurance. My friend Minna's sister was part of the Rhiz, and I was always pestering her for gossip, but it remained coiled in mystery. While I was in my Shadowlands, I had tried to placate myself by imagining their in-fighting, toxicity, ill-advised hookups, and illicit use of data.

I could not imagine queerness leading ultimately to anything more than ruin.

The Operatrix moved toward the door, carrying a small pouch that glowed in ever-shifting colors. Damn, a Biometer. Gwen had no reaction to this stranger in her home. It was as if she didn't even sense the Operatrix's presence.

"I will have a portfolio of Blithe's data sent over to prepare you. The Rhiz will also provide your airfare, accommodation, and transportation."

I stopped myself from saying, *I remember back in 20—, when the Rhiz had full integrity and no money.*

"Goodbye," the Operatrix said, and extended a ringed hand.

"Bye," I said, and took it.

I was tempted to run home and tell the Witch that she had erred, but that would only have inflamed my aggro levels. *What to do, what to do.*

I called Sid.

"Bra!"

"Hey, bra!" We forever pinged back and forth between mocking masculinity and dipping into it.

"You're not going to believe this, but the Operatrix came over."

"Shit, dude, are you having another major crisis that you neglected to tell me about?"

"Not exactly. Are you still on your Gram cleanse?"

"Yep."

I filled him in about Aiden in the city and the dual hexing.

"Gawd, Pen. What did the Operatrix want?"

"Well, apparently, the person who first looked at my post of Alice got hexed, and now this other trans guy is totally in the Shadowlands in Joshua Tree. And Aiden and I have to go find him."

"Whoa. What form did the Operatrix take? Because one of the people I'm dating met the Operatrix in the form of a *self-described* Afro-Caribbean trans goddess named Anubia. My pal Ochre talked to a computer engineer named Milton. And you had that other person back when you—"

I cut him off so I didn't have to think about my early Shadowland days. "The Operatrix was in a flowy dressing gown and also reminded me of Kathy Acker. Hard to place."

"Well, I'm starting to believe there is something like divine symmetry in the world if, after all this time, the universe has finally forced you to deal with Aiden in a real way."

"Thanks. I'm sure Sophie will agree with you."

My therapist had banned me from talking about Aiden because I turned into a totally devolved baby whenever I mentioned him.

I let Sid know that I'd meet up with him in L.A. if I wasn't too busy wrangling Blithe, and then I headed out of Gwen's apartment. My stomach lurched as I thought about what I'd done to Blithe.

By the time I got home, I was in a total spiral. Labeling it *spiraling* was not enough to stop the looping images of some young trans dude strangled by sadness and hatred of himself. I held down on the Rhiz-shaped icon on the back of my phone.

The projector raised up.

"Yes, Penfield," the Operatrix said, now wearing corduroy overall shorts.

"Blithe is going to be okay, right?" I asked shakily.

"Now is not the time for remorse," the Operatrix said.

I sighed.

"He would have gone to the Shadowlands either way. But you've accelerated the process, and that harm is your responsibility."

I was a child receiving absolution, giddy with the lightness that comes after rooting around in catastrophic thoughts. "I'll help him."

The Operatrix nodded and faded out.

That evening, R emerged. She always returned right at the moment I started to forget her a little.

I was standing in the yard at dusk before the cherry blossom tree, watching the thick buds that had formed on the branches, when I had one of those spastic twenty-first-century tics to check and see what phone-info awaited.

Come fuck me 2nite, R had texted.

I could have said I was busy, but I knew that it was healthy for me to spend time with a celebrity, or anyone, really.

I grabbed my bag of dicks and headed to the subway. I found a crimson car and waited to see if anyone would change it back to candy-apple red. The subway cars didn't change shade whimsically; there was an algorithm at play. Bio-meters were designed as orange-sized orbs that could fit in a palm. Sophie had a test model in her office, and while she refused to use it on me, she let me see a demo. She held it cupped in her hand, and the sphere turned forest green. She passed me the small monitor on her desk, which read, *8636, luminous contentment.*

"Is that you?"

She smiled. "No, that's one of the presets."

I wasn't sure if I believed her.

When corporate scientists began developing the Bio-meters, they created an offshoot that could gather the emotional data of many subjects. The subway was the perfect place for what became nicknamed the Butt-meter, which collected data from contact with riders' buttocks (or hands on poles or feet, but butts clearly had the largest surface area) and turned the subway cars various shades. In more affluent areas, the shades were often quite pretty, and there was fierce speculation as to whether the Butt-meters were designed to skew toward pastel in those neighborhoods, or whether the inner world of heavily resourced folks was full of softer feelings.

Occasionally, even in nicer neighborhoods, a disconsolate person would enter a train and everyone would glare as the shade changed from faded coral to carrot-diarrhea. Certain mornings, a screaming baby would be lifted into tender, braceleted arms and the palest yellow was restored.

The train lightened as we moved toward Williamsburg. We crossed over the bridge in a state of juicy, liquid red.

Of course, I had a fantasy that my feelings alone were potent enough to shift the subway cars, the walls of buildings, and even the atmospheric pressure of the city to my moods, whether salty or enlightened.

The train arrived at the Wall Street stop, where I could catch the white ferry. The fastest way to R would have been two buses, but that seemed an undignified mode to take for fucking a celebrity.

I walked up the station steps into the city air, onto a street with five salad shops for young lunching financiers.

I needed a snack before boarding. The last time I'd eaten dinner with R after a session, she'd pulled out cartons of dandelion greens, bean sprouts, and brown rice that her PA had left, plus kombucha and a good bottle of red wine. For a while afterward, my body felt "clean" and well, but two hours later I was ordering from the Chinese/Mexican place down the street that also served donuts that no one ever ordered and would end up in the to-go bags instead of fortune cookies. As I ate the soggy fish tacos in our dark kitchen, and then the chocolate donut with a surprising vanilla custard filling, I said *MMM MMMM* to myself. I was happy in my own little pasture without a perfect yet non-fulfilling meal, and wanted to yell at every internet article about how to "eat better."

I went to a deli to buy some nuts, a protein bar, and a pitless avocado that was possible only through genetic modification. The cashier ignored my request for no bag. Outside, I peeled off the avocado skin and bit into the fruit, passing through the hole where the pit once lived.

It killed me that my days were spent maintaining: food, serotonin, laundry card balance, low-key social vocabulary. Whatever happened to genius visionaries floating above the city, untouched by the banal, rich in obliviousness?

I had to catch the white ferry from Pier 11. I never went into the huge navy-and-yellow store in Red Hook, tho, because it brought up intense cravings for clean rooms with curtains and floor lamps that would be thrown away after 2.5 years.

I lined up behind a whole group of Hasidic Jews. As we walked up the pier, the pressures of the city dropped away. A young woman counted everyone who stepped on board, no longer delighted by the movement of the boat away from the skyscrapers at the base of the city. Counting people on a boat was just her job.

On the top deck, French people and Hasidim gathered in distinct groups, taking photos, and we pulled back, leaving the dead and glinting steel of the city. The Hasidic men's hats were swirled with fox-tip furs that lifted up in the blowing wind. The boat engine carried us toward the barracks of Governor's Island.

Out in the distance, the Statue of Liberty stood, an empty symbol.

A little boy had a hard time holding on to his yarmulke, and the dad, with grace, put it in his pocket and pulled up the kid's hood.

Maybe these people are more chill than I thought, I mused.

I thought about my sexual entanglement. Yes, I wanted more than a hookup. I wanted a lover I could share my whispered commentary with, all the eye rolls, art-feasts, pizza-eating, and hidden knolls of softness beneath them, but as a trans person, the pieces came together in a different order. I was adult and undersexed at eighteen, without a trustworthy body, and so, at thirty, I had to run around playing sex games in a guest apartment.

As soon as the boat slowed near the old shipping warehouses, the yarmulke was pulled out and put straight back on the child's head.

Off the ferry gangplank, down some cobblestones, and in through the silent lobby. My dick was hard. In the haze of my desires, I barely noticed details, like the row of tiny desert-ready succulents on the front desk. I nodded at the doorman, who picked up the phone.

He spoke too softly for me to hear, but said something like "Your fuck buddy is here, miss."

The elevator's window panel stretched all the way from the lobby to the top of the building. I was lifted up, up, without any effort as the sun set over the East River. A wooden water tower stood on top of a brick building, a hut for a secret ceremony. Red Hook always appeared as a universe apart from the city, with its dappled cobblestones and the possibility of rough sex with a celebrity. *Is this enlightenment, to be carried up above material concerns, the trash on the sidewalk, the poor people who lived in Red Hook before it gained a giant furniture retailer and a good grocery store with 112 varietals of olive oil, and toward the sky?* I asked myself.

I didn't think so.

The door was propped open. She had the whole floor.

I lined up my shoes by her front door and left my backpack

on a hook, took out my dicks, and walked down the hallway in polka-dotted socks.

R's guest apartment was empty except for tower fans and wisps of furniture. The emptiness made the space even more lavish. I was used to seeing everyone's bikes, DFW novels, winter coats, unused exercise equipment, tropical house plants, possibly bedbug-ridden mannequins found in the street, amateur paintings of solar systems, cracked lime-green Le Creusets, comforters with jungle scenes, vats of protein powder, carafes from long-gone coffeemakers, wrong world maps, saucer chairs. The stuff devoured all the apartment air and did not recycle it, like trees.

Many times, I'd walked down the corridor thinking, *What if my life was like this apartment, airy, decluttered, one part leading to another instead of like my apartment, with everyone traipsing in and out of my room in thought and scent, a building staircase that smelled like dog piss, and, in the backyard, a tableau of trash blowing every which way?*

R did always have an assistant lurking around. Sometimes her PA was standing in the kitchen when I walked in for some seltzer.

Here's the thing about being heard as I fucked R or practiced deepening my voice in the bathroom: as a trans, I'd lived under constant self-surveillance, with my own questionably intelligent, vigorous eye keeping tabs on me. What did I care if an ex-high-school-newspaper editor in chief with a walkie-talkie saw me chopping a piece of ginger for R's butthole?

She was on the bed, drinking a bottle of juice in a sheer

shift that showed her nipples and the shadow of her pubic hair. Her blond hair was French-braided, reminding me of the time my guardian, Margot, took me to get my hair yanked into a complex design at a salon for my birthday, and the stylist pulled my scalp until I cried and Margot snapped, "Why are you always so sensitive, Penfield?" and I told myself that I would get revenge on her one day by bringing my sensitivity into the world as a gift instead of a liability.

In her bedroom, R kept an antique school desk with a shutting lid where I sometimes made her write lines like *I will keep the ginger in my butt until Daddy takes it out.*

The record player was playing Cat Stevens. I returned the needle to its stand. A white curtain blew out from the window.

In some normal intimate relation, I might have laid out my whole project of hexing Aiden and being summoned by the Operatrix and then feeling bad about everything, but I knew that all she wanted was for me to spank her in the shape of her dreams and then fuck her with my longest black dildo.

"Before I blindfold you, little girl, I want you to do something."

I pulled my T-shirt over my head and slid down my workwear-inspired pants and polka-dotted underwear. She wasn't blindfolded yet and I watched her watching me, becoming famous to myself by the sheer force of her celebrity.

"Daddy wants you to suck his dick."

Usually I waited until after punishing and fucking her to put my little dick in her mouth, but today was different.

We'd gone far enough that I didn't need to add, "If you

are comfortable doing this," because she could always mutter "Eagle" in a sarcastic way that I would later punish her for.

"Okay, Daddy."

"Get down on your knees."

The desire between us was solid. Furniture could be made out of it. We'd both carved fantasies for ourselves, and when we were together we stepped into them, one aspect of childhood I never thought would come true—that you could step inside a fantasy, not like at Disney World, where everyone exuberantly goes out of their way to create an illusion, but further, the taking away of illusion, the illusion that we were rational creatures, somehow above a dick in an ass, a slap of pleasure, long skeins of skin.

She started sucking and I grabbed her head and pulled it closer. She made a deep grunt of either pleasure or disgust. I had to remind myself that she enjoyed this, that I hadn't transformed into a cis-monster.

"Suck Daddy's cock, that's it." A drop of her pussy-wetness landed on my feet. "You're going to get another spanking for being so dirty while sucking Daddy's cock," I said.

She moaned and I pressed myself farther into her mouth, and the blow job was much better than when, before transitioning, I'd have partners suck my clit, the endless lesbian sex where one person did all the work, or both people were trying to please each other, and it always felt like a food co-op work schedule, from 4:00 to 4:05 Pen sucked Reed's clit, from 4:05 to 4:15 Pen used a dildo on her, from 4:15 to 4:20 Reed said, "Enough, can I do something for you," from 4:20 to 4:30 Pen pretended that Pen was not bored when Reed started licking all over Pen's body, thighs, shoulders, etc.

She bobbed her head back and forth without pausing for air, the way I'd trained her to.

"Stop, now."

I knew that if I came, I would lose all my energy and want to cuddle with her on the bed. She sat back on her knees.

"Good girl."

I went over to the wooden desk chair and sat down. I beckoned to her, and she stood before me, giving me the downcast look that she gave the principal in her movie about teenagers who slip onto a spaceship bound for Mars. I put the blindfold around her eyes and bent her over my knee. She was taller than I was, making our positioning a little awkward. I pulled up her shift and ran a finger along the outside of her pussy to feel how wet she was.

Very.

As I began spanking her, all my cares drifted away. The only thing happening was my hand hitting her flesh, her little cries that no longer worried me. I had even more of a boner than before.

You.

Hit.

Are.

Hit.

A.

Hit.

Very.

Hit.

Bad.

Hit.

Girl.

Hit.

All her endorphins entered me. She let go of the eyes watching her, the restraint, the careful affability required of female stars. She wanted to be dirty, wet, and bad. She went through a portal to the upside-down place of dire need: pink, soft, womb-like, pleasantly dangerous, and, most important, off any record.

Sure, I could have gained internet infamy if I posted a sexy photo of her, but I wanted to help her reach this place because I needed to reach it, too. Plus, I'd signed an NDA.

I told her to go stand with her hands on her head, and I went down the hall to the bathroom.

I watched myself reflected in windows thinking, *How many layers of complacency must we shed to get to the threshold of desire?*

Naked in R's hallway, I sensed how our relationship wasn't *supposed to happen* based on the conventions that we lived in and under; most of us really *weren't* supposed to be breaking through, and yet we did, through the constant reapplication of will, over and over again, even when it felt more wrong than right, when we worried that reality might start to splinter from all the pressure forced on it to shift, and it broke and mended, and with my 2.5 trans-eye, I knew that this was the only path, the yellow brick road away from shame and not toward any great thing except that which could be found along the way.

I peed, inhaled her Moroccan jasmine diffuser, and went

back into the bedroom, where R was touching her glowing butt cheeks. I reached back and smacked her ass.

"No, bad."

"Sorry!" she squealed. "I have to pee, too."

"Go. Do you need Daddy to go with you and wipe your pussy?"

"No, I can do it."

I picked the juice bottle off her nightstand, to see where it originated—not where the ingredients were grown (surely they were from California, picked by poorly paid migrant workers), but which juice store had she gone to.

Juicemania, made in Brooklyn, Fourth Street. Park Slope.

I used to check the labels on my teacher's cardigans when they were left on chairs to find out more clues about them: *Banana Republic, how very dignified.*

R came skipping back in, totally naked, her butt cheeks still red.

I pushed her against the bed with her ass facing out.

"Does my little girl want Daddy's cock in her naughty-hole?

She moaned. She often lost verbal ability when it came to anal and, guess what, I gained it!

I slipped the butt-cock, curved without a very bulbous head, through the hole in my dildo underwear.

"Okay princess, I'm going to go slow."

"Umph."

I filled her up and gave her ass a slap.

A question I used to ask myself: *What sort of pleasure could a trans experience using a silicone cock?*

What cis people don't know is that trans people often have

the same ludicrous questions about ourselves as you do, but are simply more motivated to deep inquiry. As I fucked her ass with a cock, our pleasures mingled. We were porous, and she was held and filled, and I was holding and filling, all against the thrill of play, not pornographic because we were in motion.

In R's apartment, I shuttered my doubts and textiles spooled from our bodies.

She came a few times and stretched out on the bed, not touching me.

"Pen, have you ever been in love?"

"I had a lover who tried to save me, back in the Midwest. He was already transitioning, and I was a young queer watching him change. Early one morning, he startled me as I was about to bite into some dry toast. I'd run out of butter and didn't want to use any of my roommate's because it would be hypocritical after leaving him notes about eating my cherry tomatoes and Nutella. This lover made me put down the toast while he went out and came back with European butter and an avocado from the Polish bodega. Margot, the aunt who took care of me, didn't even eat bread. She nibbled on seeds and nuts throughout the day and when I walked up the front stairs to our house, shells crunched under my feet, as if a flock of birds had been eating out of a feeder. But as much as this lover tried to teach me such essential acts as forming attachments and folding laundry, there remained the simple fact that I stopped being attracted to him once I made up my mind to transition. I'd needed him like a child needs its peasant-mother who made the frozen-slop-bucket mornings warm with her breast."

"Jesus," she said, with pity.

"A better question would be: Pen, will you fall in love with someone once you can strain out the sludge from your dignity? And the answer is yes."

"Okay, Daddy," she said, to quiet me.

She hadn't wanted a detailed answer, and I didn't ask her about half-formed attachments to beards, illicit girlfriends, strangers. I could have checked the tabloids to find out.

As she walked me to the door, I said, "By the way, I'll be out of town next week," which wasn't strictly necessary, as we didn't fuck regularly.

Still, she was always the one leaving, and I thought it might make me seem more desirable to be less available.

"K," was her only response. Somewhere in the grand equation of love was curiosity, and she had zero interest in my mission to retrieve Blithe.

Her driver picked me up in the building garage. I always forgot to ask if I was supposed to tip. R would take care of it. In the driver's seat of his hybrid, he was too professional for me to read any of his feelings.

I walked into my apartment, bracing for weed-smell and potions and takeout splatters. There was a column of banker's boxes stacked in the kitchen.

I took the top off one and started grazing Blithe's data. The idiot must have been so despondent, he'd given the Rhiz access to *everything*. We're talking inside-of-bathroom-trash-can (some pieces of gum and, eek, a plastic water bottle), complete bioaffective feed, and certain measurements so finely graded as to be beyond human comprehension. I got overwhelmed by the accounting required, and went to sleep.

The next morning, I was out in the backyard when my phone hummed. The screen turned white, and I could either accept the Operatrix's transmission or decline it by pressing the Rhiz button.

Declining a transmission was generally a bad idea. I accepted, the air crackled, my phone's projector lifted up, and there was the Operatrix again.

"Pen, this is not the way to go about things. You have five days to write a narrative report and figure out who Blithe is. I know you've learned something about discipline from your day job."

The Operatrix said *day job* to flatter me, as if I were meant for greater things.

"Yeah, how to untangle harnesses and distinguish inside and building keys."

"We don't have time for your self-denigration."

Touché.

"We will send over the plane tickets tomorrow."

"K. But how does anyone learn about another? You must know that my parents are dead and that I lack essential bonding skills."

"Start with the first box. Boi, bye. And check your entryway for a package."

I went to the "lobby" between the building's front door and interior door, where people often discarded objects before moving out, which the super then had to throw away. A messenger had left me an almost-weightless keyboard in a normative manila envelope with a breezy green seal.

I started again, from the beginning. My insides were disorganized, so logical, linear notions, such as starting with number one and working my way forward, did not often occur to me.

BOX 1: BACKGROUND

The Rhiz had provided a lengthy background report on Blithe, which bored me. Socioeconomic status, blood type, college course list, favorite fruits, all the things you could find out about a person doing a social-justice-oriented ice-breaker. I skipped to the photos of his apartment: clean, understated, covered in weavings and climbing plants. I wasn't yet sure if I hated him. I smelled a cologne sample, floral and mossy, and I wanted to press my cheek against his.

Typical trans behavior: hate, longing, and over-intimacy.

As I gorged on Blithe, time was kinder and slower.

BOX 2: HEX-RELATED DATA

I pulled out a spongy ball, and dropped it. *Shitifical sawhorses of Schneidhorst!* A Bio-meter. I thought about all the activists who kept phones in their unused microwaves to avoid surveillance. How could I keep myself safe from emotional detection?

TBH, I was honored that they had entrusted me with an actual Bio-meter, even if it scared the hell out of me. The balls measured affect through contact with the skin or, in the case of those with Rhiz implants like Blithe, from aggregating pupil dilation, skin conductance, brain activity, heart rate, and facial movement. The labs were still working to expand both methods to include the aural composite, a person's most essential state of being, but they were always running out of funding.

TBRH, reading the Bio-meter was an imperfect art. I took off its regenerative shell (which was rumored to be made out of artificially engineered collagen) and spun the time-dial to March 10, twelve days before the hex, so I could get a sense of Blithe's baseline. The ball changed shade as the day moved from morning to night. I paused it to check the Bio-chart, which was artificially intelligent.

The Bio-chart read 8:00 a.m.'s plain orange as "exercise high" and 9:00 a.m.'s lime green as "object (person)–centered frustration" and 2:00 p.m.'s dark fuchsia as "dangerous American nostalgia." Blithe, subject to "languorous indifference," "gay frustration," and "under-justified career pride," was nothing like me. I read him like some exotic novel, thirsty for the feelings of others.

I set the Bio-meter to March 22, the day of the hex. It glowed black like a menacing night sky. The ball started to shake, and the chart, instead of naming cute and specific feelings, read only: LACK.

My nervous system started acting up. My ex, in moments of frustration, used to send me articles about attachment theory, and at night in bed he would read to me about Kristeva and lack and the doldrums of toddlers. Somehow, he thought that he could cure me, and bring me closer, by teaching me about the various expanses between parents and their children.

I didn't need theory; I needed them undead.

I turned the machine off and ate a simple lunch of crackers, Lebanese hummus with cilantro, and beet spread and went to the backyard to do some breathing exercises. The Witch was out at her temp job, but she had left something burning at her altar, which I always warned her against.

In the yard, the leaves rustled. I breathed slowly to remind myself that temporality was curved and only experienced through the body's folds.

I went back to work. I zipped the Bio-meter into its regenerative pouch and turned my attention to simpler questions, like Blithe's physical location. I consulted pages of GPS coordinates.

As I followed him down I-10W, I heard a knock at the door. A Rhiz messenger left a normative manila envelope with no seal at the door. I opened it.

A plane ticket to the other coast.

I walked a few dogs, and then Minna came over. She was wearing a thrift-store cardigan, expensive jeans, and a silk scarf. I occasionally envied the fact that she could keep the same clothes from 201–, and never had to undergo radical appearance changes. She was thin, Russo-Japanese, and every day she seemed more beautiful in her new understanding of the world.

We met because I was late one day picking up her dog for

a walk. She was getting her clinical psychology doctorate and had a special fellowship from the Future Business School. FBS's advanced monitoring technology indicated that, in the near future, the elite would confiscate most of the available wealth and the middle class would need to accumulate something else aside from capital. The FBS anthro department had been tasked with figuring out if total well-being was a viable alternative to endless toil for the pursuit of money and professional achievement.

Every year, they chose one student in each discipline as an FBS fellow, who did not have to fulfill any academic requirements. The fellow did have to rigorously meditate, collaborate with a spiritual guide, and spend at least two hours a day on food preparation and consumption. They could use the rest of their time in any way they wanted, as long as it benefited their "wholeness."

Because she was a fellow, Minna didn't go to class very often and rarely needed a walker for her French bulldog, Olivia. Early on in our friendship, her grandmother was dying, and I kept Olivia at my place while she went to Japan. She said my texts of Olivia swinging in my hammock, wearing a judge's bonnet, and eating doggie ice cream really helped.

In the kitchen, the Witch had a cauldron of bones simmering. Minna always enjoyed my roommates' eccentricities, having a more removed perspective.

"You're not going to believe what I did the other day," I told her as we sat on the couch with the TV screen pulled up.

I explained all about the hex and the boxes and the quest

to retrieve Blithe from the Shadowlands but left out the spiraling.

"OMG, Pen! You are too much," she said.

"Tell your sister to tell the Rhiz to go easy on me!"

She laughed and grabbed her phone to open the Gram. I still hadn't had the guts to check if Aiden erased my image.

"It's still there. Along with a new selfie of Aiden drinking crystal juice. The caption reads, 'Sorry a disgruntled bro threw off my vibe. Sending him muscular love + light.' LOL, you're internet-famous."

"Ugh, in some sneaky, roundabout way."

"I can see you have a handful of new followers. One is T4THotDick5."

I could have used more encouragement from her, but all the mind-cleansing had dulled her short-term gratification impulses and she was not overly invested in the sugary buzz of little hearts dancing on a screen.

"I feel great about the Gram part, but I probably need to read that lovingkindness book you're always thrusting upon me. Trying to send someone to their psychic doom, even someone as obnoxious as Aiden, is pretty harsh."

She pulled in her lips to give me a semi-reproving smile.

We always watched TV from several years ago, before VR and immersion add-ons. On the screen, a Korean nun made pickled lotus root, shiitake mushrooms in century-old soy sauce, piles of noodles, tiny colored vegetable pearls on bamboo stalks, and we were both dying with glee—I because this woman broke all the rules, creating wonder against the backdrop of blowing leaves, buried earthen kimchi jars, and low morning prayers, and Minna because the nun's constantly joyful face, body, and soul were apparent across the various distances between her and us.

Until, of course, the *NYT* food reviewer popped up, ruining all the vibes.

"Why do the show's creators think that we need a dude's narration in order to appreciate this amazing chef who appears to live blissfully in harmony with herself, fellow nuns, the wild garden she tends, the memory of her parents, and her students in Seoul, who bow to her?" I said to Minna, clutching a throw pillow with stars on it.

"Yeah, will we ever be the people that someone makes something for?"

"We are the people making things for ourselves. Well, I will be, once I stop fucking around, and you are working on creating inner harmony that is necessary for anything to not be fragile, on the verge of breaking."

The food reviewer kept reappearing, to explain:

—How the nun's food compared to that of all the great chefs at The French Laundry and Ottomnul.

—How he wanted to "down" her enlightenment lotus-blossom tea.

—How the nun had grabbed his arm on the bridge and said the single word *orchestra* in English (which had apparently changed his entire life, but not too much because he still maintained the appearance of an arrogant doofus who would spend an entire date describing how the chef at The

Blue Window gifted ostrich eggs to him after he'd helped introduce the general public to the art of dipping butter on a bronzed spoon into coffee, the way the tradition was practiced in rural Ireland).

Mansplaining went right along with chefdom, and lacked the rigor of a fricassee, jus lié, or vol-au-vent.

On the screen, the nun was a bowl filling and emptying. She had a self, but the self seemed harmoniously folded into her surroundings. There was no grasping, no bitterness, no regret, no impatience as she turned the fermented beans that would not be ready for another forty days.

Yes, I still longed to be a lesbian separatist nun, pressing my face to ancient stone floors instead of facing subway riders who didn't even want to kill me for being trans in public because they hadn't yet looked up from their phones.

A few minutes later, the nun was going into Seoul on a subway train. Hah. So she wasn't a complete purist. I was thinking about the prospect of *letting myself be* when there was another knock on the door. I didn't answer at first because I figured it was another Rhiz messenger. The knocks turned to pounding.

I went to the door, and there was Aiden. I made a sweeping gesture to welcome him into my apartment. I believe he subtly grimaced at the bone-scent.

"First of all," he said, his voice squeaking with anger, "don't ever fuck with my Gram again. It's my sacred space and you defiled it. Second, your hex didn't work on me because I've already been through the Shadowlands."

My mouth opened. "Are you serious? But you walk around drinking crystal juice all day."

What I really wanted to ask was, *Where are they? Didn't the Shadowlands leave an imprint on your person? Did anyone ever really get out?*

"You don't know shit about me."

I didn't know shit about him, and yet I wanted to dive into it. That was my job, after all, handling dog shit so that other people could go to work or travel.

"I would try to sabotage you less if I knew more about your smelly parts." That came out cruder than I wanted. Or exactly right.

He scoffed.

"Hey, I'm Minna," Minna said from the other room.

Aiden crossed from the kitchen into the living room to extend his hand. He was trying to play the "good guy." He walked back over to me, only a few steps in our tiny apartment.

"The Operatrix told me what you did," he said.

"Yes, and now Blithe needs our help," I replied.

"I find you sketchy as hell, but we need to get the narrative report going. I started a rough draft."

"I thought you wanted to drench me in muscular love and light?"

He laughed. "That's Gram-Aiden."

He was a sophisticate.

He handed me his pad. He'd made a text box for each day and started organizing a timeline of events correlated to Blithe's feelings and substances and receipts.

This went on and on, hour by hour.

"Um, this is not a narrative. This is organized data, but it's not a narrative. The Rhiz needs to know that we see Blithe as a full person. Didn't you read the zine?" I stopped myself from saying, *I would go to the Shadowlands again if this was how my life was narrated.*

He shrugged.

I fumbled in one of the boxes and pulled out the slim, stapled document.

"A narrative is a river and the data points are molecules that make up the water. A narrative is a living body. A narrative is a—"

"Okay, okay, well, this is just a start," he said, his cheeks reddening.

"You know what," I said graciously. "The only way this is going to work is if we lean into our strengths. I'll write the narrative report, and you can do the car rental and maybe find us some desert attire."

"All right, sounds good." He turned toward the door.

"You want to watch *Chef's Table* with us to continue the team-building vibes?" Minna asked.

"K," he said, smiling at her.

Minna scooted over on the short couch, and Aiden sat, blessing us with his dense, smoky scent. He was too close for me to soak in his full appearance, but I relished the clean fade of his haircut as he bent over his messenger bag.

Dashes of darling Demonides! I'd always assumed Minna was "straight-straight," but here was Aiden, performing a decent-enough masculinity that she leaned toward him on the couch as the next chef, an egoic Russian, whipped up moose-lip dumplings.

Minna and Aiden left together. I figured he was less likely to hate me if he was crushing on my friend. I lit a Bohemian Woods–scented candle, and as the Bio-meter charged in its skin, I tried to parse Blithe's gut data, because he'd signed up for one of those services to read his insides. The Rhiz had forgotten to include the analysis, and I scrolled through the universe inside his stomach, understanding nothing.

I went back to the zine article "How to Guide a Loved One Through the Shadowlands: Building a Narrative," trying to cleanse my brain with its delightful and impractical use of metaphor.

After a while, I threw it down, got a seltzer, and opened Box 3: Pre-Hex Data.

March 10 was a typical workday for Blithe. He was a writer at Elemental, whose studio head eschewed adv-tech and was known for unorthodox views about creation. Elemental was funded by a group of start-ups, and the team could make whatever "content" they desired without much worry over advertising.

I felt a quiet rustle of jealousy as I read through Blithe's wild ideas for the show's pilot. His character, Margaret, was fleeing into the Sonoran Desert with one of the eight stolen gems of Catalpa. People from multiple dimensions were hunting her.

But as I made my way through Blithe's life, I was held in by something other than my own sadness or seeking. I'd never been good at school, tho I did enjoy the structure of the day, being industrious for little pockets of time until I had to go home and make a snack in the empty house.

It's nice to do group work again, I told myself.

Using the Rhiz's special keyboard, which allowed one to type directly onto paper, I began turning Blithe into a person.

NARRATIVE REPORT:
BLITHE FREEMAN

He woke up to the gentle chimes of his phone. Sunlight poured through sheer white curtains. He stretched and got out of bed. He peed and laid out a yoga mat in the living room. He rolled his shoulders, released tension from his lower back, and did a twenty-minute core workout.

After moving his body, Blithe was opened, buzzing with life. He made a smoothie with tangerines from his neighbor's tree, adding holy basil leaves.

As soon as Saul texted, Blithe lost his glow.

"Hey, babe, I just want to let you know that we'll process this and figure it out."

Saul, his boyfriend, wanted them to experiment with opening up the relationship. The idea of snuggly, curly-haired Saul sleeping with someone else made Blithe feel like he would disintegrate, vanish entirely. Most L.A. gays accepted the narrative that they were hard-wired to be non-monogamous. At a recent dinner party, their friend Fain had brought up an article that proved men's "need to procreate diversely." People could use science to justify anything: that gays were an evolutionary abomination, that even in gay couples there had to be a "masculine" and "feminine" role, etc. Saul was not a typical L.A. gay. In fact, Saul wanted to open up the relationship and experiment with sleeping with female-identified folks, which made matters even worse.

Blithe put the phone down and tried to ground himself by walking through his apartment, passing the palm tree in its bone planter, the guest nook with its clean white-and-navy-striped sheets, the living room window facing out into the unchanging pale blue sky. At least he had the escape of work, where he could engineer stories and intrigue without going below the surface.

On his way to Elemental, Blithe played through his Line. To him, adulthood was a threshold crossed only when one submitted to the boredom of external circumstances.

So he was still a kid.

His latest project was set in the Sonoran Desert. He

took the landscape and made it into a balm, a poultice of smoky nights and elaborate self-defense mechanisms.

"Margaret has just stolen into the mine at night, and with a sputtering lantern, she chisels the gem out of the place her husband marked with chalk. Her hands shake, and she flashes back to the marauders coming into their house, lighting it ablaze, taking her husband off to the Edge of Pines. Her husband followed their plan, submitting to light torture until he told his abductors the location of the counterfeit gem, and still, they killed him."

Plenty of room for a revenge plot.

"And with the gem glowing dimly in a burlap sack, she's about to cut her hair off, dress as a ranch hand, and head into the Sonoran to meet with the Guide, who will help her to the next step.

"Only, a hooded figure with a long spyglass starts following her at Las Cruces."

He had work to do. On the Elemental Chart of Episodic Thrill, he needed to build the Arrow-Line to its Crux of Sensation Overload.

As far as storytelling, he could always count on a reservoir of confidence, a sort of rightness in his bones. When he looked at colleagues who spoke tentatively or people ahead of him in line at the café ordering with shaky voices, he tried to measure the amber liquid inside. *Could it ever run out?* he started asking himself, as he aged from a solid 28 years to 28.5.

The car ahead of him was from Maine.

"Storyboard homo whaling expeditions for another Catalpa realm," he told his phone, and his phone listened.

The studio had already started on:

Margaret, the mine worker's wife who escapes to the Sonoran in the 1890s

The Afro-futurist beekeeper

The 1980s South Korean skin diver

The Egyptian freedom fighter

A child from outer space

And the whole staff was randomly generating a list of possibilities for the last three lines.

Among his TV peers, Blithe conceptualized the creation process in an old-school way. Most of the writers had simply grown up watching enough television that they internalized the procedural aspects of plot and, beyond that, relied on teamwork and improvisation. Blithe's parents had banned TV, so he'd spent childhood reading books and doing nothing but painting pictures in his head: a lost, underground people who see with their noses, billions of miles of invisible orange film connecting everyone's buttholes, runes explaining how sharks are really the most compassionate of species.

He was a lonely and not lonely child.

Each primary writer on the Catalpa team was responsible for one line, with the beta writers fitting them together with enough loud action at the beginning and end to hold viewers. Marcus, the Guardian of Lines, told Blithe he was sure the show would go violet.

"It has this dark, juicy overabundance that everyone wants to guzzle," he'd said over video chat while he was working out with his trainer.

Blithe parked and entered the building through a set of mirrored doors, pausing to take off his sunglasses.

There was no line at the café. Everyone at Elemental could come in between 9:00 and 11:00 a.m. and work two days a week from home. Darryl, the barista, was a former C-list actor. He stirred the threat of downward mobility into every corn-milk latte. That morning, he was smiling in his black apron and unnecessary name tag. Not many could withstand the smugness of people who worked above the fifth floor; Darryl held a secret balm for a dreamy present. He had even thrown in some ideas for a Line about a wise Ethiopian coffee farmer who fled to Addis Ababa from the highlands in World War II. As he foamed Blithe's milk and then poured it up to the rim of the cup, his eyes were on the frothing. He placed Blithe's latte before him without bitterness.

Blithe always thought of Darryl as a contemporary manifestation of the Buddha, free of ego.

With coffee in hand, Blithe got on the elevator to the tenth floor, nodded to some of the beta writers, checked to see if Marcus was in yet (he wasn't), and settled into the room with a wall-sized screen. He needed inspiration.

He turned on the aromatherapy jets and leaned back against the massage pillow. He pulled up wild horses, Hemingway at a Desk Overlooking the Azure Sea, obelisks, a jungle rustling at night—and still his biodata didn't spike to the crest of exhilaration. He went to the bathroom, then got another shot from Darryl, went to the eleventh floor, and entered The Fort, a series of whimsical soundproofed cubbies that str8 people were always screwing in.

He found an unoccupied nook where he could curl up on a windowsill and look idly out over the back lot, while dreaming of his Arrow-Line.

Here comes Margaret riding into the Sonoran dressed as a man, in a hat and chaps and a suede vest.

He made a note to research hat shapes of the 1890s. That was the key to fantasy, Marcus said. As long as you assembled enough of a solid foundation for the mind to relinquish control, you could take people anywhere.

She would fall for an engineer measuring the Salton Sea levels, but as a man or as a woman?

Saguaro, boojum, javelina, he typed, to invoke the place.

His pad was set to private, so he did not receive input from the beta writers.

Traipsing through the thick marshes of his mind, he didn't want to deal with the betas' quotidian concerns about continuity, convolution, and plausibility.

Someone has lit a woodstove. The crack of a whip, or gun, echoes in the distance. She will find an abandoned cabin, bury the gem behind a loose brick inside the chimney, sleep with a knife in her hand, and dream of the Eight Gems of Catalpa.

The rough trailer opens in a dazzling pan across

the 1890s Sonoran, an Afro-futurist eco-civilization in 2100, a 1980s South Korean coastal city, the markets of 1919 Cairo, and an undated empty space galaxy with a single child in a spaceship.

The narration begins. "Eight gems have been scattered across time and space. If all eight are unearthed and returned back to their settings on an ancient wall, the goddess Oshun will return to heal the world."

Of course, treachery is more entertaining than the repair of the world, and so the show opens as Lucretine, a time-traveling seductress and thief, gathers an army to steal all the gems, melt them into primordial power, and re-create the world in her own image.

Blithe put down his pad and crawled out of his nook. Stretched. His colleague Cooper hadn't closed his nook-shade. Blithe watched him watching something on his pad. He used his key card to open a door to a deserted balcony and then shivered, thinking of the bulge between the two legs of the engineer's leather chaps.

How can Margaret take off her cowboy hat and reveal herself?

If only I could distill and market the wild bursts inside of me when Margaret throws her cowboy hat off at high speed and stops her horse and the engineer jumps off his and lifts Margaret out of the saddle and sets her down on the dry earth, and she turns and says, Not so fast. I may not be an errant ranch hand, but you better back off if you want to romance me, *the world would be a better place.*

Marcus came out, wearing his headpiece. He gave Blithe a slight nod, but Blithe was really inside himself. His biodata had shifted from anxious scanning to blissful immersion.

Blithe paused to get cafeteria sushi and to tell his division's assistant what to research. Passing the fountain in the atrium, he pushed away thoughts about the state's drought.

Keep your eyes not on what's in front of you, but on the oceans within, he chanted to himself a few times. It worked well enough. He ran his hands down the cool chino of his pants.

He sat down with a juice and some cucumber sushi at a far table overlooking the hills. There was too much haze for a good view, so he made up his own.

Birds of paradise slipping through glades; the eternal juiciness of life here on earth.

He thought about plopping down some sort of marketplace in the Sonoran, so that Margaret could run her hands over fruits and rugs and spice piles. A general store about thirty miles northwest of the sea—a day's ride—would have to do.

He skipped the producer's status meeting to keep feeding the beast. He felt rugged and drowsy. A voicemail message from Saul popped up. He listened to his boyfriend's sweet voice coming at him from far away. Still, he did not respond.

Cooper was also skipping the meeting and sat on his mobile desk throwing orange peels at the trash can. He paused to adjust the collar of his Oxford. He'd married rich, and Blithe could see that the partnering had created an invisible noose around Cooper's neck that he was always trying to loosen. "Hey, dude. Guess who's in the conference room?"

Blithe tried to create a wall of calming energy around him. "Who?"

"Rachel fucking Remedios." In his excitement, Cooper slam-dunked the skinned orange. "Shit," he said, and took it out of the trash, wiped it off with a paper towel.

A shiver of before. Rachel Remedios was part of a tacky, early-aughts rom-com quilt that taught everyone what normal was supposed to look like.

"Is she here for Catalpa?"

"Dunno. But that doesn't bode well for our Violet-izing chances if they're fishing in that pond."

Why did Cooper have to take the studio's lingo and make it even worse?

Blithe hoped Rachel didn't get anywhere near Margaret's character. She was too facile. Still, it would be a cool to tell age-thirteen Blithe, "Well, look at me now, on the same floor of Elemental Studios as Rachel Remedios."

He caught sight of his cuffed workman's chinos landing an inch above his chukka boots. *How far I've come*, he thought.

"You're not at the meeting," Blithe posed, pre-empting Cooper from saying the same thing.

"Nah, got some shit to do, don't need Marcus lecturing me on fantasy this particular little afternoon."

"True that," Blithe said, although he loved the lectures. He just didn't want to sully his ideas by having to present them to producers. Not while they were in their tender phase.

"Gotta get back to it," he told Cooper, before spending the next hour watching videos of galloping horses and wishing he were out in the smoke-filled night, at the edge of the frontier, in another, simpler time.

When he finished "working," Blithe sat in his car and called Saul. He said he was feeling lost.

~PAUSE IN NARRATIVE REPORT~

I marveled at this ability to simply state one's complex feelings to a partner without hiding them.

~NARRATIVE REPORT CONTINUED~

A few days later, Blithe was getting ready to head over to his childhood home for Sunday lunch. His phone echoed violin notes through the silent condo. He picked it up off his tan couch, where he'd fallen asleep the night before, dreaming of soft vines growing out of the ocean and crawling up the balconies toward his condo. It was Saul.

"Hey, babe."

"What are you up to today?"

He walked over to the wall tapestry that his parents brought him from Morocco, tracing the curves with his eyes.

"Not much. I have to finish up the Arrow-Line for pre-auditions next week."

"Can't you just call it a pilot? We've talked about this. I don't speak Elemental."

Elemental Studio's quirky vocabulary matched its desire to evade some of the stock features of the industry.

"Okay, sorry."

"I'm calling to see if you wanted to take a roller-blading break a little later?"

"Oh, I'm going over to my parents' house. They just got back from Rome."

A pause as Saul waited to be invited.

"Want to come with me?"

"Actually, I have brunch plans."

"Oh, okay."

Blithe made sure to sound disappointed, even though he wanted his parents to himself for the afternoon.

Outside, the palms swayed.

Blithe pulled up to the two-story stucco house shaded by acacia trees. He considered sleeping there that night, full-on digging into a cavern of parental comfort. He got out of the car and for moment forgot how much he'd wanted to leave this house, how it always seemed embarrassingly small in comparison to the Thousand Oak manses with their pool houses and meditation gardens.

He could smell sun on asphalt, dryer sheets tumbling nearby, mystical, opening the threshold to the past that came before the Before—a time when discomfort did not have a clear and fixable label.

He defined this stage of his life as "Post-transition" and he occasionally sensed that the seam was about to split, flooding him with everything he had cut off. He built higher walls and deeper holes, mine shafts, sparkling lakes, tiny cottages with underground escape routes, chalets, so many spaces to stash himself. When his thoughts approached the "Before-edge," a shiver of despair shocked them back and there was nothing like work to remind him that he was thriving, with insides more textured than the succulent terrariums popping up in every coffee shop with their burro's tails and cactus flowers, screaming about how much could bloom in brittle conditions.

He walked along the stepping-stones. Inside, the house was still, clean, polished, resounding. He took off his shoes, frowned at the large Chinese floor vase where the Eighteen Luohan were depicted up on a perilous cliff. In the front hall he ignored the table of family photographs and made his way along a "Persian" rug, which seemed dangerously close to generic "Oriental." He found them out on the patio, cutting vegetables.

"Hi, parents."

"Hey, honey."

His mom got up and kissed the top of his head. His dad put a hand on his shoulder.

They looked more worn than he would like, his mom especially. She appeared to be shrinking into her formless flax clothes. He almost wished she would do Botox or something so he wouldn't have to confront the aging process. Were they stressed about something or just old?

"Saul isn't coming?"

"No, he had plans."

"Want some seltzer or wine or something?"

"Yah, sure, I'll get it."

He grabbed a seltzer and did his quick snooping, looking through their mail, scanning their to-do lists, just making sure everything was in order, that no one had any urgent doctor's appointments.

Back outside, the sun rested above his parents' heads.

"How was your trip?"

"Fabulous. Have you looked over the pictures we sent?" his mom asked.

He had not.

"We ended up at these ruins with this couple we met at our hotel and had the most delicious cold spread of cheese and bread and olives. I mean, it was the simplest, purest food. You could actually taste the care that they put into it."

He watched his father nod at her description.

His mom started in on the artisanal cheese from goats who grazed on Greek spiny spurge, juniper, rosemary, and Aphyllanthes.

"Wow, wonder what sort of notes that diet produced." He did love geeking out on food with his parents.

"Bri—Blithe, we got you something," she said.

She went into the kitchen and came back with a brown paper bag. Inside, an unlabeled green bottle. Ancient olive oil.

"Thanks, you guys. I can use it in the lemon olive oil cake that I'm trying to perfect."

They all sat down and ate cold spread reminiscent of the parents' Roman meals. His mom had bought organic roses to top the mascarpone.

He glimpsed the three of them through the sliding glass door, the two parents browned but still white, their adopted son who neither tanned nor came from a place where they ate dairy from goats, cows, or sheep.

~PAUSE IN NARRATIVE REPORT~

This part was difficult. The Bio-meter vacillated from scarlet (original shame) to waxy blue (racial self-hatred) to a purple so dark it was almost black (lack that has been held back only by social situations). As I was thinking about Blithe's story, I realized I knew absolutely nothing about transracial adoption or being trans and transracially adopted.

~NARRATIVE REPORT CONTINUED~

"Is something wrong, hon?" his dad asked over coffee.

He stopped himself from asking if *hon* was really the word his dad would be using with a *normal* twenty-eight-year-old boy.

"No, I'm just tired, working a lot."

He wanted them to ask about his Line so he could feel like he had something to offer. They did not.

The pool shimmered. He'd longed to swim while they were away but hadn't want to email them to ask how to turn on the heater. Anyway, he figured it would be disenchanted without their presence.

It was too late to start asking them about the heater, but he could float on a raft.

"You know, in my retirement I'm just now noticing how important it is to tune out, chew the rose petals, enjoy these little things, like being with your loved ones," his dad said, and took his mom's hand.

"Um, thanks, Dad, okay. I'm going to go change and then float on the unicorn."

"You're going to have to blow it back up," his mom said.

Blithe pushed his chair in, and her glance reminded him to take his plate inside, even though he was a guest.

His parents' pool was the secret to his professional success. In the untreated salt water, he regressed into a state of wonder, contingent on his parents poking their heads out between the sliding door to ask if he wanted a seltzer, some nuts, to go out to dinner.

Wearing new red trunks, he jumped onto the unicorn's back, sending big waves toward the edges of the pool. Against the clang of his mom loading the dishwasher, he started nesting in his own colorful insides, away from the banal chatter of the world. He crossed a bridge into another world, full of hoofbeats and ridges and dragon's breath.

He pictured himself walking into the conference room with its long holographic table, clutching his light blue portfolio, knowing his new Arrow-Line would be called *kickass* and *fucking the shit* by his boss's boss, whose most notable skill was grape-skinning at cocktail parties.

Where do you come up with this stuff? his boss's boss would ask in this fantasy, and he'd shrug and blush. The mind-altering delights of a swimming pool was hardly his most shameful secret, but still, he wouldn't want to reveal his process.

It was not hot enough for him to forget his body, but he dozed off about a foot above the water, drifting slowly, almost touching the exuberant part of himself.

"Blithe?" his mom called. He started, waking up. It was chilly.

"Hon, some people are coming over soon. You're welcome to stay."

"New or old friends?"

"A mixture."

"That's all right. I have a lot of work to do," he said, and his voice sounded whiny, betraying him.

"Okay, sweetheart. Well, you better get dried off."

He changed, accepted a Tupperware of pasta. Outside, Blithe longed for Saul to hug him and remind him that he was an adult, a successful one. He dialed the number on the car screen. Saul's voicemail picked up, but Blithe couldn't bring himself to narrate loneliness from the inside of his car.

Back in his silent condo, Blithe sprawled out on the couch with his phone. He opened the Gram. The Gram made him feel competitive; it made him want to sculpt his life into its best possible version; it made him want to kill himself. He devoured scenes of palm trees and Sunday glasses of wine and annoying children and Incan ruins. He got to the dude who took daily self-portraits around L.A. with captions about self-love, authenticity, nurturing, forgiveness, evolution.

Aiden lounged in a hanging egg chair, shirtless. His ab muscles looked like six perfect sweet rolls rising out of his stomach, and his tattoo, BE TRUE, was annoying. A row of miniature succulents basked on the table next to him.

The photo was taken hours ago, so there weren't enough current viewers to trigger hologram-tech and bring Aiden's bod into Blithe's living room, with its antique kilim rug, bamboo stalks, and unused kitchen table.

Blithe touched his own hard stomach. He wasn't sure whether he wanted to fuck Aiden or be Aiden, or savor the slippage between the two desires, another flummoxing part of the city-elite gay lifestyle.

He jerked off to Aiden's torso, and then it was time to put the phone in airplane mode, open a bottle of wine, defrost a crawfish étouffée he'd frozen the other night, and turn on the internet-television for another lusty sequence of images. Blithe wanted Saul to signal that he was thinking of him without any actual interaction. He wanted to coast, partnered yet safe inside his fantasy world. Saul did not reach out. Before getting into bed, Blithe wrapped himself in his horseradish cashmere blanket.

How lucky we are, he said to himself.

~PAUSE IN NARRATIVE REPORT~

I flipped through another workweek, a blur of imaginings, meetings, and a brief attempt at sex with Saul, which ended when Blithe started to imagine his partner sleeping with a mousy white woman. And then I opened the Hex box.

~NARRATIVE REPORT CONTINUED~

Blithe woke up restless at 5:00 a.m., made his smoothie and his coffee. He meditated and then sat on the couch, scrolling through the Gram. When he got to Aiden's image, there was a scraggly aloe plant instead of a beautiful body. The caption bewildered him, and when he clicked on @fieldsofpen, he was taken to a page of aloe portraits and a locker-room selfie, a bunch of dogs. Nothing held his attention.

He got in the shower, and as he was scrubbing himself with eucalyptus wash, he felt unreal, like the arm he was looking at didn't belong to him. He'd been mildly dissociated his whole life, but this was different, because he was turning away from himself and some-how toward himself.

He did not want to take deep breaths or "process."

He needed to go.

Blithe filled a weekender bag and drove out of the city under a rose-fingered sky. Turning onto CA-62W, he briefly thought about the logistics of his abrupt de-parture, but he was always leaving people in one form or another. He could smooth things over with the stu-dio if he explained his trip as "last-minute research" and his parents—well, they had just been on their own jaunt.

Once he started losing service, the morning thickened.

He passed small sun-bleached towns of misery with missing letters on their church signs and fast-food restaurants. The desert began, cut with telephone lines, wind turbines, and unfinished pueblo houses.

He stopped at a gas station to get a seltzer. He loved the rural-urban interplay, the ringing bell of the gas station door. He could see his own desirability and elite status when the young blond cashier with tanned forearms bagged his wet drink and said, "That all, boss?"

He pictured himself gliding through the morning desert, without his boyfriend knowing his whereabouts, his charisma at a level where he could seduce a desert gas station attendant without fear of reprisal.

"Yeah, but take that out of the bag."

Blithe headed toward Joshua Tree, even though he and Saul gently mocked their friends who spent days realigning in the Integratron or building solar ovens for Bequinox. After about two hours, the road started appearing too close to the windshield. He pulled over clear his head. He stepped outside of the car and smelled the most delicious burning. Blithe had always thought of the desert as annoyingly sparse. He was wrong. It wasn't sparse but clear, as clear as a blade coming down. He was bottoming for the desert and wished he could lean against the hood of the car and pull down his pants to let it all the way in, without fear of poisonous creatures or crazed folk who might confuse his gesture.

He walked away from the road, stopping at a flowering crown-of-thorns cactus, and as he looked down at the delicate pink flowers, his entire girlhood came crashing through his body. He closed his eyes in pain and knelt down on the ground. He was an agave plant. Spiky *pencas* were removed to reveal the *piña*, the heart. Then this squash-shaped vessel was sliced open and its nectar poured into the crack.

He tried to steady his breath, think of his parents' pool, the smooth flow of confidence, the cashier's belt buckle, his own imaginative genius, but comforts were dried leaves blowing away.

Down, down, down, he went.

~PAUSE IN NARRATIVE REPORT~

The bio-affect readings stopped right at Blithe's submergence in the Shadowlands. We were so different, but I knew exactly how it felt: the terror and, beyond the terror, the need to touch the terror and pass through it; the rigid compression of feelings that were too much for a body in a single moment in time; and the beginning of a wild substance with its own laws and its own will. Sitting in my bedroom, with the Bio-meter turned to its black LACK, I wanted to send a feeling directly to Blithe, a feeling big enough to hold the desert and its strange bloomings.

He walked down the shoulder of highway and every orange streak across the sky blinked at his new form, following him to the entrance of the park, and the signs, yellow lettering on brown wood, were not calming.

He fell deeper and deeper toward the wet dark place, which demanded visitation after his long abandonment. The oncoming night was full of coyotes and scorpions, but this didn't stop him from undressing to his briefs and T-shirt. His insides were writing their own Line, obeying a logic that was not subject to the usual cloying restrictions.

Rita found him in the morning, about an hour into the Lost Horse Mine Trail, arms and legs outstretched, as if posing in some durational performance. He was naked, with two scorpions resting on his chest.

His eyes were open.

Slowly, he gestured from the top of his chest across his abdomen and down to his pubic hair, now public.

"Come on, sit up," she said, and the scorpions scuttled away.

Her eyes lingered on his crotch. She handed him a floral silk robe from her backpack. The robe felt expertly chilled. She scooped up his clothes and handed him a wool-covered canteen, which rested in his cupped hands. He stroked the softness. Blithe didn't care to evaluate if this woman in white linen was there to harm or help. As with the scorpions, he figured that if he stayed submerged in his own undoing, nothing could harm him more than that.

In the parking lot, day hikers sprayed and rubbed their skin. She put his backpack on his lap, and the car door slammed him inside.

"Do you need to call someone?"

He shook his head.

Words were no longer the units of sentences. They didn't touch. He counted on habit to hold them together.

They drove off toward the inland sea.

In Unit 2, Blithe shat out the sushi from the week before, which didn't feel chronologically possible, and opened all the bottles on the rolling cart in front of him. Smelled lavender, eucalyptus, even essence of Joshua Tree. He was grateful the mirror had been covered with a cheap red scarf because he didn't want to look at himself in her silk floral robe. He shut off the too-bright bathroom light and stepped into the tiny efficiency kitchen. The other part of the unit was divided by a white curtain stapled to the ceiling, and he could see Rita moving around behind it.

Blithe was beyond the point of concern. She beckoned him through her bedroom, just a motel bed with a large tiger blanket spread over it instead of a scratchy comforter and some lit candles, and out to the balcony.

She poured him a glass of Sprite without ice, and

they sat at a folding card table. Her movements, purpose, dwelling were all efficient and without flourish.

"You are hardly the first person I have taken from the desert to the sea," she said, as if the Salton Sea were a privileged destination and not an accident of flooding ruined by pesticides and neglect. The sea was a gray line in the distance, shoving waves of hydrogen sulfide toward him, reminding him of his own nastiness.

She handed him a water-damaged Welcome Packet in a plastic sleeve. Some letters had blurred, and this comforted him. He *was* those letters that had lost their form.

Guidelines for Rita's Resting Place

If you are trying to obliterate yourself . . .
By cutting: let me in the room with you.
By drugs: let me provide herbal balms.
I only take responsibility for moving you from desert
 to sea.
P-yment is donation based.
Maximum s-ay, two weeks.
Please respect the paying guests of Rita's Motel by the
 Sea in Units 13 and 14
-rocery run every Wednesday at 3:30pm.
You are welcome to use the kitchen in Unit 3.
Meet daily by the picnic benches for the following:
6am Morning sea stro-l

7am Simple breakfast
1pm Cathartic yell
5pm Bird-w-tching
9pm Hot chocolat-
10pm Optional tuck-in
You can find the resident mediator, Hector, in Unit 6.
I am in Unit 2

That was it, and somehow she had covered everything.

"You'll be in Unit 7. We can arrange to get your car brought over here. Also, please notify loved ones about what's going on without giving them the address."

He waited to see if she'd say anything about what she saw up on the trail. She didn't.

"What about——?" He gestured at his groin. There was sand between his teeth. His jaw was heavy.

She zipped her lips and then watched without worry as he spent a whole hour just trying to get the letters in order to send a curt text to parents, boyfriend, and work about "unplugging for a while." They were used to his whims. He was glad that he could summon enough of his functioning self to stave off their concern. The last thing he wanted was Saul trying to comfort him with a blow job or a meditation app, and he'd tortured his parents enough.

He started opening his mouth to give Rita the culturally appropriate response of "Thank you," and she stopped him.

"No need for politeness here. Politeness only constipates the air. You can start following the schedule tomorrow. Do you want me to come tuck you in?"

"Yes."

He walked down the outdoor hallway to his unit, ate some cashew nuts that were left on the bedside table, and crawled into bed, unable to believe his luck, an entire room in which to go mad. Rita knocked on the door and walked in, carrying a candle, even though it was three in the afternoon. She smoothed the covers over his shoulders.

He fell asleep in the twin bed that had been in the same place since 1962.

~PAUSE IN NARRATIVE REPORT~

The Bio-meter remained stuck on LACK, but a thumb drive contained audio files starting from Rita's arrival. The notes explained that she kept the audio files as evidence that she was not harming the resters. The files were unedited, so I had to scan through their real-time narration, including hours of Blithe sleeping and a gentle, unidentifiable hum.

~NARRATIVE REPORT CONTINUED~

The first week, as his insides turned to angry jelly, Blithe adopted a uniform of floral robe over jeans with shower slides, participated in the cathartic yells, ate yummy cans of beans and hot dogs, and learned to identify local wildlife down by the shore. He whispered *Least bittern, least bittern, double-crested cormorant, double-crested cormorant* to himself when he needed to calm down and befriended Lily and Olga, twin coders who set out glamping and ended up at Rita's Resting Place and Motel by the Sea. Together they mocked the turtlenecked tourists in Units 13 and 14, who paid seventy-five dollars a night, ate peanut-butter crackers, and had never completely lost their shit. Each night, he licked the bottom of the plastic cups of hot chocolate to get the last sandy dregs. The highlight of his day was Rita tucking him in by candlelight.

On the seventh day, the Salton Sea stilled. Blithe had gained a few pounds from cereal and the mildest exercise and had fallen out with Jennifer, a drifter who offered him one of her crystals on the first night and then tried to grab his dick on the second. He would have gone to mediator-Hector about this, but language was not useful to him, language was too finite and cloying for his breakage.

Blithe went into his room. It was the long part of the day, after the cathartic yell and before birdwatching, when most guests tried to steal internet and watch TV, or jerk off, or kill themselves.

Rita prided herself on a very low suicide-success rate.

He took a velvet pouch out of his toiletry kit and sat

on the edge of his bed. He pulled out a thick silver ring and held it under the harsh lamplight.

Encircle thrice, read the engraving.

He ran his pointer finger around the ring, sending a distress signal to his testosterone implant near the center of his right butt cheek, and then to the Rhiz.

First, nothing happened. He'd never used the ring before; perhaps the connection between silver and implant had been severed.

Then, a tiny projector, no larger than a grain of rice, rose out of the ring, like a periscope from a submarine.

Do I really want to be tethered to a bunch of queer people that I have nothing in common with? he'd wondered long ago in the doctor's office. The doctor was asking if he wanted an implant accessory with direct access to the Rhiz, and he'd said no, but his parents had said yes.

With the testosterone implant newly inserted in his butt, he'd shut himself away in his parents' house for one year so no one would have to see him in such an imperfect state, ravenous some days, yelling at his parents for keeping old photos around, checking his dick/clit size in the mirror, ordering expensive packing underwear from Thailand, wondering why he couldn't cry anymore, dreaming up horribly juicy lines for soap operas because he was living inside one—except nothing ever happened, aside from the cleaning lady coming and wondering what the hell he was doing in his parents' house, ghosting on his college friends who knew him as Brittany, failing to find any books or music or

TV that contained any trans person who was remotely un-pitiable, watching the world push him closer to his own destruction, a world that had no bright or lustrous offerings for his new being.

Now the Operatrix appeared in a hazy hologram. Blithe could make out an embossed leather belt, but the rest was a blur of pixelated motion.

"Damn, the desert is interrupting the signal," the Operatrix said with an authentic West Texas accent.

"Okay, I'm not exactly suicidal, but I think I will be if I stay here, as earnest as this place is."

Blithe spoke timidly because of course he was ashamed of being trans and ashamed of being ashamed of being trans.

"Indeed," the Operatrix said, almost flirtatiously, and without the bureaucratic emphasis one would expect of a crisis operator. "Honey, there's only one thing more pressing than trans folks not dying, and that's living. Let's get you sorted. I've been waiting for your summons."

Blithe wanted to belong to the family of queer folks, and yet he'd never really allowed himself to be trans outside of his own private, wordless understanding. He lived his life as if something monstrous was waiting at the edge of this lineage.

"Waiting for me?"

"Yes, you've been hexed. Which is not actually a bad thing. Let's first start with the Rhiz." The Operatrix came over to the bed and hovered next to Blithe.

"The Rhiz is a network of intercommunication and exchange. Queers of the world have long rejected the family unit as the primary organizing force for society and have always found ways to operate according to the ways of our guides, the great, ancient fungal goddexes."

Blithe was so sunken that he did not respond to the Operatrix's words, which would normally have set off spirals of reverie.

"I myself was summoned to the Rhiz in college. One of the Keepers called me on the telephone in my hallway dorm. Can you believe that?"

Blithe was not really listening. He traveled along the outline of the Operatrix's speech.

"When I got to the compound, the site of an old Catskills summer camp, I first had to answer the One Hundred Questions, which is no longer part of the Rhiz initiation. I slept in a tent and was not-so-secretly watched to see how I would handle the various crises and romances of rural community living and the prospect of traveling around the world, trying to help out queers in trouble, back when we only had word of mouth, zines, pamphlets, members belonging to international government agencies, rattling pickup trucks, and the currency of scrappiness, of survival. And here I am before you, somehow less weary than I was in my hard-won youth.

"Okay, time for your intake. I need to get a sense of the shape of your transition. How did it begin? This

could be a vague glimmer, an ominous portent, a for-
bidden crack, a slimy loathing, a cold withdrawal, a
green bowl—whatever form fits your experience."

Silence on Blithe's end as he heard footsteps on the
parking-lot gravel. He envied the simple rhythms of
the tourists' lives.

"Do. Not. Worry. We secure all stories of queer
shame in our archive."

Silence.

"You know what I told my parents about being
trans?" the Operatrix asked.

Silence.

"First of all, I didn't transition until decades after
joining the Rhiz. I didn't know that was a possibility for
myself. My parents had vaguely tolerated my dyke years
and had sort of given up on me performing their way of
life. I texted them because, while I love talking, I don't
have a great track record with them listening. I texted:

> Do y'all know the best part of being trans?

> So many people lament:
> Oh, I wish I could start a farm with a
> hydroponic mullein grove, maybe when I'm
> retired.

> Whereas trans folks ask,
> So where are the shovels and the AP-100
> air pump?

See, there's no cushion of toleration, no
boring nest of succumbing.

The status quo is a guillotine and it's
positioned at many junctures along the
body and the parts remain alive and numb
and if you take a look at a cutout of a cutoff organ, the veins have looped back and
formed a new, different circuitry of pain.

"It was kind of emo, but they make me feel like I'm
thirteen years old."

"Wait, what?" Blithe was annoyed at the Operatrix's digressions.

"How did it all begin for you?"

Blithe was not ready to go there. To begin, he would
have to start in the aching place of absence.

The hologram began to crackle with impatience.

"If you cannot vocalize, there is another way."

The Operatrix explained that a messenger would
drop off a scroll and the Rhiz's special keyboard. "Sign
over your well-being to us, and we'll send help," the
Operatrix said.

Privacy has kept me lonely, Blithe thought.

"Wait," he said as the Operatrix's outline began to
fade. He wanted to descend further without any entan-
gling ties to normalcy. "Tell Saul it's over."

Even inside the Shadowlands, he knew this was

a terrible task to outsource, especially when his boyfriend so prized "face-to-face contact."

The Operatrix did not respond.

THE END

I found Aiden at the airport gate with his feet on top of compression luggage, drinking adaptogenic water. He had special celebrity security clearance. I'd checked my clunky duffel suitcase, and my feet were still sweating from my encounter with the airport scanners. I knew they saw I was missing a big dick.

I was always surveilling myself.

"Hey," I said, trying to sound lighthearted.

Aiden looked up from his phone. "Hey, man."

I was proud to see original Aiden Chase content without needing to look at the Gram. He wore a white woven poncho, soft brown pants, and leather sandals. His toenails glinted in the harsh lighting. His hair had been newly cut and faded; a long swath swept over the top of his head like a wave, and it got shorter and shorter down his neck. Mine was growing out from a fade because I didn't always have the courage to go into a barbershop and bro it up with guys who called me *boss*.

"Okay, I think we need to process some things before we get on the plane," I said, sitting down next to him. "I don't want to go try to help Blithe when there's a veil of resentment and distrust hanging over us."

Sophie and I had role-played a whole dialogue with Aiden that could be adapted to varying levels of hostility.

"Pen, are you fucking serious?"

"Good. Thanks for starting us off. I think that your very existence brings up a lot of self-hatred for me, and the more that I can hold myself in loving imperfection, the more—"

"Aiden!"

A young dude with a nerdy bike-courier look and bad barbed-wire tattoos around his upper arms interrupted me. He stood expectantly in front of our seats.

"Hey?" Aiden said.

"My bf is over there—he's transgendered like us—and he'd really like to meet you. Do you mind saying hi, hashtag OMG, I can't believe I'm standing next to you!"

"Um sure, that's cool."

He went over to pose with the trans couple, and I was left trying to remember the techniques Sophie had reviewed with me:

> —*Coat yourself with love.*
> —*Feel the contact of your feet on the ground.*
> —*Daydream about Aiden experiencing minor life difficulties.*
> —*Remember that Aiden's "authentic self-perfection bullshit" is just another garment, like Wolf recycled-wool sweaters, that he puts on for attention.*

Aiden came back and threw himself down on a cold airport seat. "Listen, whatever you think you know about me is wrong."

What a melodious ring those words had, even if they implied my own dimwitted nature.

"I'm sure you're right. In fact, I'm counting on it." I paused, giving him space to show a little shadow.

"Great, well, I brought some desert outfits for you to borrow."

Having grown up with Margot, I was used to such redirections whenever a fraught topic emerged.

"I do hope you know that your entire internet presence is actually quite harmful to some people. And no desert outfits are going to change that."

He looked at me with mock concern. "Have you seen my desert blanket hoodie?"

We laughed and laughed, the only cure for certain madnesses.

The Rhiz had booked us seats next to each other. A middle-aged businessman sat at the aisle with headphones in. I wanted our presence to make the fellow traveler's tentacles stick out, but he did not seem interested in others. I tried to catch Aiden at unflattering angles in my periphery. As the plane took off, he dozed and I flipped through the notes I'd written down on actual paper, even though it wasn't cool with the Rhiz to keep confidential info.

Before we left, I'd placed the narrative report in its appropriate sheath outside my apartment door, and then gone to add an extra layer of succulent soil to Alice's pot. The Witch said she'd watch over her. When I passed through the living room, I saw that someone had taken the Bio-meter and left the boxes. I was sad that it had been confiscated before I could try it out on myself or Aiden or my roomies.

There was a square note on the kitchen counter, stamped with a neutral seal.

Your synthesis is fine, but the depth is off, was all it said.

When the plane reached its cruising altitude, I nudged Aiden. "Hey, how far back into Blithe's files did you go?"

"What?" He had a little spit on the corner of his mouth.

"Blithe's life, how much did you read?"

Aiden sat up. Rubbed his mouth. "Uh, not too far before you told me I was doing a shitty job."

"Okay, well, let me catch you up. Blithe was adopted from China by white American parents. He had a tomboyish childhood—you know, long basketball shorts and big tees. He tried to assimilate into girlhood until he was seventeen, followed by a raging lesbian college phase, a post-college year of deep depression, then a year working in TV and trying to be an escapist who didn't have a body. He started medically transitioning at twenty-six. The files called his transition form *the slice.*

"He cut off all friends and went into seclusion in his parents' very nice home. He didn't even have to see a therapist because the Rhiz covered his hormones and surgery. He wrote for TV shows from his old bedroom. He rejoined the world when he felt like he could pass. And met his boyfriend, Saul, whom he has apparently just dumped.

"The Bio-metric report also said that some parts of him don't yet know that he's trans, and that his adoption had probably led to *inner disorganization*. He's rigidly protected himself and will probably hate us for confronting him with this new knowing."

I tried to sound overwhelmed with the task ahead of knowing and saving Blithe, but really, I loved digging into this guy's life. It was way easier to enjoy the messiness of someone else's transition, like watching a film up on a screen, in air-conditioning, with popcorn.

"I'm pretty jealous that he could convalesce in his parents' house, although something has clearly gone awry. Were your parents cool with your transition?"

"No," was all I got from Aiden.

"You should release all your info to the Rhiz, and then I can dig into your past," I tried to joke.

He didn't smile.

"Come on, what's the deal with them?"

"Damn it, Pen, I don't want to get into it with you." He grabbed the seat in front of him and shook it.

"Well, my parents died in an avalanche," I said, pretending that I wasn't offended by the *with you*. "And I was raised by my non-emotive aunt. Like, her bioaffective readings would be in the gray area, unless there's some magenta spot hidden at her core. I basically tried to avoid everything related to bodies or families, and the fog lasted all the way through college—even though I think some of my blackouts occurred on important family anniversaries. I stuck around my college town with my lover, who was transitioning and working on a PhD. I learned how to give him a shot and how other people responded to his transness.

"I lived in this cute bubble with my older trans lover until he went to Thailand to do his research. He was racking up thousand-baht bar tabs talking to *khon kham-phet* folks about gender performativity and dissolution, and in his absence, I knew it was time for me to transition. He was so certain about his transness that mine always hid away when we were together. He returned with another lover he wanted to bring into our relationship, and I had to leave.

"I moved from my midwestern college town to this city, and everything collapsed. The glue that was holding together my sanity (denial?) did not travel to the Northeast. Parents holding their children or yelling at them, the notion of cooking dinner, writing a security deposit check, visiting a doctor, buying more toilet paper—every single action and thought and association was frayed and imperiling to me as soon as I arrived. And yet, as I've learned, the symptoms often include their own cure, and the city, while maddening in every visceral sense, demands that our threadbare nervous systems get rewired.

"Everyone is an ass-wipe during the beginning of their transition. Luckily, I was dog-walking and didn't have much human contact aside from the Witch and the Stoner-Hacker, who are lost in their own worlds. Still, I was mean to the dogs, not in any direct way, but my inner dialogue was constantly bitter, like, *Why do you assholes get to be fed and applauded for every small thing, played with, caressed, treated with warmth while I am the lowest of the low, and I am a*

*human, which is supposed to be higher than an animal in
some fucked-up hierarchy?*

"That first Yom Kippur in the city, I tried to atone for all
the bad vibes I had unleashed into the world by washing my
hands in the radioactive waters below the Metropolitan Avenue Bridge, even tho, arguably, the bad vibes didn't belong to
me. They belonged to the existence of social norms.

"At first, my former guardian, Margot, was all uptight
and weird, but then I was, too. Now she sends me articles
about every state that legalizes a third-gender option, which
is her way of expressing love."

"Good for her," Aiden said.

I was hardly satisfied with this reaction. I had just dumped
all of my whole story onto him, and he'd let it slide off.

I certainly could not do that with the stories of others!

"You know, I think it will be good for Blithe if we're open
about our complicated feelings," I said. What I meant was
that it would be good for him if we arrived in Joshua Tree
newly bonded.

Aiden shrugged.

To my right, the businessman played a game involving
jewels. He made no sign that our conversation had reached
him.

The palm trees waved at me through the windows at
LAX. As we walked to the baggage claim (Aiden brought
a ton of material possessions), we passed travelers in straw
hats, holding their succulent carriers. I found myself believing that things could be different in a new, drier climate.

We picked up our luggage, found Aiden's hatchback in

Lot D, and headed east toward a motel in the Californian hinterlands.

The more hours I spent with him, the more I was able to destroy his perfect tableau. He was super anal about driving, checking all his mirrors before he switched lanes, keeping the car just under the speed limit. He had a folder with him in his waterproof tote that contained every piece of documentation about his transition, in case airport security, some stranger in the bathroom, or a potential sponsor needed to verify exactly what was going on with his genital situation. Inside his wallet, antimalarial tablets.

He glanced furtively at the road as he passed a car, and I expanded in the dry air. I sat in the passenger seat, relishing the ugliness of California and surmising about Blithe in a gossipy way, as if we were entering a melodrama of easy feeling and action.

Aiden had brought along frozen smoothies that were starting to thaw. We pulled into a rest stop, and he handed me a deep green one before checking his tires.

"Thanks," I said. "I'm gonna get a hot dog, too. You want?"

"Ew. No."

I shrugged, and he went off to a patch of cacti with his tripod. Maybe there was something restorative, if not 100 percent accurate, about the Gram, about framing a tableau with only the choicest cacti and leaving out the rest stop with its uniform offerings of hot dogs, cotton candy, coffee, and gender-segregated restrooms.

We got back in the car and drove through faded land-scapes. I thought about myself as a girl, how I used to pretend to be mad when kids teased me for having a boy's name. I had no recollection of wanting to be a "boy" as a child, as tempting as it is to try to revise history. I simply wanted to be a girl who was wild. My parents were almost androgynous to me in their matching T-shirts and jeans and boots, so the question of gender did not become poisonous until after they died and Margot tried to be a good guardian, draping outfits and accompanying tights on my bed before a celebration or party. Every time I was forced to put on a pair of tights, they chafed both my inner thighs and my soul, and yet I needed to prove to the world that we were *okay*, Margot and me, that we were still *normal* even after an avalanche.

After miles of emptiness, I spotted neon palm trees flash-ing across the front of the white box of a building in ma-genta, yellow, and orange.

"Let's pull over," I said.

"Pen . . ."

"Come on, it says *diner* in tiny letters. We can get coffee. You won't be forced to eat saccharine pie with cherries from a can."

"Fine."

We entered through a curtain of hanging crystals and I praised my intuition. Servers of all genders wore checkered aprons and black platform shoes and posed by the host stand, braiding one another's hair.

We were led to a sticky booth.

Our server, Lionel, had a nose ring, aqua glitter-nails, and a copy of the *Inferno* hanging out of their apron pocket. They set down a glass pitcher filled with what looked like bioluminescent water.

Aiden and I raised our eyebrows at each other. The liquid tasted like water with vague notes of moss. *What sort of aqueduct had this come through?* I asked myself, not yet ready to let Aiden into my inner whimsies.

Two ceiling fans turned slowly, and there was only one other occupied booth. A pile of black hair pooled down the vinyl booth-back.

We ordered coffee and it arrived in a silver pot with a slender spout. The coffee was as disgusting a drip as one could find anywhere. I didn't mind. I diluted it with indeterminate nut milk. Aiden took his black.

Lionel brought us dishes of pickled veggies. The menu was written in loose scrawl on the back wall. I asked for pie, even though I wasn't sure they served it.

As I waited, I stared at my bud. His eyes were tired. I was greedy with new information about him. Somewhere in between the city of height and wealth and the city of sunlight and fantasies, my hatred of him had changed form.

Lionel wheeled over a glass box, and inside I could see perfect neon spheres resting in trays. They reminded me of edible lil' Bio-meters.

No explanation was provided, and I chose a pink one. *Why travel in the relative safety of another trans guy and not relish the opportunity to fuck with gender?*

With an oven mitt on, Lionel reached in and grabbed it. "Hold out your hands."

The sphere was deposited.

It was creamy without having any particular taste. I nibbled at it like a wary bunny and hoped that a queer diner would not put too many weird chemicals in its desserts. I couldn't eat it all, and finally Lionel came by in rubber dish gloves to remove the orb from the table.

A pink spot remained.

When Lionel brought the check, a note was paper-clipped to it.

Get moving, was all it said, stamped with a green seal.

We pulled up to a dilapidated motel. A hand-painted sign depicted what could be Rita surfing on a wave. The sound of our car doors slamming summoned a small group of people in sweatpants. After spending years in a city of wealth, I found it strange to see such unkempt and unhurried folks, all holding plastic travel mugs. A pioneerish woman in a white dress and hiking boots came up behind them, without a mug, holding a lit candle. Her hair was braided, and she reminded me of the frontierswomen I used to fantasize about as a child. She walked straight up to us with a sort of vigor the others did not possess. The flame shook with her steps. She was probably forty-seven, or sixty-seven and well preserved by the desert.

"I heard you were coming. Welcome. I'm Rita. Let me show you to your unit. Guys, these are Blithe's friends. They are coming to get him."

We introduced ourselves. I scanned the group for someone who could be Blithe, but I didn't see anyone in the shapeless semicircle.

She led us up to Unit 13 and unlocked the door. There was a musty smell and only one bed.

"As I said, Unit 14 is the only other non-resting room, and it's currently occupied by birders," she explained.

"That's okay, it's just one night," Aiden replied, and I wondered if he was trying to renegotiate our relationship with a revenge fuck.

"Put your stuff down and I'll take you to him."

Aiden picked up a laminated copy of guidelines for guests to follow when interacting with resters, amounting to: *Leave them the fuck alone.* He took a picture of it.

"You're not going to post that, are you?"

"Of course not," he said, and looked down at his phone, lit up with praise for his cactus shot.

Blithe was lying on his bed in a floral robe, looking up at the constellations of stains on the ceiling. I wanted to whisper to Aiden, *Shit, is he de-transitioning?* but I didn't want Blithe to hear.

The files did not prepare me for Blithe's actual face. His pained eyes reminded me of floating through time without hope. His hair was fine and light brown, reaching the top of his shoulders. I realized that he would have been one of those effortless and pretty girls.

Would it have been hard to give that up?

"You know, you three could almost be confused for

triplets," Rita said, chuckling with the earth-worn detachment of a farmer.

The three of us were short, with prettily handsome faces and decent builds, although Aiden was definitely the most muscular. And Aiden and I were white, him in an All-American earnest way and me in a cozy, nonthreatening Jewish way. Blithe was Chinese and Californian. I could see him on a rooftop in L.A., wearing the floral robe, dancing in that club-kid way with hands gesticulating as if he were on molly.

"Hi, I'm Pen, and this is Aiden. We were sent by the Rhiz," I said slowly, leaving out the part about how we had hexed him in the first place.

"*You*," he said without turning his head. "*You*," he repeated, in a conversational way, as if we understood.

"We're here to help," Aiden tried.

"*You*."

"Okay, Blithe," Rita said. "It's almost time for you to leave the Resting Place."

She turned to us. "So you both know, he has started shifting linguistic parameters, which is completely normal for someone in distress. Think of it as him regressing in order to evolve. He's really moving forward, but it might look like he's moving backward." She put a hand on his shoulder, right on top of a fat flower.

"We're going to take you back to Aiden's in L.A.," I told him.

In principle, we could have gone anywhere and charged a hotel room to the Rhiz, but an article in a zine ("How to Guide a Loved One Through the Shadowlands: Logistics") left on our motel bed had clearly stated that intimate spaces were better than sterile ones. It also recommended simplicity: "For further reading, see the archive's file on PL and JH, who tried to bring RF to PL's family house in the Maldives to recuperate and the logistical, political, and judiciary issues that ensued given RF's fragile condition." Returning to L.A. was the easiest plan.

"*No wallpaper.*" Blithe was shaking his head left to right, clearly agitated.

"Where would you like us to take you?"

"*No wallpaper.*"

"Okay, plan B," I whispered to Aiden.

The zine also explained that taking people back to where they were high-functioning was generally a bad idea. Blithe needed a place where he would not have to function. I certainly didn't want to spend any time among the celebrities, astrologers, and health goths that Sid always texted me about. He'd recently slept with a health goth who shamed him for his choice of nut milk.

"How would you feel about us taking you to New York? I have a cozy apartment; you won't know anyone."

"*No wallpaper,*" he said, softer.

"Okay, then, we're going to New York. Do you need anything right now?"

"*Sushi.*"

Thank god he's a little coherent, I thought. I started to wonder if he was just fucking with us for attention, but the zine said that assuming the worst of people will only draw out the process.

"Okay, bud, we'll get you some sushi in New York," Aiden said in a sweet voice.

"*Sushi*," Blithe whispered as we closed the door.

"So what are we thinking?" I asked Aiden as we headed to the sea. Rita sent us off with a moldy bird identification guide.

"He's in pretty bad shape. What do you think about her?" Aiden carried his tripod over one shoulder and brought an extra linen shirt so he could take a scenic photo for the following day.

"IDK, does anyone pick up unstable strays in the middle of the desert without some sort of ulterior motive, or are we too jaded?"

"Good point."

"I know this seems really fucked, but are you sort of excited by how out of it he is?"

"Yeah, I know I shouldn't be, but it makes me feel needed. And sane," Aiden said.

The smell of rotting eggs rolled toward us.

"Why would anyone call this a sea?" he asked when we reach the gravelly shore.

Water stretched out to the horizon, and the shore had gathered fish heads, a rusting metal stool, some boat carcasses.

"It is saline."

We walked in silence for a while, listening to the birds diving into the water.

"What's our plan?" I asked.

"Well, we take him to your apartment. Get him on a schedule, see if he wants to video his parents."

We didn't have anything to do except text the Rhiz to send Blithe a plane ticket by desert-motorcyclist courier. We sat at the shore. I made circles in the sand with a stick. Aiden waited until the sun started to set, then changed into the linen shirt, which filled with the light breeze. He posed by the water's edge. Another solitary photo.

"What's the caption?"

"Something about stillness," he said quietly.

The desert chilled at dusk, and Rita came around with musty blankets. A rester named Claudia made a vat of pasta, and we all ate dinner at picnic tables. Blithe sat with the other resters. We watched over him from afar. For once, life wasn't dictated by my own failings or motivations. It was not mysterious to me why someone would enjoy themselves there. At nine, Rita rang the bell for hot chocolate, served in hard plastic coffee cups with floating marshmallows. One of the resters passed around a bundle of sage. We cleansed ourselves.

The next morning, I was irritable after a night of sleeping next to Aiden, who rolled back and forth across the mattress, knocking into me. Even the desert outfit that he'd brought for me, light linen pants and a heat-stabilizing T-shirt and soft leather sandals, hardly soothed.

He had woken up at six to run around the lake. Instead of going back to sleep, I decided to meditate in the comforting strangeness of the motel room. Minna and my therapist had recommended the practice, but because of the pressure to somehow succeed at meditating, I'd always declined. At Rita's, I was freer.

Aiden and I went to breakfast. We sat across from each other over our plastic bowls of cornflakes, sipping shitty coffee. Blithe was ignoring us from over at the rester table. In the sharpness of my fresh mind, I realized that he might think of us as I thought about Aiden, these bright and untainted beings. Shit.

"Hey, man, how do you keep up all your regimens? Where'd you learn all this discipline?"

"My father," he said flatly, and a whiff of pain curled under my nose. "My whole life he's gone to the boxing gym every other day at six thirty a.m. He was there when my twin and I were born. There's a picture where he's holding us in a hospital gown with a sweatband around his head."

I didn't want to say *cute* if his parents were now estranged from him.

"But, like, *how* do you do it?"

"Well, I do it because when I don't, I fall apart. If I don't work out, I become unbelievably depressed. As much as waking up early sucks, it sucks less than the alternative. And this Gram stuff, let me ask you: Why do you think I photograph myself in favorable lighting every single day?"

Whoa. Even though I'd begged for it, I wasn't ready for his realness.

"Because of all the frames that never fit."

•

At the airport, I requested a wheelchair so everyone would know something was wrong with Blithe. Aiden was dropping off Blithe's car at his parents' house. His celebrity status meant that he would not have to go through security. I texted him that things were going smoothly and asked if he could get us into the special airport lounge. He didn't respond.

At airports, it was always a shock to see so many normal families at once, screaming at and ignoring each other in matching airport sweatpants.

I was *almost* nostalgic for the wrong future, which would have turned a Bio-meter sickly red.

Blithe and I reached the security desk, and I handed over our tickets and IDs. Mine was from two years prior, when I'd begun dog-walking in the city as a new trans. I'd grown my hair shoulder-length, put it up in a man-bun, wore ribbed Henleys with a button open to flakes of chest hair, and joined a climbing gym, trying to evoke some long-forgotten adventurer. I put my fifty apartment keys on a carabiner and went to an REI outlet to get climbing pants and a synthetic Scylla fleece that Margot would never let me buy as a kid because it was "over-athletic," even though now, in the 20—s, she wore yoga pants over her narrow hips like you wouldn't believe, along with those high-performance gel clogs that had holes in them.

My adventurer's persona did not last long; it reminded me too much of my nerdy geologist parents, who wore sporty pants with elastic waists that could be unzipped into shorts, and black all-terrain sandals streaked with yellow, like ugly wasps.

"Penfield Ruth Henderson?" the airport security guard asked with skepticism.

A shame blanket draped over me as the uniformed man uttered the *Ruth* aloud. *Why hadn't I packed a waterproof document carrier like perfect Aiden?*

"Yes?"

"The name printed on your ticket doesn't match your ID."

On my ticket, it said Penfield R. Henderson.

"How important is the middle name to national security?"

He ignored me and called for a manager.

A manager wearing cargo khakis came over, adding insult to injury. He asked to see all my credit cards. Blithe started getting agitated, tapping the side of the wheelchair, whispering, *"Wallpaper, wallpaper, Ruth, wallpaper."*

After the manager scrawled a series of symbols on my boarding pass, we were waved through to the next embarrassment.

Inside his pain, I hoped Blithe noticed that I, too, had all sorts of problems.

2

The kitchen looked new to me after a few days away, with its dried herbs and animal bones hanging down from the ceiling and the three stools lined up below the counter.

The Witch floated in, wearing layers and layers of shawls and her Melusine skirt with a tailed-woman appliqué.

"Welcome, welcome!" she said, warmer than I'd ever seen her, twirling around in a circle. "Please use this dwelling as you wish, only do not disturb my arrangements. You may cross through to the backyard during my morning chants, from nine to ten; when I'm temping from one to five in the evening; or during the Descension, occurring in the evening from eight to nine in the spring."

The level of awkwardness was not yet intolerable. I pulled Aiden and Blithe into my room to explain.

"Okay, I know she's weird, but when I interviewed people to see if they wanted to share this tiny-ass apartment with me, only a few responded."

It was hard to speak in my room with the door closed because the S-H's takeout-and-weed residue formed a thick cloud.

"An artist couple, a neuroscience PhD student with a

snake, a perfect quiet ceramicist who bailed on me, a cis white str8 guy who used the word *hella*, and a baby-boomer divorcée. I think my compatibility test scared away most folks. I asked them about condiment usage and how likely they would be to squirt some of my ketchup onto a bun if they'd run out.

"The crazy thing is, I didn't even care about condiment usage. It was just because of a story I heard about someone threatening to put laxatives in his ketchup if his roommates kept eating it . . . Okay, you really don't care."

Blithe had wandered over to my mood board, and Aiden was scrolling on his phone.

I knew my voice was taking on a high, shaky tone. "But do you understand how I ended up living with the Witch and the S-H?" I couldn't refrain from asking.

"Hey, we're not here to evaluate your life choices. I have to pee," Aiden said, and before I could warn him about the Witch's cleaning aversion, he was off down the hall.

Blithe and I scanned the photos of hamburgers, "bohemian" living rooms, and geology labs until Aiden came back.

"I'm not comfortable with this," he said quietly, referring to the bathroom's green sludge jars, old pubes, dust, poorly tied bundles of burnt sage, the S-H's cologne, and a Toftbo bath mat that was always left sopping and moldy.

I sighed. "The Witch believes cleaning is a form of violence—"

The door opened. The Witch poked her head into my room.

"Yes, a futile act that humans practice to ensure some

sense of power over the *elements*. Cleaning is an extreme delusion. You sweep the floor, and then you throw the dust ball and bread-bag plastic cinch into the trash, and the trash goes to the landfill, as we all know, and the landfill will never be cleaned unless scientists release plastic-metabolizing microbes, which will surely get out of the landfill and come back to eat our flesh. More often than not, cleaning makes things dirtier. Bleach, antibacterial soap, idiots who throw their compost into plastic bags . . . By trying to eliminate ninety-nine percent of germs, we're adding in toxicity." She finished the diatribe.

Copious coffins of cuttlefish! Now my new trans companions were really going to know how weird things got around here.

"I hear ya! It's just that I'm super anal and I'm going to have a panic attack if I have to use the bathroom near those . . . containers," Aiden said, trying to keep his tone low-key, as recommended by psychologists when confronting others about their disgusting lifestyle habits.

"Woosh, weesh, wash," the Witch said, with a flick of her hands, and removed herself from the doorway.

I gave Aiden a look, trying to remind him that the Witch had great hexing powers.

"I'm sorry, I have to clean it. Do you have rubber gloves?" Aiden asked.

"Under the kitchen sink."

As Aiden cleaned, I cooked us eggs and toasted English muffins and the Witch walked by and sprinkled chervil on the plates when my back was turned. Breakfast for dinner was the ultimate comfort in a world that had turned upside-down more than once.

We ate quietly, and then I set Blithe up on the couch with my special gravity blanket and inflated Aiden's air mattress. It was almost like summer camp, except for Blithe's suffering.

I went into my room, and on my linen duvet cover I found a pastel purple zine stapled twice across its thin spine.

How to Guide a Loved One Through the Shadowlands: Emotions
When you love someone, you will want to pull them out of the Shadowlands, to rescue them from the terror. And if you love someone, you will let them stay. You will keep your gaze steady; you will hold out a bucket for their despair without dunking your head into it.

The words were so true that I could read only a page at a time. I rationed it.

In the middle of the night, I went to pee. My slippers did not stick on the bathroom floor, the sink had been wiped down, and the air smelled of lavender.

The morning was bright and domestic. Aiden ran to the grocery store, and then we took Blithe outside through the Witch's room. We sat at the little table and had coffee and yogurt with blueberries. We asked Blithe what he needed. For a while he said nothing, just looked toward the train tracks.

After the monotony of the desert, the yard vibrated with greens and growth and tiny creatures. It had changed from the depressing plot I'd found when I first moved in. The landlord had razed the yard when renovating the building, and the former tenants had done nothing aside from adding plastic lawn furniture. I'd complained about this to Minna, who brought over her FBS Agriculture colleague, who planted vines and a young cherry blossom tree.

"You know," she'd said, "it's all well and good to have a pretty backyard, but if you clean your consciousness, the tiniest cell (as in where a monk sleeps) can become the most expansive field."

I nodded and then dismissed her on the basis that such wisdom was only applicable to someone who had the luxury of time, organic produce, beauty, stability, and a legit mentor. I bought a woven hammock and set it up against the death-gray back wall. Eventually, invasive weeds began to grow. A few stalks of wildflowers emerged, and one day a monarch appeared and I was a girl again, running through a butterfly garden.

I would never regret those delights, even the feeling of a cotton dress against my young legs.

Aiden went inside to get his selfie equipment, and I headed to the cherry blossom tree for my morning meditation. I set my phone timer for ten minutes and closed my eyes.

I could hear the branches moving and the rustle of little birds hopping around on the ground.

Beep, beep, beep.

I set Alice on the table so that a tendril could witness Aiden's butt crack as he leaned over to adjust his phone.

I sat down at the table, and Blithe said, "Sushi."

"Sushi? You want sushi?"

"*Sushi.*"

Aiden came over.

"He wants sushi."

"Shit, we never got him any at the airport, did we? I'll order some," Aiden said.

He went inside to get his computer and order, even though it was hardly the appropriate American hour for rice, seaweed, and fish. Twenty minutes later, the doorbell rang, setting off the dachshund on the third floor. Aiden returned with a brown paper bag and placed a few trays on the table.

"*Sushi,*" Blithe said. He wouldn't touch the food.

We tried not to take it personally.

"Maybe we're interpreting him too literally."

"*Sushi,*" Blithe said, with a little more enthusiasm.

The Witch banned TV in common spaces but made an exception for Blithe. She perked up around him. I mean, the fact of his existence in our apartment did verify her powers. We played a nature documentary about the desert, and everyone fell asleep before the part where the giraffe escaped from a pride of lions. I woke up first and turned off the movie. Aiden's food-delivery page was open on his computer, and I went to his history. Days of breakfast sandwiches, nights of Thai.

I still ached to know him.

•

"I'll cook dinner, but is there a better grocery store?" Aiden asked when he woke up.

He was judging my entire unhealthy existence. "There's a bougie health store by the train," I said sharply.

I dug into a sticky drawer and pulled out bamboo shopping bags.

He came back looking like a hot stay-at-home dad with arms full of groceries. His large brown eyes were pretty under the denim cap.

"I went to a vegetable stand and found some good avocados. Help me chop some veggies."

I started hacking at an onion, and he had to show me how to cut it properly. As Aiden leaned over me, for once I could not smell anything. He chopped peppers, mushrooms, and carrots into almost-perfect strips and slices.

"Where'd you learn to do that?"

"From an ex."

"Who's taking care of Agatha?"

"My bro. Not bio bro, bro bro."

I wanted more info, more than adv-tech could provide, deep, chunky layers of his life, and he wanted to simmer vegetarian chili in the Witch's second-best pot/cauldron.

How nice that our first day back is structured around sleep and food, not work or processing boxes of data, I thought, and went to read another page of the zine.

Aiden and I messed up a lot in the first few weeks. We talked at Blithe as if he were trying to speak our language and misusing it, when really he was speaking a variation. We tried to buy him what we thought he wanted, and our failures stared at us, unused, untouched. The Witch did not know how long the hex would last, and the Operatrix beamed into the kitchen every other day, observing our fumbles, measuring Aiden's bio-levels and mine (Blithe's were still unreadable), reminding us the queer community is nothing if not

Revolutionary

Scrappy   Operatic

Obnoxious   Toxic

. . . and that we had to combine all of these qualities to help Blithe.

I tried to retrain myself to have positive associations with Aiden's face. The Bio-meter flashed its reading too rapidly for me to discern whether I was coral with object-centered rage or peach with vague hopefulness, but I didn't want to end up on the Rhiz's maladjusted charts. It really skewed your chances of them recommending a compatible person to date.

Aiden took care of the more detailed-oriented paperwork, noting how long Blithe slept, what he ate, what his range of vocabulary was, how often his parents called, how he reacted to various stimuli. I thought about using some of Blithe's data, telling him to remember his parents' pool, and the softness of their voices, but I knew that the zine was right. When you're in the Shadowlands, attempts to comfort are the worst balm. I simply sat with him.

One easeful morning while Aiden was off at a sponsorship

meeting for a new SpaceShoes style, Blithe, Alice, and I sat out in the backyard, admiring the sky. I was glad to be alone with him. Aiden's early rising and smoothie pulverizing and impromptu push-up seshs were messing with my energy.

The cherry blossom tree had bloomed, and the wind scattered its petals across the lawn, like an unimaginative str8 lover strewing rose petals.

"Aloe, aloe."

Blithe rubbed Alice's arm against his face. I cut a small part of her tip and he took it. I was meeting with Sophie later and tried to think of how she would help him. He'd plateaued at my apartment, speaking in one-word mysteries, often staring into the distance with a look of disbelief.

I wanted the Rhiz to know that I had learned *something* from all of my pain.

How could I transmit any of it to this young person, tho? I didn't want to pretend that I was an expert in the Shadowlands; in fact, they still scared the shit out of me.

"Blithe, you know, maybe the one thing I can do that a therapist, shaman, or bioaffective data analyst cannot is tell you about my own messed-up path."

"Aloe," he said, seeming interested.

"It wasn't terribly long ago that I was off in my own Shadowlands, getting my wagon wheels stuck in the same ruts, hating myself, like hating myself beyond the level of hatred that any transphobic person would care to reach, imagining a thousand lost futures, experiencing moment-to-moment reality as a constant plunge into humiliation, a receptacle of the underside of an entire culture's anxieties about trans people . . .

"I mean, not to discourage you, but every day I have to drag myself away from its magnetic pull."

I was getting derailed. I didn't want Blithe to think of the Shadowlands as a geographical location that you could use GPS to get out of.

"Anyway, I'm going to start to tell you about how I've emerged. And guess what, even if I hadn't hexed you, you would have ended up here. I mean, not in my backyard, but in the Shadowlands. For god's sake, you tried to transition by slicing everything off and hiding in your parents' house."

Damn it, I should not use his own data against him.

"We all do the best we can. No one prepares you for this. Even well-meaning other trans people with lots of exposure."

I had to go to therapy, so I left Blithe listening to rain sounds on my bed. The timing worked out because I wasn't sure I knew how I had "emerged."

I took a charming purple train to Chelsea. In Sophie's office, I regressed into a whiny baby as the strong, wise adult listened to my complaints about Aiden's perfection, Blithe's oblivion, the fact that one could soon pay to sit in a "comfort" subway car, the receding of my hair.

"Let's pause here, Pen," Sophie said, leaning back in her deep, padded chair.

I'd skipped a session when we were in the desert. She was wearing bright red lipstick, and her motorcycle jacket hung on the door. She was trans, and although she surely had her own suffering and her own past and her own rage, when we were together, she was like a smooth stone surface, warm with sunlight.

"Because this is a really interesting moment for you to observe Aiden in a new light, which is the only reason I'm letting you talk about him right now. Instead of going down those same muddy, stuck, mossy tracks that always mire your wagon"—she became a third-rate poet when speaking of my pain—"can you get your neural pathways to fire in a different way?"

I took a deep breath and stopped myself from asking if I shouldn't just get a better job so I could buy the tech for that. This healing business was hard.

"Fine. I noticed that Aiden is anal about a lot of things. He shares his bod with everyone, but he never talks about his family or a gf or bf or g-qf or poly situation. He can't write a narrative report, but he did let me borrow a desert outfit, which was a nice change from these weird preppy ensembles I'm always throwing together out of nostalgia. I prefer that he doesn't spend too much alone time with Blithe, because I don't want Blithe to feel pressured to be perfect when he should be free-falling into the Shadowlands. He's been flirting with Minna—"

"Okay, let me stop you there. Instead of framing the negatives about Aiden, can you turn those into positives about yourself?"

"Ugh, I'm not *that* anal unless my boundaries are askew and I'm close to an anal person. I'm trying to repair things with Margot and celebrate the lives of my parents. I'm dating someone—well, you know, it's a *cas* hookup situation, but it makes me feel alive and famous to myself. I really hope you don't think I'm delusional and making up this fake celebrity to—"

"Stop."

And on and on we went, flying one minute through new cutaway paths in wildflower pastures, getting mired in deep ruts, getting out.

"Remember the time on the roof with the microscope and telescope?" I asked as we neared the end of the session.

"Oh yes," she said, smiling.

Things had gotten so bad with my Aiden-obsession that she made me come to her office at night, to the roof, where we occasionally went to fight each other with long sticks (really to fight my depression). She'd set up a microscope on a table and pointed a telescope toward the heavens.

"Go," she said, and walked to the edge of the roof.

When I looked up at the Manhattan sky, I was tiny and awed. "Venus is out tonight."

She must have enchanted the telescope.

"Now go to the microscope," she said.

I looked down into the lit-up lens and saw stained purple circles, with darker spots like little raisins.

"It's a flake of skin," she said. "It's corny, and I certainly didn't come up with this, but one way of looking is love and the other, envy."

Riding back on a light pink subway car, I thanked the Rhiz for setting us up. At the time, I thought that by pressing the never-before-used Rhiz button on my phone and summoning an Operatrix to help me, I had failed in some elaborate scheme of self-reliance. When the chubby Latinx Operatrix in a long printed caftan had given me their tablet of recommendations with Sophie's starred name, I'd expected to encounter a weepy and patronizing cis woman who signed a lot of online petitions in her free time. And yet the Rhiz had succeeded like its namesake; I was a tree in distress, and the network had sent out a signal to bring in reparative nutrients.

Aiden was home, on the couch with Blithe.

"The cis women in marketing thought I was this cute, unthreatening stud and asked me really invasive questions about my dick size. And, voila, here's our compensation," he reported. Three SpaceShoes capsules—one silver, one red, and one teal—sat by his feet. He unboxed the Jupiter for us, all temperature-stable mesh with a pronged gap at the top. The defunding of NASA had released all this cool gear into the fashion world. We let Blithe choose first. He picked the silver.

After we'd eaten ramen that we'd ordered in, Aiden and I sat out in the backyard, sipping ashwagandha tea. I hadn't slept with R in over a week, and she grew clearer in my mind. The secrecy around our relationship was a vine-covered wall that I wanted to scale. I figured Aiden could handle it.

"What's the strangest hookup situation you've ever been in?" I asked, knowing that he wouldn't want to answer me.

"Pen, you know I don't like to talk about this private stuff."

"Can I tell you mine?"

"Sure," he said, without enthusiasm.

THE STORY OF R

I went to the Cape last summer to have a breakthrough in a bungalow, to finally cut through all my bullshit as a chorus of seaside insects chirped and dolphins flipped into the air.

I took a bus from Penn Station, switched in Boston, and took another one all the way to an outpost called Howard's Way and found my friend Minna's cousin's cabin behind three tall stripped birches, as described. The little dwelling smelled sweetly of pine and had an ant problem and a straw mattress oozing onto the floor. Once I got over my initial horror that there was no plumbing and that an orange extension cord siphoned electricity directly from the boatyard next door, all I could think about was having sex.

It was only my second summer on T, and the first summer I'd been so hungry and worried about being a believable *dude* that I didn't go on a dick-bender. I let all my anxiety and energy ferment into a disastrous brew, and then it was late August and the time of sexual frenzy in the city had passed.

The cabin baked in the sun. Once I sent Minna's cousin my daily email trying figure out the logistics of bathing (at the showers on the next beach) or eating (at the diner or from the tiny grocery store that still kept produce in wooden boxes), I would walk to the ocean, which was emptied out of all its rejuvenating power because I was so fucking tense.

I called Sophie, my therapist, to give her a typical "I think I'm going crazy" report and when I told her that all I wanted to do was have sex, she said, "Thank god, you're finally turning into a person."

"But you know I fall apart when I'm not working."

"So think of sex as work."

"Well, what am I supposed to do?"

I was being one of those girls I always heard on the subway whining to their parents about insurmountable issues: understanding APR (okay, I had no idea), taxes (my former guardian's accountant does mine), separating white and dark clothing (no segregation, just cold water).

"Uh, go on Tinder, go to Provincetown, come back to New York and cruise, jerk off, do you need me to keep going?"

"No."

I took a rickety bike and rode to Stallions, the one gay bar in P-town that was not cis-only.

Going to a gay bar hardly made any sense. I would end up getting hit on by a bear seeking a cute cub or an otter and might have to end up explaining that I was str8 in a queer way, a trans guy who needs to sleep with femme women to prop up his half-assed masculinity.

But a str8 bar? Those were not my people.

I locked up my bike in front of an ice cream shop and showed the old bear in an embroidered vest my ID, ordered a beer from a cute twink wearing rows of jeweled studs in his ears.

As he handed me my change, he said, "I'm Amber,

by the way," and he—she—tossed back her head, so maybe she was trans/femme. What did I know?

I settled into a booth to stare at the nautical homo-erotica: a huge mural of Billy Budd, a collection of dried sea cucumbers. Only a few patrons were around at four in the afternoon on a Wednesday, old men not stooped over like in str8 bars but sitting erect, in crew-neck long-sleeve shirts and printed shorts, speaking of a certain queen's adventures in Italy.

"Did you see *her* on the Gram with that gnocchi-maker?" one of the gays sneered, which caused the gold chain against his chest to shake.

"She certainly does not go in for *gnocchi*," another laughed, referring to her love of big D.

She sounded very Genet, and it seemed like they worked in PR.

I sipped my beer. I didn't see how I was going to find anyone there to have sex with. I ordered another beer. The bar started to fill.

I was about to leave when a hooded woman came flying into my booth, sloshing her drink onto *my* table.

"Do you mind if I sit here?"

I looked around. There was one open booth left.

"Um, I guess not." I did mind, but I didn't know how to say that. Blame girlhood socialization.

She pulled down her hood, and there was R in front of me, but also not in front of me because we were in the valley of the real, and her face was not so smooth as on TV.

Not only was I *not* star-struck, I was annoyed. Don't celebrities have plenty of private islands and bungalows to throw themselves into?

"What are you doing here?" I said, not straining the annoyance out of my voice.

"Hiding."

"From who?"

"Beard. He's str8 and would never come in here."

I didn't follow enough celebrity gossip to know which B-list actor would have been assigned to her. I figured R was probably the type of glamorous lesbian who only dated beautiful women whom she could share Ari-Efi purses with, stuck in a nineteenth-century fantasy of lesbianhood, only vaguely sexual, and more concentrated on a bosom-buddy friendship, the trading of flower crowns.

She did not interest me in the slightest because her life was so readily available, in some form, on the internet.

"Glad I can be of help," I said sarcastically, and took out my phone. I wanted this celebrity to feel ignored, for once, to meet the indifference that awaited Pen everywhere, from my own caretaker's face to the barista who would never understand that asking for a top-off took all of my daily allotted courage.

She sipped something in a plastic cup, really slumming it. I did want to see her carrying out an unstudied movement. I glanced over as she ran a hand through her hair, those expertly tousled ringlets, lustrous with argan oil. As a Jewish person, I'd never really been that exposed to blond hair—it was so white, so American—and I was drawn to its promise of sunny, ignorant afternoons spent running around cornfields.

Across the table, R's mane had a dark patch along the part.

"You dye your hair?" I asked.

"Well, not personally."

"Of course not."

"What's your prob?" she asked.

"Why would you even care if I have a prob? Aren't you on another plane of existence?"

"I seem to be sitting here in this bar, just like you."

"Not just like me. You're taking cover in here on a whim and I'm—"

"You're what? Trapped in here?"

"You know what I am? I'm a trans guy who is desperately horny, and this is the closest place I can go to find someone—not just any tattooed queer, but a cis femme woman who I can be a daddy to, who I can act out all of my strange ambivalence about my own girlhood with, by punishing her and maybe dressing her in little nightgowns, and making her sit on my knee, leaving a wet spot on my pants."

She did not frown. She did more than not-frown; she smiled.

She started separating her hair into two pigtails. Her face retained a glow of innocence, which led her to be cast in high school comedies well past her twenties.

"Tell me what you would do to me if I was your bad little girl," she said, and leaned into me with imploring eyes. She took the straw out of her plastic cup and licked it.

Stop it, Pen, you're about to be topped by capitalism, Hollywood, the whole spectacle of beauty, came the warning, but I kept going. I was shy and rigid around other queers, afraid that they were all trying to out-queer me with their chosen names and elaborate origin-story tattoos taking up their entire bodies, but with R I could relax because I felt that I *knew her* from watching TV, and she didn't belong here any more than I did.

"I would take you over my knee and spank you," I said, leaning back to achieve the illusion of power.

"You sound like a mean daddy."

"Only to little girls who deserve it."

"All right, we're going back to my place," she said, and chugged the rest of her drink.

I wanted to grab her wrist but didn't know how to signal that as part of the scenario. "You don't get to make the rules," I said, but of course she did.

"Okay, Daddy." She waited.

Well, I wasn't going to bring her back to my ramshackle cottage.

I took a long, slow breath, giving myself a moment to catch up with the fact that she had gone from a disinterested glamour-lesbian to a willing little girl.

"You're going to send Beard away for the night and call a car for us to take us back to your place."

"Yes, Daddy."

"That's better."

With other queers, I was a half-convincing daddy, always afraid my partners would think I was actually an asshole, but with R, I tried harder.

An SUV (*Ugh, I'm going to have to spank her for ecological reasons*, I thought) picked us up, and the driver, a generic white guy in shorts with an earpiece, opened the door for her and then for me, even tho I wasn't sure how the code of chivalry extended to fuck-boys. As we drove down sandy paths, passing sunburnt families with canvas tote bags, I traced her clit through silk panties. The divider was up.

"Oh, Daddy," she moaned. "I've been so bad."

Our roles were scripted and inviolable; we were free inside of them. I didn't have to pretend to be suave; she didn't have to pretend to care or be down-to-earth. It was just her juices dripping through the fabric, the cold leather seats, and her skin, which close up did not belong to a celebrity at all—it had all sorts of irregularities, disordered hair follicles, a freckle all by itself, veins close to the surface.

Driving through a wooded tract, branches slapping the car, we had our talk about safe words and limits.

"The safe word is *eagle*," she said, and I consented, although it sounded nationalistic.

We pulled up to a restored farmhouse.

"It's my grandparents' old summer place," she said.

We walked through a sunroom covered in art and

old photographs and vintage floral fabric. My grand-parents stockpiled canned goods and jugs of water, while hers kept old pinecones and tartan tablecloths. I looked at the pert ass that I had seen so many times on TV as we went up a dark walnut staircase covered in portraits of her bony ancestors.

"We used to come to Neena and Poppy's place as kids," she said, kicking off her shoes in the doorway of a bedroom with sun pouring in.

Her grandparents sounded like seventies lesbians, and I wanted her to stop talking. The WASPiness of the room was stifling, even if the chairs were covered in relaxed linen.

Once I pulled her to me and kissed her, I didn't need my own biting commentary anymore.

I positioned her on their great wooden bed with carved ducks on the headboard and took off my belt. Just then, her assistant came in, wearing a pair of com-petent slacks and those flats with triangles emblazoned on them.

"Marcy," the assistant said.

She held out her hand, and I had to put down the belt to shake it.

"Step into the study for a moment."

For a second, my fear impulse kicked in and I thought about all the sketchy things that might ensue, some sort of trans guy snuff film. She took me into a sun-shaded room with comfy chairs and gave me a stack of papers to initial.

After I'd legally sworn that I'd never whisper a word about fucking R, or risk going to both the Rhiz-Port and the celebrity Gold Court, we took our positions again, R with her feet on the floor, bent over the bed.

She turned to me.

"I have one request, Daddy. Will you blindfold me? I don't want to have a face when I'm having sex. I want to be closer to my body."

I wrapped a silk scarf around her eyes that smelled like old-lady Estée Lauder.

I started whipping her, as if I knew what I was doing, doubling the belt over in my hand and slapping it down onto her flesh, as if I'd been whipping women my whole life.

"Um, do you have any obligations, such as that you don't want marks to show?" Somehow, my nervousness found its way into formal language.

"No, just fucking hit me."

I was pissed that she tilted the dynamic, so I went harder. I focused on her butt, which was whiter than the rest of her body, and then branched out to the back of her thighs.

An old pro-domme had once given me a short impromptu workshop in her bedroom after one of my partners complained that I was too timid. She made me practice on one of her many subs, hitting the crease where the butt meets the top of the thigh. The sub was all tied up and gagged, which was not my favorite; it's like, how fragile does a top have to be to want to hit an immobile lover? I always wanted my bottoms to challenge me. It was thrilling because they could very well outmaneuver me and then I'd have to think of a way to regain control.

"Bad girl, being punished on your grandparents' bed by a stranger. What a little slut!"

First, she was quiet and gave a little grunt when I hit her. As I kept going, she started to yell, "Yah, Daddy, punish me, punish your slut, hit me, hit me harder, HARDER!"

"Eagle!" I cried. "I'm starting to feel like an object," I told her as she lifted up her blindfold.

"Ugh, you're one of those sensitive queers."

"Yup."

"Okay, Daddy. Do what you want to me," she said with a bored, bratty air, which made me hit harder and harder until the backs of her legs were bright red— but not sadist purple-red—and she was wailing, "I'm sorry. I'm sorry. I'm sorry," tears and pussy juice pouring onto an antique quilt that would have to go to a very discreet dry cleaner.

I had to stop and ask her where the dildos were. We paused and she pulled out an Hermès shoe box. I chose a purple dick and laced it through a harness.

It was really when I fucked her in the ass that I started to feel close to R. I watched her butthole swallow the purple sparkly dildo, as she moaned, "Daddy. I can't believe you're fucking me there, oh, Daddy," and

I slapped her ass and told her to be quiet. Of course, I couldn't believe it either.

We both came together, which almost never happened when I fucked anyone because my dick usually needed its own special attention, and we lay, me on top of her with the dildo in her ass, until we heard the far-off tinkling of a bell that seemed to cross centuries.

"Oh! Go slow!" she said as I pulled out, and I didn't know what to do with my frustration that she was still telling me what to do.

"Sorry." I winced for her and it plopped out.

"That was the dinner bell."

"Am I invited?"

"Yeah, silly," she said, exactly as she had in the film about teenage animal rescuers, and I had to wonder if her personality had seeped into her film. What if there was a limit to how much superficiality one can effect, even at a high-grossing level of acting?

We went down to dinner. I was in my J. Crew faded women's boy-cut jeans. I'd kept them from before the transition, and now they were much baggier on my man-legs, but they were so soft and preppy I couldn't get rid of them like all the rest of my girl-things. With a white T-shirt and Birkenstocks and a red dad cap, it was the best Cape outfit I could pull off. She'd thrown on a white sundress, but all I saw was the point where her legs emerged, and I wanted to put my hand down there, but we were seated across from each other in straight-backed

Puritan chairs and served clams and melon and red and white wine by an old servant, Mr. Sims.

"What's the name of the butler in *The Simpsons*?" I asked her when he'd left the room.

"Smithers!"

"Yah."

As a trans kid unknown to myself with dead parents and an almost-silent aunt, I hated pop culture because it never included me, not even as the butt of a joke. Now this rainbow you see in an oily spot in a parking lot after the rain—beauty so cheap and toxic that it offers the tiniest bloom of delight before turning to disgust—opened to me.

And we were sharing it, me and R. Even if I'd only watched *The Simpsons* before my parents died because Dad liked it, and not after because my next guardian, Margot, said it was "everything that's wrong with this country."

Maybe R could get me my own TV show. Trans visibility as a service to cis viewers? Okay, I was drunk. She put the sorbet spoon on her tongue, and I was worried she'd want to keep having sex when I was so full and delighted with myself that I couldn't really summon my daddy-mode, but she said she needed to go meditate (after three glasses of wine, I didn't know how that was possible). She sent me to the den to amuse myself.

I fell asleep curled up in a blanket watching that old film *A League of Their Own*, with ocean air entering through the screen door.

I woke up on a faded denim couch with a cashmere

throw draped over me. Not a sound went through the entire house. My dick throbbed. I found a bathroom and peed and lathered my hands in kelp soap. I went up the old stairs as quietly as I could and knocked on R's door. The driver had confiscated my phone and I didn't know what time it was.

"Pen," she called.

"Yeah?"

"You looked so cute on the couch I didn't want to wake you last night."

For a moment our roles shifted, and I was the child and she was the mommy.

"Have you been a good girl?" I said, to flip things back.

"No, Daddy. I've been touching my pussy without you."

We played our very real game for a few hours until the bell tinkled again, all the way from the nineteenth century, and we ate poached eggs and drank coffee on the porch. She pointed out a dent in the wood where her drunken aunt had thrown her mother's engagement gift, a heavy crystal vase, against the wall. The vase was so fancy that it didn't break.

"Today I have to run some errands, but feel free to stay here and go to the beach, and I'll be back around six."

"Is my D really that good?"

"Yeah, your D and your anonymity. What are you, like, a student?"

"Something like that."

"Perf." She went back to typing on her phone.

I took a bath towel and went to the beach. I was scared to ask Mr. Sims for a beach towel because he wasn't *my* servant, for god's sake. No one was around. That is a function of money: no overly public beaches like the one in the city where the old gays go to fuck in a tent with flags of various nationalities flying around, really the most patriotic thing I've ever seen for all the countries involved—Cuba, Norway, the United States—and you have to listen to reggaeton and see all the queers from tepid OkCupid dates, including the girl who said I wasn't enough of a top for her. After she left the bar I'd texted her, Well, obv, I mean when I'm meeting someone on a first date I'm a scared nervous child, what do you want from me?, which I then regretted and asked myself:

Haven't you learned anything about masculinity?

Play it cool!

Say nothing!

Don't have any sort of vulnerable reaction!

I drifted off to sleep and awoke to Mr. Sims standing over me in a polo shirt and jeans so carefully casual that they looked fancier than any of my fancy clothes.

"Here you go," he said, and handed me sunscreen, a bag of grapes, a striped folding chair, and a beach towel.

"Oh my god! You didn't have to do that!" I shouted.

"I know I didn't. And here I am," he said with a wry smile.

Had he noticed my scars? Had he ever served a trans before? Damn, if only I had that kind of steadfastness, to be thoughtful to someone else without all this accounting. If I were in his place, I'd wonder, *Does he want to be disturbed? Does he like grapes?* But he was able to execute a simple human action without all the noise.

I walked among the dunes, following crabs in and out of their holes, picking up pink stones and throwing them into the sea—my old gender costume, good riddance!—writing PENFIELD in the sand fifty-five times so someone would notice me. My skin cooked, I ate some grapes, and, once the sky started deepening, I walked back to the summer home and took a nap in R's bed, my first completely quiet, structurally sound bedroom in ages.

R leaned over me to wake me up, and the smell of synthetic perfume made my dick hard. I wanted to fuck luxuriousness out of her and into myself, getting a temporary bioaffective kick. She wore a drapey silk blouse.

"Beard is downstairs waiting for me. We're going to a wedding, and then tomorrow we have to go through JFK and LAX together. It's in our Scroll."

She whispered this in my ear, and I felt more betrayed than I'd expected. And still horny.

"My driver will take you wherever you need to go. And, Pen?"

"Yeah?"

"I could use a daddy to keep me sane in the city."

I nodded, having no idea if she was serious or not.

I took the back staircase, like the help that I was, and got into the SUV, with its too-cold air-conditioning.

THE END

"And then you really kept seeing each other in the city?" Aiden asked.

"Yep. About once a fortnight. In her Red Hook guest apartment."

"That's a great story, Pen."

I refused to let myself think he was implying that I'd made it up.

"Yeah, it is."

For a moment, I saw myself through Aiden's eyes as a hot dude who had been sleeping with a celebrity.

Ew, I was so much more than that, but in my early days of transitioning, I was clearest to myself in the pleasure I could give to others.

The next day, I took Blithe out with me on my route. The "Emotions" zine article said that movement is vital, even if it's the last thing the subject wants to do, even if the subject wants to watch TV all day in the bathtub with their computer perched perilously on the toilet seat.

We both wore our SpaceShoes, and I hoped no one thought we were really rich.

On our way to walk Louise, I pointed toward a street of

brick fortresses warming in the spring sunlight. The grass patches in front of the apartments were kept trimmed and chemical-green.

"Okay, up there, between 54 and 63 Palmetto, old Polish women in headscarves and sturdy wooden shoes sprinkle lye and baking soda on the grass patches in front of their building, which burns the dogs' feet. Even when I cross to the other side of the street, they still chase me with old-school brooms made up of bundled branches."

At one point, I would have said, *Of course they want to protect their two-foot by three-foot square, they've lived here all their lives, they have no suburban pool to lounge in. What do you expect?* But I no longer apologized for strangers. I spent less time occupying their hypothetical insides. I didn't care to imagine how they saw me: as a girlish boy or a boyish girl, a blossomed fantasy of freedom, someone trying to muddle God's perfect creation, a phallocentric lesbian.

We crossed Linden. In thirty-eight days, the lines of trees on each side of the street would blossom, suffusing the air in the sweetness of another era.

"And if you keep going all the way down Linden, Latinx families have woven a covering. Suspended from the trees, it hangs down to the sidewalk, and we are not allowed in. And around that corner"—I gestured toward Madison—"the Scorpion Café. Don't ever go in there thinking you are going to find cheap well drinks and smoke-stained air. In fact, I would cross the street instead of walking by," I warned. "If you need coffee, go to Chronos two blocks from here, but to get in the door, you have to be able to pronounce the names Hegel, Kant, and Goethe."

By that point, we were almost to Louise's. Trash blew by. I had a rule that I could only pick up dog shit in plastic bags that I'd taken off the street. On windy days, I collected at least fifteen and took them home to sterilize. Sid had chosen this neighborhood in which to start The Dog Walkers because there were enough affluent people around to pay us, but they were not so affluent that they would install grass-sensors to ticket you when a dog peed on a patch of lawn.

"The neighborhood weed is bought and sold on the rooftop of the old button factory over there. You simply yell Tawanda as loud as you can, and a Black lesbian named Block will throw down some keys. She sends her girlfriend Persephone to our house when the S-H texts that his dread is higher than a fourteen on the Crisis Chart and he can't leave his room."

Since Blithe and Aiden arrived, we had only seen the S-H poke his head out a few times.

I wanted to show Blithe how being a dog walker could mean many things. Who else got to travel in and out of homes, like a thief in the night, and roam the streets all day? Who else could take stock of the faces carved into nineteenth-century façades on fried-chicken shops and cell phone accessory stores, of wind-eaten plastic bags, and of a never-open window where a vine had split through the vinyl shades and was spreading across the glass, asking for help?

As soon as we entered her recently saged apartment, Blithe hugged Louise, a Great Dane. We had a good day.

Only one person took a poop bag out of their trash can and threw it at us.

Back at the apartment, I cooked rice and beans and debated whether drinking wine in front of Blithe was appropriate. Aiden didn't drink. He was with his new trainer, someone his L.A. person had recommended. I poured from a bottle of rosé that I had opened before the hex. The wine was less juicy than before. Blithe sat on the couch watching a nature documentary about coral reefs. I hoped that thinking about global warming would not push him further into the darkness, although I often wondered if human activity wasn't causing the Shadowlands to move from the psychic to the natural realm. No one wanted to hear my unfounded theories.

I brought the two plates into the living room and went back for my wine.

The TV displayed the delirious color of reefs.

"You know, when I was growing up with my aunt, she never let us watch TV while eating dinner, which is weird because she also didn't know what to talk to me about. She was a heart surgeon and always said the only people who could truly understand her were other heart surgeons, because they were such a difficult bunch. And that because they were such a difficult bunch, she never wanted to spend any time around them. I always felt like life was made of these impossible binds. I didn't want to be around her, either, I wanted to be with my dead parents, and there we were, with no distraction, eating pasta."

I turned to Blithe on the little couch.

"Snippets," he said neutrally.

I sipped some wine. It was quite enjoyable using Blithe as a sounding board. "I guess if we're really going to start talking about my Shadowlands, we'd have to go back to my parents' deaths. That made the landscape particularly putrid. Can you imagine something organic dying and then sealing it up in an airless room and returning to it almost twenty years later?" My voice cracked.

"Mondo," Blithe said, and pulled his knees to his chest. His plate sat on the coffee table.

I started to tell him about the first day I could identify being in the Shadowlands, when I went to sign the lease for the Ridgewood apartment. I was sitting in the management company's trailer (yes, I wanted to rent directly from an owner, but that didn't happen), and as I handed over the forms with both Margot's signatures and mine to my future landlord, who wore an oversized construction hat so I could barely see his face, the taste of shit entered my mouth.

I side-eyed Blithe to see his response to such a wild detail.

He slept with his head against his knees.

I took our plates into the kitchen and covered his with foil. I topped off my wine and Aiden came home.

"Hey, man," he said, and opened the fridge.

I smelled him. Woody. "There's more rice and beans."

"Cool. How's Blithe?"

"He's all right, sleeping. He went out to walk the dogs with me."

"Sweet."

I took my wine into my room, practically a cupboard. It was tiny and yet, once Aiden and Blithe had descended, it had become my snug refuge. I put on some ambient music and stretched out on my bed.

Soon after, Aiden crashed into my room.

"Pen! Pen! He's unconscious. What the fuck. We need to call—"

"What?"

Aiden's eyes were large with alarm. "I don't have service in your fucking apartment."

I ran outside through the Witch's room, through a pool of smoke.

The EMTs only let one of us ride with Blithe, and Aiden's silence forced me to volunteer. As they were strapping Blithe onto the gurney, they'd asked me what he ingested, and I told them that he'd left his dinner untouched and was only out of eyesight when he'd gone to pee.

"Medications," the EMT asked.

"Testosterone," I replied.

The Witch pressed a stone into my hand as we headed out into the sirened night. Had he tried to kill himself and then listened to me blabber about other deaths? I tried to focus on the tiniest details, the shaved back of the driver's head, the still trees outside that were not experiencing any major upsets.

"You have to take him to Poncy," I said, jolting out of one form of panic and into another. "He's trans, and the last thing he needs is typical medical establishment bullshit."

The driver shook his head and made a jerky U-turn at the next light.

I didn't tell the EMT—he was stuck in the fluorescent realm of emergency medicine—but people don't generally try to kill themselves within the first few days in the Shadowlands.

A new Operatrix met me in the waiting room. This one wore a long white robe and black platforms, a nightlife monk. I bet they didn't have a Gram addiction and attachment issues.

"Hello, Pen." A kind hand on my back.

"We at the Rhiz want you to let us know if there's anything you need. Blithe has insurance through his parents and through us. However, because Rhiz members were responsible for at least part of Blithe's deteriorating mental state, we cannot cover Blithe's medical expenses if this was a suicide attempt. Liability and such. We access Blithe's medical records through more unofficial channels, and we ask that you refrain from mentioning the Rhiz in any correspondence with medical personnel. All right?"

I was annoyed that this person was so benevolent.

"Can you get them to turn off the TV? I can't deal with the news and this real news."

The nightlife monk bowed.

"Also, will you explain why our old Operatrix is gone?"

"We decide when to go out missions based on our own individual needs and capacities," they said, and their outline faded.

Time did not pass. A nurse turned off the TV and no

one argued. Children behind me were drinking soda and I wanted to scream at their parents.

Aiden arrived much later than he should have. "How's he doing?"

I held up my hands.

Aiden started pacing and then swung around to the front desk. "They don't know anything. He's stable, though," he told me.

I grunted.

The lights hummed, and I knew that if the hyped-up kids behind me jostled my seat one more time, my self-restraint would evaporate.

"I'm gonna grab a coffee," Aiden said. "You want something?"

I glared. "Yeah, I want you to fucking just be here. Not sauntering around, not coming an hour late, not trying to save the day."

He didn't move. "It's the hospital, man."

"What? What's the hospital? Yeah, we're in the hospital. With Blithe. Blithe is in the hospital, and we are supposed to sit here and completely lose it while we wait."

He leaned over and put his head in his hands. "I was in one. For a while."

Damn it, Pen. Guns-blazing anxious rage was not helping.

"Fuck, I'm sorry."

He didn't say anything.

"If it isn't obvious by now, I'm scared," I said.

"Yeah."

"I'm going to call his parents," I told Aiden.

I went outside and called Margot.

We had a standing phone call every Sunday evening, which I'd skipped while at Rita's.

Normally, I made sure I had enough anecdotes gathered in case the silence started hurting. Not this time.

"Penfield, what's wrong?" she asked, and I could picture her sitting on her chaise longue, playing with her tablet. She refused to talk to me via video after six.

"It's my friend. The one I was helping in the desert. He's unconscious."

"Oh, Pen. Which hospital are you at?"

"Poncy."

"That's good."

"Is it possible for someone to go unconscious without taking something?"

"Without overdosing?" She always disarmed me with her directness; Margot never couched anything in the casual sloppiness of contemporary conversation.

"Right."

"Well, it's unusual for an otherwise healthy man in his thirties—which I'm assuming he is—to go unconscious."

"He's trans, if that has any bearing. And he's not exactly healthy."

"What's going on?"

"He has some mental health things." I needed my vagueness.

"I see."

"Do you know anyone here? Anyone who could check in on him?"

"I do have an old friend who's sometimes at Poncy. A surgeon. I don't really know what she could do—"

"Just. Come on."

Aiden had his hang-ups about hospitals, and so did I. Before my top surgery, Margot and I stopped speaking after she'd refused to come to New York for the operation. Sid came, as did Jillian. I'd woken up from anesthesia, put my hands over my numbed new chest. The whole region shook. What would happen if I lost my substitute guardian?

"Okay," she relented.

"Also, make sure you get the head night nurse to keep the notes."

"I will. Thanks."

"Call me tomorrow and let me know what his status is."

"K, love you."

"Bye."

I walked to the small park around the corner from the hospital to get away from the sirens and the people in pain. I petted the leaves on wet bushes without pulling them off. Someone was yelling into their phone, "Don't you fucking know who I am?" I thought of how I'd spoken to Aiden. Wasn't that what men were supposed to do? Act like dicks so that other people respected them? How much poison had I swallowed? When I made R suck my dick, was I just acting out a patriarchal script? Did Blithe go unconscious because

I'd had some wine? Or, worse, because I'd sent him too close to his own poisons?

Stop, Pen.

I went back to the hospital.

Aiden was staring at the ground.

"Okay, so I was going to call Blithe's parents," I said, "but then I realized that they might fly over here and take him back to L.A. and our mission would be over. If he did try to kill himself, though, we're going to have to figure out their insurance info because the Rhiz won't cover it."

I left out the part about my responsibility for his possible suicide attempt.

Aiden looked at me, his face drained of its usual color. He nodded.

We sat together, thinking of Blithe's loneliness.

A nurse came out, her white sneakers squeaking against the floor, and told us we could sit with Blithe for a while. Hospitals had revised their visiting policies after it was definitively proven that personal contact was its own medicine. The Rhiz had advocated for changing the "family only" dictum, and it worked, although the older queer community was melancholic. "If only a billionaire's child had joined the Rhiz at the height of the AIDS crisis," they said with sarcasm and rage.

Blithe's room was shaped by white curtains. He looked like he was sleeping. His cheeks were flushed.

He had not woken up, nor was he in a coma, the nurse said, picking up a clipboard. "He's completely stable."

"Was there anything in his system?"

"We'll know more when we get the blood tests back, but his body seems to be at homeostasis, which means in balance."

I did not say that I knew what homeostasis was.

"Can we talk to a doctor?" Aiden asked, which was foolish. Nurses were generally more competent.

"The doctor's been in, and these are her notes. She'll be back for the morning rounds."

She left after checking some of the machinery. We pulled two chairs up to his bed. If Blithe died, he would die unknown to me.

"You're gonna be okay, bud," Aiden whispered to Blithe.

I wondered who had been with him in his hospital.

After the nurse came by again, I kissed the top of Blithe's head and squeezed his hand. Aiden whispered something in his ear.

We went home in silence.

Back in the apartment, I saw the stupid wineglass sitting in my bedroom. I took it to the sink and smashed it with a plate.

I checked my phone.

Margot's friend had texted in usual surgeon shorthand: Will b at Poncy tom 11am find me on flr 10

And my old college friend Sara K. had texted, Cya tmrw for round 2.

I'd completely forgotten my second court date for a name change!

THE FIRST APPEARANCE OF
PENFIELD R(UTH) HENDERSON AT
NEW YORK CITY COURTHOUSE,
111 CENTRE STREET

A wordless clerk handed me a pile of paperwork and a beige warning slip because I hadn't worn proper footwear. The courts still used the old bureaucratic ways of endless documents. No one could rewrite the law fast enough to allow surveillance tech to supply all their informational needs.

When I was finished offering two to three anecdotes about why my name definitely needed to be changed, I slipped the paperwork into a metal bucket at the edge of the bench and waited with the rest of the silent room.

"Penfield Ruth Henderson?" a young man in a long coat called out. A tall, slippery fellow, he practically vibrated with restlessness.

I stood, ready to declare myself a trans who deserved to take three letters out of his name.

He beckoned and I followed him through a door next to the judge's bench. Above the empty judge's chair was a portrait of a severe woman in a bonnet, standing in a moving field of wheat. I started shrinking down without my crew in sight. Sid and Minna waited in the courtroom.

He took me into a windowless vestibule with velvet-lined benches and motioned for me to sit. His face narrowed with seriousness, and he started undressing, setting down his collegiate-striped scarf and long wool coat and kicking off his shoes. In a white ribbed undershirt and men's slacks, this irregular arm of the law bowed before me.

"I'm Tommy, the magistrate. You're going to have to step it up here, Penfield. You gave us this very dry Explanation of Name Change petition, and we're used to dazzling tales of violence, exploitation, assumed identity, and mental breaks causing one part of the self to splinter off, assume dominance, and rename the entire subject. Give us something juicy. Trans is juicy, trans is mind/body split"—he jumped back—"and then reunion."

He did a back handspring, which the adolescent Pen could never master.

"Trans is people kicked to the curb"—he kicked a small hole in the wall for emphasis—"by their stupid"—another kick—"loved ones who hate the gendered system of dominance but feel the only control they have over their lives is to play out the role they were assigned, wipe the countertops with bleach spray and paper towels, and force their offspring to do the same; trans is 'I don't give a fuck about the public gaze averting itself from me as I transition and then gluing itself to my new form, begging for me to perfect, enhance, and moisturize myself back into being a good boy.'" He thrust out his chest, ripping through a flimsy undershirt and splitting it in two, and I saw that his chest had no scars. He was not a passionate trans guy, just a bad actor.

My first thought: *Does he really want the juice?*

Usually, people greeted us trans with a weak smile because their minds were too busy calculating, *Okay, you are actually a girl, but through the wonders of pharmaceutical intervention and liberalism, you are able to transform yourself into a boy*, and here they get very distracted because as long as the biomedical technology is available to help trans people, that low rung of society, couldn't it allow rich people to transmogrify into birds, great winged predatory people who can fly across the land unhampered by conscience, gravity, taxes, or common sense?

My second thought: *Oh, he's a failed artist who has ended up as some finger of the Law and is taking every opportunity to pour his frustration into the sundry duties assigned to him on a whiteboard to-do list.*

"You want juicy?" I said.

With a sigh of relief, he threw himself into a chair.

"My parents were killed in an avalanche, seeking a rare mineral deposit. They named me Penfield Ruth Henderson because they looked Jewish but wanted their child to fit it 'anywhere,' and perhaps they mystically predicted that the pendulum would swing backward against the Jewish, and so they started this whole name business, and I'm happy to keep the Penfield and the Henderson, but the Ruth, it sits on top of me, a large-breasted pale woman who reads *The Red Tent*, with dirty ringlets running down her back, wearing a faded shift that barely covers the top of a gaping vagina."

"You crazy." He raised his eyebrows and glanced at the clock. "Okay, let's move this along," he continued, reverting back to a civil servant who still had a long list of people to press for juice. "The dead-parents part is a little tedious. It's really less charming and more devastating outside the realm of a Dickens novel. If we had more time, I'd push for some sort of 'turning over a new leaf' narrative: By wrenching the *Ruth* from your name, you are able to become your true self, a spirited and emotional young man with a hard bod."

Pressing my biceps, he squirmed with delight, then made some notes on a form.

I was led back into the courtroom. After hearing the judge, a Jewish man with wiry strands sticking out from his bonnet, grant a number of name-change petitions on the basis of familial breakage, TV-character obsession, and domestic violence, he took a look at my petition and said, "Ms. Henderson, I'd like to ask you something. Let the court note that we could all recount some childhood folly where we put on Nana's high-heeled shoes and clomped about in the living room, or got a unisex bowl-cut, asked for implants for Christmas, or switched the arms and legs of our secret Barbie so that at least she, too, could be grotesque. Why, I ask, are you allowed to switch genders? Who has granted you the moral grounds to bring into adulthood the urgent caprices of childhood?"

Under his scrutiny, I wished I was in the UK, where judges wore serious wigs and robes to make sure everyone knew they were the body of the state. Sara K. was too confused to advocate for me, so I started to speak. "Well, that's a great question, actually—" and then a security guard came and put his hand over my mouth.

"Do whatever you want, Ms. Henderson. Call yourself Hieronymus Bosch for all I care," the judge said to me while the security guard's institutional-pink-soap-cleaned hand was blocking my air flow. "But do *not* open your mouth in my court. Trans are children begging the government for luxuries, and they should be seen and not heard."

It was refreshing to hear someone speak the truth about their feelings. In fact, it made me feel sane, substantiating all my anger-floods in the entrails of his disgust.

The judge might have granted the petition, all reservations aside, but before he could, a bell rang, closing the courts for the day.

"These proceedings have gone on far too long," the judge said. "You'll have to return next season."

THE END

Two seasons had passed before they granted me a follow-up visit. I'd put the date in my calendar, where it had gone unnoticed with Blithe's various upsets.

I'll try 2 advocate for you tmrw if the judge says anything weird, Sara K. texted.

Last fall, when we left the building, she said she couldn't believe the judge's non-impartiality.

"I was taught at a highly prestigious institution that the law is fair and orderly, blind and righteous," she told me in a heavy voice.

"Welcome to the other side of naïve faith in establishments," I'd said.

I wasn't sure if I could go through the humiliation of court while Blithe was in the hospital.

I found the Witch hanging upside down off her bed.

"Hey, can I talk to you about Blithe?"

"Yes." She didn't move, although her face was flushed red with blood.

"Have you heard of someone going unconscious soon after they enter the Shadowlands?"

"Yes."

"What happened?"

"They went to sleep. They woke up again."

She closed her eyes, reversing the process. Her hair pooled on the ground, and her hands were folded on her stomach.

I felt better. I texted Sara K.

9am, I'll be there.

Before I went to bed, I put my head between my knees and braided the top tuft of my hair as though I were eleven years old.

The court threatened me not only because they might reject the name change but also because they might approve it.

I had lost so much in my young life, and I didn't want the *U,* *T,* and *H* to be another severance.

A secret that I wished I could tell someone without rejection or more madness: I wanted to transition enough to "male" that I could reunite with certain girlhood parts and not have to explain myself.

If only I had my old diary with a lock and key.

If only Blithe were under my gravity blanket right now.

Aiden and I walked into the brick-cube courthouse together. Sara K. met us in room 112 in the basement. She wore her steep red high heels, which meant she wasn't fucking around. The room was full of somber, age-old wooden benches and plaintiffs in the most thoughtless earth-toned business-casual outfits. We sat together in the front row. Aiden looked hot and weary, wearing his SpaceShoes. That pretty much summed up the contradictions of our lives: being able to wear the trendiest accessories to a hearing where someone in a bonnet would decide your fate. While your friend was in the hospital, stunned into unconsciousness by his own hand or something else. As I thought of Blithe, I straightened up. When he woke up, he would need something other than flip and backhanded comments about what it felt like to be trans.

"All rise," the court officer said.

We stood.

The judge entered and sat down under a portrait of herself, or perhaps an ancestor.

"Honorable Justice Wendy Arcana Williams," the magistrate declared.

The judge bowed and we bowed back. Had she authorized her own middle-name change? Did judges have to subject themselves to the same humiliating process of three DNA samples, fingerprints, butt prints, notarized petition, character reference from an almost forgotten acquaintance, and the wearing of court-appropriate clothing palettes? Prob not.

"Penfield Ruth Henderson, approach the bench."

She loomed up on the dais as I walked toward her. She began lifting a giant long-sword over her head. Shakily. The metal glinted, even under dead civic lighting.

"Kneel," she ordered, and I did, one knee on the pea-green carpet, a position I might never again take because I would not humiliate a woman by kneeling to ask her hand in marriage when we all know that marriage emboldens the man to tower, grow, rise, erect, flourish, and the woman to sour, grow brittle, fill with venom, get fat, take up gardening, and dream of lost solitude.

I didn't know how she was supposed to knight me from up above, but luckily, Tommy the magistrate came in. He was also dressed in an earth-toned button-down shirt and slacks. All that was left of his whimsy was a glinting shield pinned to his shirt. He went over to the side of the dais and was handed the sword.

"Penfield R. Henderson, I knight you Penfield R. Henderson, in the guise of the name-wielder Fiacha Sraibhtine, from now until eternity, neither snow nor rain nor heat nor gloom of night stays these couriers from the swift completion."

He hit me quite hard with the sword.

I pictured myself virile and boundless, no longer held back by the *UTH* in the center of my being.

I rose. The judge came down to press her wax seal onto my forehead, and Aiden gave me a hug. I saw that Minna had showed up, and she blessed me with her hands folded on her heart.

The magistrate ushered me to the cashier. The hallway was all brown and municipal yellow, and I loved that no one had tried to make the building sleek or user-friendly. The civil courthouse and elementary schools in poorer neighborhoods were shabbily insulated from modernity.

I found the cashier on the aged eighth floor and handed over my records and the eighteen-dollar check that would grant me a new persona.

The cashier, a Black woman with a pug calendar next to her computer, said, "Sir, I need a proper check."

"Excuse me?"

"It says that your name is now Penfield R. Henderson and that doesn't match the name on the check."

"Right, because I just got it changed."

"I need an accurate check."

"Should I come back?"

"No, you cannot leave the building with the valise."

Before I could open my mouth to protest, she said, "And yes, I've read Kafka, Solzhenitsyn, and Achebe. I'm well-versed both experientially and in a literary sense in the serpentine nature of bureaucracy and how it is designed to subjugate—to smoosh, as Jewish mothers say—the ordinary citizen, and especially"—she winked—"the non-ordinary ones."

I was almost ready to concede when Sara K. rushed up.

"Damn it, Pen, you shouldn't try to do anything without your lawyer present. That's for poor people who get totally chewed up by the system."

Without waiting for any instruction, she took out an ink stamp from her bag, pushed in two truncheons to shorten it, dipped the stamp in ink and pressed it down on top of the *U*, *T*, and *H*.

Before the cashier could object, she whipped out a calligraphy tool and inserted a period next to the *R*.

"Are we all set," she asked, although it was a statement.

The cashier sighed, peeled the seal off my forehead, and dropped it into the valise. She handed me three Declarations of a Changed Name.

"I'll be in touch," I told Sara K.

"Yeah, you must come up," she said, referring to her five-bedroom house in Westchester, the end of a trajectory she briefly abandoned during her college stoner phase. As she kissed me on the cheek, I smelled her perfume, unchanged in ten years, the musky scent of Stella: rose, balsam, and amber mixed with parabens to maintain "freshness."

If only I had the luxury—or was it a curse?—to keep any part of myself for ten years.

I found Aiden and Minna in the lobby. I showed them the official document. Behind us, the security guards were growing their piles of guns, liquids, metal-studded shoes, and other banned objects.

Outside, the sky stretched over everything without a break, a jagged tear, a lapse, or a lessening of soft, limp blue. The palette was kind, predating Pantone, which had separated every color into an upper-class shade, marring looking forever with Fig, Moss, Leaf, Prune.

I rlly am a new man, I said to myself, and carved out a little gem that I could share with Blithe, the soft freedoms that blow in and out the door.

Minna came with us to the hospital. In the waiting room a new nurse with puppies on her scrubs told us that Blithe was still stable.

"Is the doctor around?" Aiden insisted on asking.

"I'll page her."

Blithe's neighbor was blasting a soap opera, and there was no Operatrix around to shut it off. Blithe looked the same.

Don't die on me, man, I said inwardly.

Minna did not know Blithe at all, but she whispered him a koan and then went to sit by the far curtain.

Aiden held Blithe's hand. "Do you think it's right to keep this from his parents?" he asked.

"No, but do you want to lose him?"

"No."

The doctor in her lab coat came sweeping in.

"Hi, are you all friends, family?"

"Both," Aiden said.

"Okay, well, I'm Dr. Garamond. I've been looking after Blithe here. It's quite interesting; his blood tests came back completely normal. We can't find any medical cause for his loss of consciousness. Can you fill me in on his life these days, any stressors, abnormalities?"

I bit down on my lips so that I didn't giggle with tension.

"He's been having some mental health issues. Depression, mainly," Aiden said, and that word was so small against the scroll of our lives.

"I see. Also not a cause. Well, from a medical standpoint, he's in good shape. We're going to keep him here today, but if he's the same tomorrow, it would be more cost-effective to send him back with you in a cab and have a home health aide pop by."

She left after checking Blithe's vital signs.

"Do you feel better?" I asked Aiden.

He shrugged. Minna pulled at her sweater, stretching out the sleeves.

In the bathroom, I splashed water on my face and reminded myself that I had changed from Ruth to R.

When Aiden left for a coffee, I asked Minna, "Are you crushing on Aiden or what?"

"What?" She looked surprised. "I mean, I like him, but I'm not trying to date him or sleep with him."

"You're around more, though."

"Well, ever since Aiden and Blithe have come to the city, you've loosened up. You're not always complaining to me about your doom."

"Huh."

•

We went back to see Blithe the next morning, and the nurse from the previous day greeted us. Her scrubs had flowerpots on them.

"I'm glad you're here. We tried to call you," she said. "We wanted you to know that Blithe has regained consciousness but had to be sedated."

"Wait, what?"

"He awoke extremely agitated. He was experiencing symptoms of delusion and persecution."

I could have gone on a whole diatribe about how Blithe's "craziness" was most likely the absolute truth, but I held back.

In his partitioned area, he was sleeping like a child.

The nurse said that we could either take him home with us or have him sent to the psych ward. "Which is quite full at the moment."

"We're taking him," Aiden said.

Again, I wondered what had happened to him.

"We need to process the paperwork and get some more insurance info."

Blithe's parents had sent tilted photos of their insurance documents, which I'd printed on the S-H's printer. I handed them over.

We sat down to wait. I tethered my phone and saw a text from Margot's friend, the surgeon. I told her where we were.

Thirty minutes later, an older butch woman with a buzzed head and orthopedic loafers walked in. I assumed she was an Operatrix.

"What's going on in here?" she said bombastically.

We stared.

As if responding to her energy, Blithe awoke. "Two people took me from my home," he said.

"Blithe, holy shit." Aiden turned to him.

"Is one of you Penfield?" the woman said.

"Yea, me, oh, you're—"

"Margot's friend. Natalie. Nat."

I could not mentally link the person in the room to Margot.

She hated masculine women!

"Hey, thanks for coming to find me."

I did not have time to do a complete historical revision of my childhood and Margot's responses to my feeble attempts at masculinity.

"He's no longer unconscious and it seems like this is more of a mental than physical thing," I said apologetically.

"No difference. No difference whatsoever. I should know from all the fat, stressed, angry, loveless men whose hearts I'm supposed to unblock."

Wow. I was crushing, too, aside from her fatphobia.

"Well, any advice for him?"

"Keep him close," she said, walking over to his bedside, where he was glancing around the room. "I have to go, but here's my card. I'd love to get coffee and hear about how you're doing. Margot has told me a lot about you."

She what? I had this whole story about how I was this obnoxious kid always ruining her career and moments of solitude with my needs.

I took the card and put it right behind my subway pass in my wallet. She squeezed my shoulder.

Something passed from her into me and she left.

"Two people. Took me from my home."

I went to Blithe and sat at the end of the bed. "We know, we know. We're sorry, Blithe, but you would have ended up in the Shadowlands anyway," I said as his legs thrashed around under the covers.

"No, not you two," he said, and closed his eyes.

Blithe was cranky and itchy when we got back to my apartment, demanding that we let him go home, to his real home. Aiden had to go to a meeting, and I dreaded being left alone with the patient, who had gone from subdued to unconscious to unmoored.

"What's your real home?" I asked him in the living room, and he stared at me in disgust.

"They know, but they'll never tell you."

In the kitchen, I crushed up some Xanax and mixed it into his hummus, which I served with carrot sticks.

When he was asleep on the couch, I texted Margot that Blithe was so-so and that I'd met her friend Nat. I pulled out my phone and held down on the Rhiz button.

The nightlife monk Operatrix appeared.

"I have something else you can do for me," I said.

They nodded and the light caught their earrings.

"I need some more files. The ones about his adoption."

"I'll check in with our archivists. You're doing great, Pen," they said, and they were gone.

How secure in yourself do you have to be to tell someone else they're doing a good job? I wondered.

Something moved in the doorway.

"You know, you could just ask me directly about Blithe's adoption," Blithe said. His tone was murderous. For a moment, I thought he might have a weapon.

"Okay, Blithe, let's sit down."

I gestured for him to come sit on my bed.

He came over and stood.

"What's the deal with your adoption?"

"These white people took me. And they wouldn't let go." His voice remained like stone.

"How old were you?"

"Young."

"Do you remember your bio parents?"

"Call the Rhiz, call the Operator, and tell them to deliver an important message for me, okay?"

He started squeezing the cold cast iron of my headboard.

"Tell them."

He hit it with his palm.

"Tell them."

Hit.

"To tell my parents."

Hit.

"That they gave me up."

Hit.

"But I am."

Hit.

"A boy."

He started hitting his head on the wall and I had to pull him back. I held him and he didn't fight me.

Aiden came home after I'd convinced Blithe to take another pill. I told him what had happened.

"Oh shit. The one-child policy."

"What?"

"I watched a documentary about it. Chinese parents had to give up their children and always kept the boys."

"Omigod." I hadn't made the connection.

We sat in the kitchen, soaking in Blithe's tale.

A messenger dropped off an envelope. *Your request for adoption materials has been denied.*

I was hesitant to leave Blithe and go out with Jillian, but it was time for Aiden to do some caretaking.

I always forgot that when I went to see my old high school friend, all the old Pens threatened to come tumbling back. *Can you hold it together with a specter from the past or will you revert into a timid, accommodating girl who will not correct Jillian when she says "Yass, bitch" to you, or asks about dildo technicalities?* I asked myself in a cornflower-blue subway car.

In my fantasies, people from all parts of my life could come together at a giant party, but there had not been a socially acceptable occasion for this since my bat mitzvah.

We were meeting at Piastres, the old blacksmith forge at

Metropolitan Avenue and Port. I'd texted her about it, and first she texted back, You know, historical frisson is complicated for most Black folks.

A few minutes later: Fine. I heard they have good Manhattans.

While many old buildings repurposed into bars had an obsequious, self-conscious feel, always winking at you when your wine at the old shoe factory arrives with a submerged shoelace, Piastres was dark and unfinished. The forge still stood in a once-neglected corner, and the building hadn't been sold because the already-wealthy children who inherited the building from their grandmother could not be bothered to venture past Bedford Avenue, for fear of ending up in lands beyond the reach of their car service.

I wanted to celebrate my name change but didn't have the energy to fill Jillian in about Blithe and the hex.

I spoon-fed her pieces of my life, morsel by morsel.

Outside the bar, I heard low chatter and glasses clinking.

By the door, a dog's paw print had been pressed into the cement. BLOOPIE, 2005. I caught sight of Jillian's bun and felt the usual hesitation about entering a place I used to go to before I transitioned.

Head to toe flow, head to toe flow, hands on pants. I started my mindfulness exercise.

Oh, fuck it, I'm not that fragile.

I tapped her shoulder. "Heyy."

She put down her drink and turned. "Hi, Pen. You're looking good, hot actually, except for the fact you're wearing a polka-dotted sweater and striped pants. I would do you."

I tried to let my irritation and the phrase *power-clashing* float off into the noisy bar.

"You look good, too."

She did, in a generic straight-woman way, with a white button-down shirt and black dress pants, no hint of hipness about her, and that was what I admired about Jillian. She was something of a constant in my ever-shifting universe. She'd even kept a Clayton High School Greyhounds sweatshirt and had worn it one Sunday morning when I stopped by her apartment with coffee. She was hungover and wanted to complain to me about cis dudes.

"It's better than girl talk, you know, because you've seen both sides. You could be the ultimate negotiator."

I was already too cozy under a fleece blanket watching *Clueless* without any Witchy burnt-sienna smells to start arguing about how I was not Switzerland in the battle of the sexes, that in fact I had my own battles against the entire gender system, as well as an ever-growing need to assert my sexed-up masculinity and press all my discarded feminine objects (an old purse with lush flowers painted on it, a horse poster) between waxen paper. Her parents had bought her an apartment in the city, and the womb of parental comfort had stunted her emotional intelligence.

I ordered a glass of champagne from the bartender who used to ignore me for about fifteen minutes before I was on T, and occupied the no-man's-land of not passing as a man, woman, radical no-fucks queer, or anything, really.

There had been freedom in that impenetrability.

"Is champagne girly?" I asked Jillian.

"Only if you're giggling while you drink it," she said.

"Let's toast to my name change," I said, hoping she'd feel a little guilty about missing the court date after my last-minute text.

"What should I call you now? Bubbles?"

"I took the *Ruth* out and left the initial."

"Not terribly dramatic. How's Margot dealing with all this these days?"

My jaw tightened. She always took Margot's side. "She says she's grieving for the old Penfield, which is shitty to me because in all the years after my parents died, she never once let me see her sadness, and now here I am, alive and trying to flourish for fuck's sake, and she's wearing a mourning dress and covering all the mirrors. She started following my Gram, but now I'm not using it that much."

"Well, it's a new era. Give her a break. She's trying."

Jillian was talking about herself, how I needed to make space for her stupidity. Where was the middle ground, the mythological bridge between experiences? A certain lightness, a way of turning things over like compost, letting air in . . .

"Well, it was a sort of breakthrough when Margot told me that she started watching the TV show where people cut vegetables into animal shapes really quickly and that there's a *transgendered* person on it."

"See, it's a start."

"I think I understand the smallest fraction of Black rage

at all the missteps white people make in trying to become allies, accomplices, actual human beings."

"Yeah," was all Jillian said.

The bridge was not sturdy.

The first conversation where we dug into race came during college after another police shooting of an unarmed Black person. I, overcome by horror and guilt and wanting to bring everything together and closer and up to a soulful fever pitch of no more bullshit, texted her to say, I'm with you, which I somewhat hoped would be followed by I'm with you, too, Pen, but all I got was a K, and then at brunch, after I made a long heartfelt proclamation about how I stood with Black Lives Matter and had made a sizable donation, like any good white person, she stirred her drink and said, "I want to be more than the visceral abstraction of another Black body."

Around that time, she had started speaking with a forcefulness that betrayed how tense she had become, how being the only Black person in her office had not radicalized her in the political sense, but in the fleshier beingness of existence. She wanted to be more than not-dead; she wanted to be living.

"Even tho Black Lives Matter is presumably about the living, the movement is situated in the endless deaths of Black people at the hands of police and the entire white system of power," she'd said, and tho I had been waiting all of my twenties for her to bring up race, in order to link all my reading and theorizing with her *real* experience, once she started speaking, I did not know what to say. I was afraid of her hating my whiteness and I froze up, letting guilt wash over me in an annihilating wave.

I had to keep pushing, even if I made a thousand shitty mistakes, even if the patrons sitting next to us were discussing the newest nut milk.

"Why don't you like talking about this stuff with me, when I'm trying to be open with you about trans things?" I waited for a most scorching retort.

"Why don't I like talking about Black stuff with you?" she asked, and my question sounded absurd. "Well, I used to think I didn't want to talk about race because I wanted to take comfort in midwestern propriety, niceness, low-hanging upper-middle-class perks—Van Leeuwen pistachio ice cream and steak-frites at Balthazar—and I presumed that if I went too deep into Black reality, I would lose it entirely, would break down, and nothing that my parents taught me about hard work and courage would mean anything and it would fall apart and there would be no consolation, just the cold hard stabbing edge of truth amid the Shake Shack wrappers.

"But that's bullshit. What I really mean to say is that I'm uncomfortable when you regurgitate all these notions you've picked up by trolling the internet, whereas I am doing a lot of heavy lifting simply by existing in a PR office, online dating, getting on the subway, going to the hair salon—if I want my hair relaxed I have all the sisters hissing that I'm a self-hating Becky and that I need to decolonize my beauty regimen, and if I leave it natural, my boss's boss asks me if he can touch my hair at the annual pub crawl, and wants to know my opinion of Kara Walker's *bugaboos* that he saw over the weekend in Munich. So yes, I feel proprietorial about my Black experience, which is always being explained to me, and I'd really rather that you not mansplain it back to me as you compare it to the trans experience."

"Got it."

We sat in silence.

A Bio-meter would have beamed marigold with "social-justice-related awkwardness."

Yes, as a trans guy with dead parents, going to the hardware store, the barber, the swimming pool, the grocery store, the airport, the car rental agency, the gym (which I hated anyway), and the clothing store was fraught with everything lost and gained, the constant crashing of memory into future joys, of girlhood training into unexpected manhood, of a body still as stone turning into a living organism, but it was not at all the same as being Black. My whiteness had protected me from violence and poverty. These were simply facts. It was up to me to start digesting reality.

"What do you think of the last *G+T*, OMG, when they did that faerie orgy flashback from the time before Fae Luc got sober?" I asked, moving back to safer territory.

First she ignored me and ordered another drink, further putting me in my place. The bartender handed her a shot of tequila, and she finally said, "Ugh, I was dying when they broke into a conga line with all their dicks in each other's asses," and we were friends.

I longed to solidify our friendship by telling Jillian about R, the very actress of the cult comedy in which two nerdy girls move to China, where they are suddenly popular, that we used to love. But I'd signed papers in Cape Cod stating that if I ever disclosed personal information about R, I would end up in celebrity court, and who knows what would happen to a normal civilian there. They could rescind my name or gender marker change, or worse.

We talked more about the shows we were watching, who from our high school class had divorced already, and her parents' trip to Spain, sketching over our old map with new details.

Finally, she said, "I've gotta get up early for spinning."

I stood up to hug her, pressing my body into hers and inhaling the scent of her closeness. She walked out and took with her the painfully sweet town of Clayton, Missouri, and its careful brick houses, trees everywhere, very few Black folks and queers, and Jewish deli with better corned beef than Katz's.

When I was alone again, I briefly considered getting wasted and taking a hangover day because having an honest conversation with Jillian had bowled me over. Watching both of us go to the edge of tolerance and come back was not warm, not inevitable, but frightening, and if such tension existed between the two of us, wouldn't the rest of my life be a gauntlet of partially understood dialogues, yelling over a gorge instead of meeting on Monet's bridge? Didn't I deserve some peaceful oblivion in a dark former blacksmith den? I was already tipsy enough to see the other side. Couldn't I slither over there and collapse?

Naw.

Sophie was right. There were too many forces working against me for self-sabotage to take on more than a fleeting glow, and as sexy and self-evident as the television tried to

paint alcoholic bliss, if I got wasted, I would feel terrible trying to watch TV on my computer without Blithe noticing,
worried that he might take my plunge into alcohol as an en-
dorsement of meaningless abandon.

I was already moving against habit, standing before Jillian in my stripes and polka dots, newly renamed.

"Hey, man, do you want to start a new tab?"

"No thanks."

I grabbed my jacket and my bag and headed toward the
mouth of the forge, scraggly rock framing darkness.

What I longed for was the unseen and the unknowable,
the cave that still stood.

The whole apartment smelled of actual lemon and lavender.
Aiden was sitting on the couch. He had gotten another haircut. He gave me a little smile.

"How's Blithe?"

"He wouldn't talk to me," Aiden said.

"Did you do this?" I asked, gesturing at the stove no longer splattered with sauces, the scrubbed trash can lid, the
row of shoes by the front door, a vacuumed rug, the vanished
row of fish bones that always stank.

"Yeah, I talked to the Witch about it, and she agreed,
as long as she could bless the nontoxic cleaning products,"
Aiden said.

"Wow." I hadn't known she was willing to compromise in
any direction. I went into the bathroom to pee. The sludge was
gone. Aiden had stuck bamboo caddies onto the wall, bursting

with the Witch's glass tinctures, Blithe's fancy men's elixirs, my low-brow natural products, the S-H's normie shampoo and conditioner, and Aiden's sample-size bottles from his sponsors, along with a large Head and Shoulders. Next to the toilet, there was a stainless-steel box with Aiden's and my hormone vials and needles and alcohol wipes in sealed pouches. Blithe had his hormones delivered in implant form. He was a man of the future, while Aiden and I signaled to the Rhiz with our phones, which were *almost* parts of our body.

Blithe had dragged the air mattress into my room and fallen asleep on the floor. Inside my pillowcase, I found a lavender sachet.

When I needed to take a break from the domestic situation, I went back to the pool, a beleaguered parent finally getting some downtime. I swam behind a slow older man with a white ponytail hanging out of his swimming cap. It moved through the water like a furry eel.

Aching and breathless, I decided to return to the sauna and ask for another appointment.

"Hi. I had to go out of town to help someone and I missed my appointment with the Grandmeister," I told the new gatekeeper, who was reading a book in the humid anteroom.

"Was he a brother?"

"Like biologically?"

"A brother is any man you would share half of a sandwich with."

"Sure, yes."

"Then there's no problem."

"Can I make another one? I told the last guy that I would be happy to give myself a shot and celebrate masculinity."

"It's a slow day. You can come in now."

I was not prepared for my entrée.

"Just repeat after me: *No bitches here. No bitches here. No bitches here.*"

"What? Seriously?"

"Well, yes, it makes our brotherhood more potent when we cast out any bitches."

"Fuck that."

At other, more cowardly junctures of my life, I might have calculated: *Is it worthwhile to say something you don't believe in to gain access to a pore-opening spot?*

No longer.

I took a chartreuse car, and when I got home, the Witch had burnt something and dumped it into the newly cleaned shower, Blithe was nonverbal in my bed, and Aiden was out in the backyard posing—again—against the plastic textile art on the fence.

Wanna get a drink? I texted Minna.

Can't 2nite. Sorry! she wrote back.

I thought about calling Sid in L.A., but it would take a lot to explain the situation here. Plus, I felt like I was cheating on him in terms of intimate trans friendship. I texted Jillian Whatsup and she said Hiii back, and I left it at that. Finally, I reached out to R, not expecting anything, and she told me to come over.

•

We started to go through our spanking scene and for some reason, neither of us were into it. My dick shriveled up and I could tell she was distracted.

"Why don't we take a bath?" she said.

I agreed, although I was hesitant to step out of our scripted roles.

Her bathroom was naked compared to mine. I wanted to press my cheek against the coolness of the black-and-white-tiled floor. She took off her schoolgirl skirt in front of me, and I unclasped her bra. Even though I fucked her in the ass all the time, I felt shy watching her slip off her underwear. I sat on the toilet, clothed, as she ran the water and dropped in bath pods that curled into little jasmine-releasing flowers. We got in together and she leaned against my chest. For once we were completely still.

I woke up in R's bed, confused. I'd only slept over once before. We had both gotten wasted, and the next morning her assistant had given me a coconut water and a coupon for a restorative IV.

I padded down the hallway. R was already in the living room, working out. I was not at all turned on by her leaning over an exercise ball in a sports bra and yoga pants, but I enjoyed watching.

"Hi, do you want breakfast?"

"Sure."

She made eggs and toast and orange juice, and we sat out on the balcony, looking over the water where ships used to sail.

"Next time, maybe you could come to my real apartment," she said.

I set down my fork. I knew what it looked like from her PR Gram account. She had a giant oil portrait of a black horse hanging in the entranceway.

"Really?"

"Yeah. I mean when we first met, I think we were in very different places. Hell, I was still with my beard, and you seemed uncomfortable when we weren't in the middle of a sex game, you know?"

She brushed my hand with hers.

"You mean like me 'forcing you' to suck my dick?"

"Yeah," she said, and got down on her knees and unbuttoned my pants. Below, the waves played as well.

When she was done, she kissed my cheek and went back to her chair. Wiped her face on a linen napkin.

"Wait, now I feel like we just switched back into our sex games," I said. "Tell me something about you. Something I wouldn't know from the tabloids."

"My family is really messed up," she said, and let her sadness touch the air.

On the way out, the doorman tipped his hat to me. "Good day, sir."

Outside, the cobblestones clicked under my feet and the city pulsed with possibility. Wow, R could go from a disaffected actress to a warm lover—it was positively Proustian!

The next time, we met in public, at a rooftop restaurant. The night was thick with promises of summer and the roses budding on the trellises. She ordered a bottle of Sancerre and I ordered zucchini frites. She wore a shapeless white tunic and I wore a striped shirt and nice black jeans without worrying that our styles did not complement each other. We spoke of nothing serious. The night was loose and open and long. Stepping out on the sidewalk with her, I assumed that we would go back to her real apartment.

"I want us to start over. Let's pretend we haven't been fucking for a year."

She pulled me in, and we made out with a new ferocity. When she stopped, I was ready to fuck her in the street, in the car, in any type of apartment, real or fake.

"I want you to woo me," she said, and I was floating off to another plane, a softer one.

R texted me every night—Sweet dreams or Xoxo or Hope youre thinking about me—and arranged elaborate dates, after which we would kiss and head to our separate bedrooms. As my initial excitement subsided, I started to feel like she had initiated a new game, one that I had not agreed to, one with no safe word.

When I told Sophie about this "new phase," she grimaced.

"I'm just wondering what will be left of the relationship if you take out the sex," she said.

Sometimes, I hated her directness.

On an early Friday evening, R texted me to meet her for oysters in Soho. After the server verified that she was really expecting a guest, I found her sitting at a small table in the back of a brasserie, no makeup, old white tank top, white jeans, dykey boots. Even in her college-sophomore-lesbian outfit, she still exuded the type of charm that had the maître d' running over, pouring us little glasses of calvados from Bretagne.

When I opened my mouth to speak, she put up her hand.

"I can't. Not right now. I just want to sit."

Everyone around me seemed immersed in their despair, which was odd for a low-key fancy restaurant.

Was I the only one slowly finding my way out of it?

Pen, in a crisp white button-down and teal SpaceShoes that were not even available to preorder.

R ordered oysters and Aperol spritzers and frites for us both. She was already drunk.

I wouldn't have minded eating in silence with her if she hadn't been manipulating me for the past few weeks. A couple next to us argued about splitting the housework fifty-fifty. ("Well, it's more like Esmerelda does eighty percent and we're arguing over who takes care of the remaining twenty percent," the guy chimed in.)

I thought that roommates represented a uniquely horrible arrangement whereby you were subject to the domestic whims of strangers, but choosing to live with a partner who reasoned that he should be responsible for only 5 percent of housework to your 15 percent because of the relative ardor of his *real job* was definitely worse.

Over tea originating in the Himalayas, which I convinced her to order instead of another spritzer, R looked at me with guilt and secret knowledge, as though she were about to end our liaison.

"Penfield, will you marry me?" she asked.

I waited for a clue. She didn't slide a ring across the table, which had been cleared of crumbs by a man with a file. But she definitely didn't laugh.

"Okay, so my grandmother Neena, the one whose bed we fucked in, is a dumb bitch."

I was not attracted to this snarling side of her.

"She's petty and calculating, and she uses her money—some of which comes from mining in the Congo—to control people. Blah. Blah. Blah. She's getting really old and she hates my parents and last time I was in Los Angeles, she point-blank told me that I would inherit, along with my brother, as long as I got married. To a dude. My brother will take the money and use it to build AI robots that will fuck him. As much as I don't want to get married to win her over, I can't let him prosper from my queerness."

"As happy as I am that you've actually used the word *queer* in my presence, no. I can't believe you would dangle the possibility of a real relationship, one based on, IDK, oxytocin and trust, while you were cooking up this scheme. I mean, I can believe it, but it's not okay."

I got up to storm out, as I'd always wanted to do to someone.

Unlike in films, the volume of the restaurant remained uniform even as I pushed back my chair and walked past cis people, sprayed with various aromatic chemicals, who most likely would not propose to each other in such a manner.

"Excuse me," I said, pushing through the waiting diners, and my voice came out as girly as ever.

My life was in disarray. I turned my phone on Do Not Disturb and walked all the way home, past the neighborhood where girl gangs rode skateboards while swinging Bluetooth speakers on long ropes to ward off catcallers, through the Lower East Side where my Jewish ancestors ran a vegetable stand, across the bridge, along the streets where wealthy bros felt exotic every time they entered *Brooklyn* into the city box at their online shopping checkouts, down the Plaza of the Rose, carefully avoiding the Scorpion Café, and then over to the street below the train tracks, where Linden and Palmetto met.

Aiden and I sat out on the back steps drinking iced coffee. He'd already taken his daily selfie beneath my cherry blossom tree. I remembered how my insides used to curdle from looking at him all those dead mornings ago.

The blossoms on the ground were the color of the potty seat my parents had when I was learning to pee on the toilet.

"How's it going with the Gram?" I asked. I didn't go on it much anymore and found myself craving a distraction.

"Just this morning, I was eating an egg-and-cheese sandwich outside a bodega and did not have time to run away from a group of canvassers. One of them walked up to me and said he was taking a survey of this rapidly gentrifying area to see if any of us newcomers had stable jobs that could endure outside a frivolous bubble. I wanted to lie and say I was a lawyer or accountant, but I was wearing this"—he gestured to his tie-dyed T-shirt and billowing light blue pants—"and knew they wouldn't believe me. I said that I modeled. The survey was thorough; he wanted to know for whom. 'For myself,' I said, 'on the Gram.' 'Think about where you'll be in twenty years, son,' the guy said, and put a hand on my shoulder. He was full of pity. He said that since I was ripped, I should look into construction work. I need to get my life together."

I felt a little better about my choices.

"We should ask the Witch what's going on astrologically. Everything is falling apart. You know, Rachel and I just broke up because she asked me to marry her."

"Huh?"

"Yep, Rachel has a rich, sickly, mean grandmother, and in order to inherit her money, she's got to marry a man. She asked me, which I guess I should feel flattered about, but it's so fucked that I don't."

The following day, Blithe and Aiden went out. With them gone, I thought I would bask in my disappointment with Rachel but grew bored after a few minutes. I opened the bubble wrap and pulled out the pad that Blithe's parents had sent us. I connected to Wi-Fi and opened Elemental's network, where Arrow-Lines were sculpted, colored, cut, upped to 133 percent drama level, obliterated, braided, and ultimately sent out into the world in episodic spurts.

I lit a candle in my bedroom, trying to draw Blithe's realm closer to me.

When all eight jewels are put back into the belt of Catalpa, then Oshun may return for the healing of the world, read the tagline on the home screen.

The eight Lines could be tracked at once, each in a different color, but I chose Margaret's and minimized the others.

Hers was cobalt blue. I had read the background on Margaret from Blithe's files: five foot five, hard blue eyes, long brown hair, perpetual frown on her handsome face, born on a wagon moving west, hardscrabble life in a settlement outside Las Cruces, escaped from an arranged marriage and met a miner in Colorado.

Her Line stretched out in a row of blue boxes that the beta writers had been reshaping according to the Elemental Rubric of Satisfied Desires. The boxes were changing as I watched. It was a Thursday and the regular world was working.

HN33 commented, If Margaret wears "men's" clothes, but it's still clear that she's a woman, our audience SD quotient will go up by 2 points.

Hey, where you been?

Shit, they could all see that BF45 was online.

I disconnected.

There was one chunk of writing still in pastel purple. This part was kept private, written in Blithe's handwriting, a finger pressed against the screen.

Water spurting from the pump onto a bed of mosaic tiles

Scratchy woolen underwear against muslin skirt and saddle

Long blade of the men in long capes who will come to bring her back to her family to be wed

Jewel in soft sack

Frisson—Margaret seduced the Salton Sea engineer so that she could steal his Echometer, a tool that will track the history of the other gems through the soil. Yes, fuck yes. If you dig a spike into the earth, a—

Tapestry will emerge from the ground?

Reading will come up with precise past latitude and longitudes?

Spirit will start to narrate?

The Echometer cracks the earth around it to create a map, and on the map each gem location is marked. The Echometer doesn't follow the conventions of modern geopolitical boundaries. The map has sixteen circles, each about the width of a wagon wheel, and on eight of them, a shallow hollow has been carved out. When a hand is placed in the hollow, a gem-bearer's memory emerges in a cloud of dust, smudged and incomplete. Margaret will have to flee from the engineer and find someone who can read the marks in the earth. She sketches the map in her oilskin journal, where she keeps track of her provisions. In a burst of feeling, she runs around putting her hand in all of the hollows. Eight memories crowd the air, bumping into one another.

As I read, I thought of the pink sphere at E-M-E-R-A-L-D's, the diner in the middle of the desert. He was going deep here, in a way that satisfied ancient, archetypal longings for meaning.

Sinking into the outlines of his words, I fell asleep.

Later, I was sitting on my bed, about to jerk off to an imagined scene between Margaret and the engineer when I heard the front door open. I shoved a pillow on top of Blithe's pad and pulled my shirt over my opened pants.

"Well, how'd it go?" I yelled into the hallway.

Blithe poked his head into my room.

"We went to Flushing and ate a shit-ton of dumplings and walked around," he said matter-of-factly.

One morning I woke up early, inexplicably optimistic. I jumped out of bed instead of lying there, ruminating in dread-circles. I went into the kitchen to make coffee. The Witch was standing in the kitchen, cloaked and dropping rose petals onto a hand mirror. She did not acknowledge me, and I let her do her thing.

Desires poured into the dark, narrow space with rosemary branches hanging down from the ceiling, mortars and pestles with half-crushed insect shells and bird-poop tinctures on the counter, spice jars that held flakes of gold and mouse skulls, takeout containers full of spring water (even tho the plastic leeched, the Witch still used them), spindles of twine, a pot of algae. The air was permanently stained with mandrake root, eucalyptus, burnt hair, and something that must have been natural but smelled like wet dry cleaning.

"The Strawberry Moon is on her way," she said.

"Maybe I'm feeling it."

"Maybe," she said, skeptically.

"I think I need to grow up," I said, and she didn't respond.

I would start by making myself, and everyone else, breakfast.

I walked a few blocks to Food Carnival, bracing myself for the extreme stimulation of death-white lights and flour-sack-shaking bachata.

Every aisle was an algorithm of my hunger and nostalgia and dumbness:

Kraft mac and cheese
Hi-C

Froot Loops
Choco Tacos
organic polenta
avocados
guava nectar
mantecadas
harina de maiz
enchonadas
lard
hindquarters

Someday I could go strolling down the coast of Maine and plunk blueberries into a pail and stir my batter near a hearth, but I had to start where I was. I grabbed a plastic container of blueberries and paper sack of flour and went home to my brethren.

Blithe was in his sleeping bag on the couch, talking to his parents on speaker.

"Honey, no matter what's going on, we'll always love you," said his mom. "And you don't have to worry about getting back to work too soon because we called and the beta writers can patch up the rest of the story line for your pilot. But we did send you the pad just in case."

"You did?" His voice lacked affect.

"Yep, and I've been keeping it for you," I said loudly.

"None of you understand me at all," he whined.

"Honey, you're going to be fine," his mom said.

It wore on my body to listen to such love expressed to someone who had expressed his hatred mere days ago.

I made the pancakes and we ate outside. Blithe chowed

down. The Witch picked out all the blueberries and ate them, leaving holey remains. Aiden suspended his carb avoidance and didn't comment on my technique. We left a plate for the S-H covered in plastic.

Without being tangled in Rachel's celebrity vibes, I had all this excess energy—I was not overdrawn—and while Aiden loaded the dishwasher, I went running through the neighborhood, down streets that appeared shrouded in desolation when I was transitioning without anything as disruptive as hope, past the bakery and the chiming church bells and the pork store, all comforting because they'd been around since before the neighborhood trended, down toward the industrial warehouses, under blooming, arching trees that I hadn't registered before, around people walking their own damn dogs, and into a hazy stupor of long strides on hard ground.

Back at home, Aiden leaned against the counter.

"Hey, I need some more clothes, bro, let's go to ift," he said.

"I'll get Blithe ready after I meditate," I responded, happy to be a capitalist for a day.

In a sour-green subway car, a mother was explaining to her child, dressed in all polka dots, like a young Pen, how to avoid the *wrong* cars.

"If you see some depressed or poor people about to get on, just move down a few cars so you don't have to soak in some horrible color. But they should know better than to walk into a perfectly pleasant pastel car," she said, glancing over at the angry mother with three screaming children who were probably keeping the train's interior in the limbo of lime. "Often, white kids in their early twenties try to sneak into dying grass or algal bloom cars, but they end up returning to the *tasteful* colors," she added, pushing the child's hair back from his face.

We reached Mulberry Street and passed consumers who did not have the privilege of mind-cleaning, who only wanted to find the perfect acid-wash jeans to go with their despair. I saw our reflection in a storefront and wondered how anyone could ever want to hate-crime us.

We were looking so hot and unified!

Inside the over-lit store, techno throbbed and Blithe and I fished complimentary ear plugs out of a mesh basket. The overstimulation didn't seem to bother Aiden, who wandered off without us. The *edgy* retailer sold three items, all unisex: enormous T-shirts, long shorts, and a pair of sweatpants with legs four times the size of a usual leg, designed for a monster. The colors rotated every three weeks. That week's: Fragile Violet, Renaissance Gold, and Horchata.

"I miss those shiny Adidas track pants," I told Blithe.

"I'm nostalgic for every single part of my life that didn't feel like a pit of despair," he responded, and walked away.

I started spiraling, thinking how feminist cis-dudes out there would be scoring major points for wearing genderless ift sweatpants in their dating profiles while all of us trans who wanted actual fitting M or F clothing were told: *Just wait a little longer for the next stage of capitalism to bring strange new forms into the marketplace.*

Trans desires still counted for about fifteen cents on every dollar, unless there was easy entertainment value. All these well-meaning fools were sitting around a boardroom table in a smart office with whiteboard floors for creative juicing, thinking up a thousand new, disposable ways for cis, straight, skinny women to dress themselves.

Oh, but look at these giant coral shorts on sale!

The color-archives sale rack had a pair that was *très* cute. I decided my furry legs and olive skin would look great in the shorts against a sea-blue yoga mat or riding in a sherbet subway. I held up the shorts to my waist, as if these sizes would ever fit properly.

Brain and creature desires do not need to align, I told myself.

I don't need to be a pure trans of ideals, wearing only Levi's from the thrift store that still carry the ball sweat of some skinny graphic novelist in his forties.

After a few minutes of trying casually to make eye contact, I got the sales associate's attention. This gender-nonconforming person (I presumed, given their shaved head, huge orange pants, and two nineties lip rings) made no facial expression as they registered my presence and took me into a dressing room with a curtain that stretched only halfway across the stall. *Fuck it.* The world could handle the sight of this short guy with a beard—*what a cute face*—his stomach muscles visible under a slight layer of fat, a tattoo of an osprey on his upper thigh, a slightly wary look on his face no matter how hard he tried to be delighted.

I got down to my underwear and took out my phone. I ignored a text from Margot, How r u. It had been a while and I opened the app. I temporarily stepped into Aiden's selfie persona, even if the lighting in there was unflattering enough to make someone buy twenty pairs of peony-shaded leggings to feel better about themselves.

@ift with @aidenchasestruth. <3

I left Blithe out of it because he was developmentally under eighteen.

My bod was still buzzing with desire. I showed Blithe and Aiden my shorts. Blithe shrugged and Aiden smiled an approving-parent smile.

We walked out into the street, and right at the corner of Houston and Broadway, a new Operatrix appeared, a Black femme in a jean jacket and crinkly green skirt and necklace that read *Mar'iah*.

"Hello, you merry three transmen," she said. "I've noticed a spike in all of your bioaffective data—even yours, B—and I wanted to say, soak in it. Soak in the joy, soak in the warmth, soak in the winning of the tiniest battles. But don't become complacent privileged bros who make a man-cave of safety for themselves and shove a boulder in front of the entrance. That is all."

We all nodded solemnly, and Mar'iah left us.

We ate dosas for lunch, and then I went off to Turquoise Yoga, where I'd been absentee for some months.

"Does anyone have an injury I should know about?" Kaya asked our intermediate class.

I was illumined from head to dick to toe in radiance, and my new shorts only made it better. I always imagined this was what antidepressants would do to the body—light up all the dark corners, chase away the shadows, leave me bathed in new skin—but they made me sleepy and numb, so I stopped taking them.

"Yes. I'm trans."

"Excuse me?"

I'd taken her beginner class many times but had never spoken to her. She squinted from the front of the room and walked over slowly, elongating each step.

"I'm trans and I bound my chest for ten years so I can't properly do boat pose and I want you to know this lest you take my ineptitude compared to all these lithe bodies as a personal failing and not a dense web of causal links and betrayals."

She bowed. "Thank you for gifting that to us."

I could see some eye rolls through the mirror.

We went through our flow faster than in the beginner class, with the usual farts and sighs. The pancakes rumbled around in my stomach as I inverted and watched the sweat-stained back of a long person, who had to be a ballerina, extending her leg back in dancer-pose.

I was always half-aware of Kaya hovering around. Before I started taking T, I hardly looked at str8 women—we lived in a world apart, without any sexual value to each other—but after, I could get lost in their scent and our feminism and how they looked at me curiously.

When it came to bridge pose, I couldn't hold myself up with my arms. I caved in and thought of Aiden and all his weightlifting, and how I was hardly the muscular dude that trans men were supposed to become.

Phew. Thank gawdess I'm a bad trans, came the new refrain.

During shavasana, I dreamed I was on a tiny boat floating in the ocean.

Kaya rang a bell and the room filled with palo santo smoke.

I awoke with a fresh feeling.

We all hummed *Om* together in a cacophony, my voice cracking. I was trying to slip out the door when Kaya came over and put her hands on my chest.

"I feel the surging here," she said, with eyes closed. "All that movement, stiffness, tissue."

Am I comfortable with this? Do I want to punch, crumble, roar, or accept her touch?

Sophie always said that being an adult means having options. But sometimes our options were all second-tier shows available to stream instantly, while the option we needed had been removed due to copyright.

Or our options were all the foods at bicoastal food halls, from ramen burgers to burrata ice cream: As long as you were white and rich and didn't mind waiting in a line of ift clothing and bamboo textiles for thirty minutes, you could chow down on all the earthly delights.

"You know, trans people have an extra chakra," I told her, deciding to accept her touch but also educate.

She nodded.

"Equidistant from the third eye and the throat. Thanks to all the bullshit we have to process on a daily basis, we are at least gifted with a portal."

"Do you mind if I put my Reiki fingers on you? You're transmitting really hard."

I shrugged.

She ran her fingers across the scars, and a solid mass started rising out of my skin. She worked her fingers along the side of my chest and said, "You are seeking entry into the Piscean age, when the very foundations of the universe shift toward the dignity of all people."

I nodded, enthralled by all things fluid and dignified.

"Also, for what it's worth, the surgeon did a good job," she says, giving my chest a pat.

"Thanks."

I went into the bathroom to change. I pressed my hands against my pecs, which were still flabbier than I would have liked, but way better than boobs.

THE OFFICE OF DR. GARTH

Dr. Garth was the surgeon who did *everyone's* chest. A robust, cub-like man, he had the mannerisms of a trans guy but was not, as far as anyone could tell, trans. Some patients chose to hang out in his waiting room after hours because it was the only place on earth where T-guys could speak among themselves, and the nurses obliged, installing a card table. They sometimes hovered on the fringes, jotting down their anthropological findings about this curious demographic. (*T-guys are way sweeter than cis guys,* a standard finding.)

When I went in for my first appointment, I, too, was amazed by the existence of these characters: a luggage handler, a kindergarten teacher, two servers, a visual artist who used his old menstrual blood as paint. I wasn't sure I could find *common ground* with them, tho. If I said I was a dog walker, they would forever identify that job—the least important thing about me—with Pen R. Henderson, and if I said my future was still unformed, they might think I was full of shit, just another frivolous artist who hangs out in the neighborhood where everything was built from newly harvested bamboo and recycled bottles.

When I heard Stuart the teacher talking about his two beagle "sons," I thought, *What if everyone thinks all trans guys are as bubbly as him? Or as nebbishy as Clive, the sloppy bike messenger who drinks water with chunks of garlic in it for his immune system?*

I'd been well conditioned by solitude and waited to be called from the back of the room. When I came back for a presurgery consultation, the guys were talking about the cliffhanger of *Goblins and Trolls*, and from my lonely chair, I blurted out, "I wish they had done a better job foreshadowing that Medusa was going to turn on everyone," and the five sitting there threw me a nod and I was grateful to join them for some seconds.

That day, the only other trans person outside the circle was a trans kid with his parents. I wanted to murder him. His mom's arm was around his shoulders, and he had dark black hair growing at the top of his lip and was wearing metallic purple low-top unbranded sneakers. This kid had bypassed the whole ordeal of wearing women's clothes and then looking back at them with fondness. He would be named prom king, and the school parents would feel liberal and accomplished. The PTA moms would even forget their initial exchange:

PTA Mom 1: Does Ryan really need to use the men's restroom?

PTA Mom 2: What about the fact the he used to sleep over with my daughter, well, he *was* she *then. Should I be retrospectively alarmed?*

I said to myself, *Maybe one day I'll find a place to put all of this commentary. It would be economical. I can't refrain from making stories out of the raw materials that come my way, three people sitting contentedly in padded office chairs, leaning into each other under photographs of three dudes with surfboards, hyacinth leis covering their scars.*

THE END

I sat on a bench outside the yoga studio, happy to be in a neighborhood with seating that didn't send up spikes after fifteen minutes. The Witch texted that the Strawberry Moon was rising. We were leaving the hex's astrological quartern.

The seeds are thrown, the seal is 'orn, the door is shut, the house, a hut, she wrote. Of course. Ending my hookup arrangement, buying a pair of shorts, and taking a yoga class certainly could not explain my sense of well-being.

That night, I went through my gratitude list and

uncharacteristically included many people: Blithe, Aiden, the Witch, and our many Operatrixes.

"Blithe still passes much of the day inside the Womb, a sleeping bag on my floor. He orders American Chinese food and then explains to me how it does not resemble anything cooked in Chinese provinces. Some days he speaks to his adoptive parents, and some days he won't answer and then they text me asking about him. Often, I resent him because I went through that stage all on my own, I mean except for you, but obviously, you couldn't be there with me every moment, except you always were because you helped me reshape my thoughts," I said to Sophie during our appointed hour.

"How beautiful, to give that experience to another," she responded.

A new vase of water lilies sat near the edge of the table and I had no fantasies about smashing it.

"Ya, you right."

"Maybe there's a way you can try to tell him about some of the advantages of being trans, so that it's not just a dark hole to fall into."

"That reminds me of what the Witch said when she moved in."

Sophie smiled. "What did the Witch say?"

"She came in to see the apartment, and she stood out on the back steps and said to me:

You trans, you make the mirror see its error.
You take the shame, cast it out.

You husk nuts waiting for your return and there it comes,
Curling over the fields as serpent's love.
I bow to your truth.

"And she bowed, asked me about the dimensions of her bedroom and the dryness of the kitchen, and left. I didn't know if she was making fun of me or not, and I would never have asked her to move in if the perfect ceramicist hadn't backed out at the last minute."

Sophie was trying really hard not to laugh.

"Oh yes, the mythical ceramicist. Okay, so that's how the Witch would phrase it. What about you?"

"Well, when you're trans you can look back and see how every gut sensation that told you something was off, too tight, wrong, airless, and incongruent was a beautiful curling script toward the future."

"I bow to your truth," she said.

Sophie was wearing a clingy T-shirt, and I could see the rather large breasts she must have demanded.

The surgeon probably said something like, *Are you sure you want grapefruit-sized breasts? For your body type?*

And she knew exactly the contour she wanted.

"Hey, are we having another Unfuneral next week?" she asked before I left.

God, I always blocked out the anniversary of the avalanche.

For the last few years, Sophie and I had been holding an Unfuneral for my parents. We went to the park at night with trowels, buried a handful of the stones they left me, lit a ritual candle, circled the burial ground twice, and then dug them back up. Their dewy, nerdy, quiet-but-full-of-love presence came back to me; I swore; we opened a door with a gesture. After that, they visited me at night, in waves of remembrance, and I knew that the flat world where they were truly dead was not the real one.

"Yah, let's do it."

I usually sent Margot a postcard invite with the Unfuneral date and time on it, in case she wanted to join. She never acknowledged receipt.

Aiden was meeting with another trans Gram influencer in our backyard, and I went down the street to the bookstore to avoid them.

An embroidered sign on the Chronos door warned, NO ADV-TECH ALLOWED.

The old red-cheeked bookseller waited for me to enter with arms crossed. In another era, he would have been the type of professor to give wild talks under trees and sexually harass female students, universally beloved by all who had agreed to overlook his faults.

"Magic words?"

I mumbled, "Kant, Hegel, Goethe."

Flanking him were two or three young disciples who smoked herbal cigarettes and longed desperately for a father figure.

I perused Coetzee-laden shelves until I found something that I was thirsty for, set among the acacia trees and the futile priests of New Mexico. In spite of my knowledge, the mythic American West still appealed to me.

Gun belt. Horsefly. Saguaro.

I sat down in the café area and ordered a coffee from a silent barista. It came in a tureen-shaped bowl, and I pretended that the drink was brewed in a heavy iron pot over an open fire on the western frontier instead of in a smudged glass Chemex.

I started reading. I wanted to be transported, to walk the harsh paths, to cheer for the Hopi and the Navajo, but all I could think about was Blithe, and his night in the desert, with scorpions.

Headphones were banned, so I picked up on the disciples' whispers as they shelved new arrivals, wearing linen gloves.

"I really don't know how I can keep working here at fifteen dollars an hour when I have 90K in student loan debt from my undergrad years and philosophy master's."

"Don't let him hear you say that."

"I know, I know. *Thought above all.*"

"Think of honor as a currency. It is an honor to be invited into this den of thought, the oasis in a desert of ignorance, plastic, non-English speakers, television watching, and emoticons."

"I'll try."

I wrangled my attention and tried to read another page, but it was useless.

What was bright and hot on my brain was Margaret, on the verge of stealing a precious tool from a lover in the Sonoran. I saw horse hooves kicking up dust. And she was not alone: there was a man smoking a pipe in an Ethiopian coffee grove, a beekeeper scraping honey in the future city-state of

Hente, a skin diver who had expanded the capacity of her lungs beyond science, all hovering close to the gems.

When the cuckoo clock struck three, the bookseller sat down at the table next to me. His disciples ambled over. One removed the bookseller's shoes while another grabbed a bottle of apple cider vinegar. The third applied the ACV to a towel and started rubbing the bookseller's feet. The first then retrieved a bottle of coconut oil. I left without buying the book before they reached the moisturizing stage.

Blithe was on my bed, eating saltwater taffy.

"Hey, so I happened to read on your pad the part in your Arrow-Line where Margaret is going to find the Echometer so she can track the gems and memories and I love it, that gives me the chills, like the part of film previews where the drama and the music come together in a crescendo—"

"Yeah, that's called the Pinnacle, or, informally, the orgasm. It's very cis-male-centered."

Oof, Blithe was starting to enter the "identity consciousness" phase.

"Well, why don't I help you work on the Arrow-Line and see if we can get the Echometer in there?"

"Pen, all that Catalpa shit is meaningless. It's like expensive perfume that makes you want to buy things. It's a complex blend of chemicals that approximates something pleasurable. I can't. And they must be at least halfway through the season by now."

I flushed.

"Well, I want to buy the desert and the jewels and the guns and the smoke."

I went into the backyard, and there was Aiden and Egret sitting side by side, furiously coloring.

Egret wore a crop top and baggy purple cargo pants. I wanted to congratulate her on picking a name that so perfectly suited her tall and graceful form.

They both looked up.

"We're trying out these new pheromone crayons," Aiden said.

"And also trying to stop from boning each other right here," Egret added.

That Sunday evening, with the ice cream truck song looping in the background, I called Margot, a duty like injecting myself with a needle and sending hormones into my bloodstream.

"Hi, Pen, how's your friend?"

"He's okay. I'm taking pretty good care of him."

"That's good."

"You know, the Unfuneral is coming up."

"Yes, it is."

"Could you visit their grave for me?" I didn't know this was something I wanted until the words left my mouth.

A long pause.

"All right."

"Really?"

"Yes, Pen, really."

"Great—and bring marigolds. Mom loved them."

"I know. She had our dad plant a whole patch at the house on Morris."

"And bring a Mexican bottle of Coke, you know, the kind Dad would only drink once a year."

"Yes, on Father's Day. All right, Pen."

I was afraid to use up her goodwill all at once. "Okay, tell me about surgery this week."

"Well, I had a hard one."

"Did he die?" Her patients were invariably older men, and often hated to see female cardiologists.

"No, he didn't die, but it really took something out of me."

"I'm sorry, Margot."

I was sorry and relieved at a break in her invulnerability. She usually gave a brisk summary of her surgical procedures, omitting any mention of deaths or strain.

"Me too. I think Nat is going to fly in and we'll do something wild like go down to Nashville."

"Nat—I met her. Did she tell you? She was not what I expected."

"I felt the same way when she first entered my life."

After we hung up, I stared down at the phone, trying to figure out what had changed between us.

The night of the Unfuneral arrived. At sunset, I traveled to the big park above Manhattan. On the train, I passed revelers who were heading to the pride parties. Aside from an upswing in Aiden's sponsorships, and his presence at certain required events, we were not observing Pride. We were living it in another form.

The Unfuneral could only work by candlelight. I carried

the stones my parents left me in a leather pouch and brought trowels and candles. The sounds of boom boxes and food trucks dimmed as I carried my candle toward a shadowy spot that we marked with a survey flag. The flag was often bent down to the ground when we returned each year, but no one bothered to take it. That night, it was at a forty-five-degree angle. Sophie was there in her long cape. I lit a candle for her. We didn't need to speak. I gave her half of the stones.

"How about I dig part of the hole and then you finish it?" I asked.

"Sure."

In years past, we dug together and, nervous about getting too close to each other, we ended up creating a shallow, oblong shape.

I dug straight down and pulled up clots of earth. I smelled the wet freshness. My parents' bodies had never been recovered. When I told Margot to bring them marigolds and Coca-Cola, the gesture was symbolic, as are all gestures toward death. I let Sophie dig until the hole was about two feet deep and then we dropped in the stones, one by one. We buried them and circled the plot.

I found myself shouting, "Mom, Dad, Mom, Dad," and Sophie joined in.

I liked watching her get weird in the candlelight.

We dug out the stones and sat on the cool ground with our hands touching them. I closed my eyes. There was my mom, making me puppy chow in a big plastic bag, her hair stuffed into a baseball cap. And my dad, sitting me up on his broad desk and showing me the cracks of oolitic limestone through a magnifying glass. And they stretched, stretched across time, so that they were not stuck in these moments, and we were not stuck in the present moment, missing them.

I was singing to Alice in the kitchen when Aiden walked in, wearing a pastel T-shirt and cutoff jean shorts. While he often looked hot and pensive in his photos, I'd never seen him look this relaxed, like he'd lived inside a Korean spa for a week or two, eating nothing but kimchi and going into the hottest bath, where they cook eggs.

"I have to tell you something."

His face was shifty. His aqua shorts were tight along the outside of his packer, and his mesh running shoes were so hip they were unbranded. He pretended to examine one of the herb bundles overhead.

I raised my eyebrows.

"I happened to look up Rachel on the Gram after you told me you two were breaking up."

I didn't say anything.

The words *commitment, your kink phase, partnership, cuddling, never thought I would, financial precarity, stability,* and ultimately *marry her* came floating by me.

Part of me wanted to tell him, *Our fam is not ending like this. Let's go to the beach and process this like good queer folks and sort it out*, and the other part wanted him to fuck off.

"Fuck off," I said.

"I know, I know, I mean, I am, actually. I'm leaving for

L.A. tomorrow with Rachel and she's going to start shooting for that show Blithe was working on before he conked out."

"Conked out? You know what? Nothing makes more sense than you fake-marrying a fake-ass celebrity. It's the most consistent thing you could possibly do. Now your whole life can be one giant fake tableau where you get to cut out anything inconvenient or repulsive."

His mouth opened as if he were about to say something real. Instead, he shut it, took a deep breath, put his hand through his expertly faded hair, and said, "You know, spending time with you and Blithe made me realize that there's this whole world outside of the internet."

"Well, *praise the Dionyesian deities!*"

I was so angry at losing R and Aiden, I couldn't even curse correctly in the Witch's style.

When I woke up the next morning, I found that Aiden had slunk out, leaving his bedding in a pile on the deflated air mattress. Blithe was still asleep on the couch, under my gravity blanket and the old sleeping bag. I went to boil water and heard a knock on the door. I opened it, but no one was there. An envelope was at my feet. Another one had been left across the hall, where two sets of straight early-twenties couples lived, so it couldn't have been from the Rhiz. In the kitchen that Aiden had rubbed down with the Witch's neem and tea tree oil, I read that we were being evicted so the building could be sold.

The premises must be vacated in the next 45 days for the purposes of luxury reoccupation.

The letter's wording made it seem as if there were no human subjects involved, just the value of the building and the relative lack of value of the inhabitants.

Blithe stirred. I told him what had happened, with Aiden and with the building.

"We can go back to L.A. and you can stay with me," he said.

I wasn't quite ready for him to be well enough to take care of me, but I nodded and slumped down on the couch.

After all my complaining, the other coast was the only option. This city's romance had dimmed. My romance with my own misery had dimmed.

As I packed, Blithe spent hours talking to his parents about his job situation. He decided that he needed to quit Elemental. He said he could try to get me an interview

When I told Sophie I was moving, she started to cry. Her lipstick smeared. Then she composed herself and said, "You will always be a part of me. All I ask is that you don't remain a secret to yourself. Also, simple tech does exist that would let us continue seeing each other. If you want that."

I cried for everything that had passed between us, and for the necessity of crying as a man. I told her I needed to recollect myself in a new clime and then I'd reach out.

The landlord came over to inspect the building and told us we were not getting our deposit back. The Witch's potions had formed a thick layer of oil over all the surfaces in the apartment. The building would be gut renovated, but we were being penalized for our negligence in maintaining proper hygiene. After I got off the phone with the landlord,

I went into the kitchen and threw one of the Witch's potion jars against the wall. I was terrified of leaving the den I had dug myself into. Once I'd calmed down, I prayed that the Witch would not use her power against me.

I said goodbye to all my dogs and gave them each a sustainably collected animal tusk. Buford pranced around the apartment with his tusk in his mouth, farting.

Jillian came over to help me finally donate an old box of "women's" clothes. As she sat on my bed, holding up clothes that no longer fit me, we played music from our high school days and danced around in my bedroom, kicking tape guns and rocking out on a floor that would soon be destroyed.

"I hope you can find the bright future I know you have," she said at my door, gently implying that this future had not arrived in the city of wealth and angst.

Minna and I took a yoga class together, and afterward she told me she could sense the shift in my aura. We said we would video each other and keep up our TV dates from across the coasts. She was going to come to L.A. during her summer break. I could not promise I would return to New York anytime soon.

"Even with my hundred-day meditation streak," I added.

Margot was neutral about my decision. "But you need to think about getting a *real* job, Pen, no matter where you choose to live," she said.

Blithe and I completed our regional exit interviews with the well-bearded Operatrix, who interpreted my light purple Bio-meter reading as "geographical optimism." Blithe was stuck in a gray-streaked green.

I tried to ask the Operatrix if he'd interviewed Aiden as well. I wanted to know if Aiden's Bio-meter showed any hints of fermenting-grape repression or lemon-colored deep satisfaction.

The Operatrix looked at me and started to sing in a low, cis-male voice. *"Down, down, down in the archives, down in the archives we bury all the answers, all the dirt, all the tar, all the answers. Down, down, next to the bunker, through the deep tunnel, close to the uranium, that's where you go, that's where you go when you must know."*

3

Blithe and I walked up to his parents' front door draped in the insect-chirping serenity of a California suburb. I had déjà vu from composing the narrative report, but Blithe's sensory associations were now a mystery to me; I did not know if the smell of barbecue would bring up nostalgia, giddiness, hatred of American backyard practices, or regret.

His mom met us in the front hall. She pulled Blithe to her and then hugged me. We walked past the Chinese vase that irked Blithe, through the kitchen, and to his dad, who was grilling on the patio in a long apron. He hugged us both, too, and I smelled his scent, smoky-citrus aftershave.

Blithe's dad had tears in his eyes when he stood back. "We were worried about you, bud," he said.

His mom stepped out onto the patio. "Pen, we really want to thank you for taking such good care of Blithe," she said.

"Of course," I said.

Blithe didn't interject to explain that I had hexed him and that he remained in an advanced stage of misery.

As they grilled steak and salmon, we both enjoyed the pool. I held a noodle under my armpits and kicked around while Blithe floated inside an inner tube. Was he mourning the lost universes he had created in the languor of these waters?

His mom called us to the table, and we put shirts over our reconstructed chests and sat down to eat.

"So what are you going to do with yourself in L.A.?" his dad asked me as we passed plates around.

"Blithe said he would try to get me an interview at Elemental."

Blithe's parents looked at each other, as if worried that the name of his former employer would set him off.

"That's great. I'm happy to help you prepare for their kooky questions," his mom said.

Blithe pouted through most of the dinner while I basked in parental attention.

I wondered if he had told them my parents were dead.

After dessert, the two of us went up to Blithe's bedroom, cleansed of all signs of his earlier life. It was just a room, with a four-poster twin bed, striped wallpaper, and a reading chair by the window. We sat on his bed, relaxed and yet distanced, like siblings or exes.

"Do you want to see my box of remnants?" he asked.

"Obvs."

He went to the closet and pulled out a shoe box of earrings and old photos.

"This is as titillating as when I'd go into my parents' bathroom as a kid to spray my dad's cologne—all fir and tobacco. I'd sit on the floor in the closet underneath his pants, soaking in the scent."

"Yeah, it's insane how much pressure there is to just

pretend like I never had a crush on myself when I was covered in Sunshine Splendor from the mall."

"Is it in there?" I pointed to the row of bottles.

"Yeah, it's so chemical it's probably still intact."

We sprayed his old perfumes on ourselves and spun
around in Sunshine Splendor, Gardenia Moonlight, and the
fancier Octavia, recalling those days when objects of girlhood delighted us. Then he sat on the floor while I perched
on his bed and braided pieces of his hair, the purest therapy.

When we came back down, drunk on the past, his mom
asked if I wanted to do the Elemental demo.

"Mom, leave him alone," Blithe said.

"No, it's fine, I'll do it."

She dug a small whiteboard out of a drawer. "Okay, I will give
you a prompt and you'll quickly jot down notes about how you
would create episodic thrill. You have sixty seconds. Okay?"

"K."

"How would you create conflict in a village of sailors'
widows?"

I glanced over at Blithe to see if he would understand that
I telepathically needed to know if it was okay to make them
all lesbians. He raised his eyebrows. Fine.

I wrote:

*The captain's wife falls in love with the cook's wife, and her
son threatens to tell the constable.*

*A psychic rolls into town and tells the women she can
communicate with their husbands, who are not dead, but ma-
rooned on a distant island—some set off to find them.*

This is feeling very patriarchal, so we would not even worry about the dead husbands but follow one character as she spots a large hole in the ocean from atop her widow's walk and rows out, only to get sucked into a portal to another dimension.

The timer went off. I read my notes aloud and amused everyone. Then I had to come up with resolutions to a Line in which a young man has to give up his humanity to live as a fish with his lover, and finally his mom gave me three potential Lines and I had to guess which one had the greatest Violetizing potential. As we went back and forth, I wondered if Blithe's mom did not have some hidden wishes to create that had been squashed.

We left their house with a paper bag of leftovers.

"Your parents are great," I said to Blithe as he drove.

"Do you think they have any remorse for adopting an Asian baby?" he asked as we pulled onto the freeway.

"Probably not, but you could tell them about how hard it's been."

"I don't know why I have to do all the work."

Blithe let me stay in his guest room and it was different from the Rhiz's files.

The decor was the same, but I wasn't.

In the mornings, I meditated with Alice in my guest nook, then stared out at the palm trees brushing against the sky, embarrassed by how narrow-minded I'd become in the other city, dreaming of ruin and degeneration. Blithe would make me a California smoothie. Then we'd go to the gym and he'd drop me off at the university library before he went to see his healer. His father had gone to the U and let me use his alumnus library card to get in. I didn't want to sit in a café with all the other "creatives" trying to break into television.

One morning, I was reading a crime novel because I longed for every loose end of a story to get tied up, and I saw her. She was sitting two tables over in the large reading room with her back to the cylindrical windows. A newspaper was sprawled out before her. Newspapers used to trigger me—new acts of destruction and violence every single day—but as she turned the pages, she reminded me of the soft eternity of daily habits. Her hair was wavy and fell down her shoulders. She wore a light blue button-up shirt, and I could see rings on her fingers. She wore clothes so well I couldn't tell if they were new, old, fancy, heat-maintaining. She exceeded them.

A removed observer might have been able to read her, but I couldn't.

She seemed unaware of the frenzied world outside her gaze.

The gauzy lightness of that moment did not turn to any sharper texture.

Was it her beauty, languor, or discipline that drew me in?

I was stunned. Smitten. I didn't have any fresh language for the encounter.

I couldn't envision talking to her, but I returned to the same table every day. I read crime novels or wrote spastic and incomprehensible lines about the skin of plants. She surrounded herself with piles of books, and once she opened one, she did not furtively check her phone like the others.

•

I sat on the front stairs of the library on an unhurried after-noon, waiting for Blithe to come get me. It was midsummer, but there were few signs of it. I hadn't seen the reader in the library for a few days; her absence had solidified the crush. I basked in the seasonless sun and watched groups of under-grads without even worrying that they were headed toward a brighter future than mine.

Blithe pulled up. His head was newly shaved. He had taken to wearing a gray linen robe everywhere.

"I like this look," I told him.

He nodded.

"How's it going with your healer?"

"They are helping me retrieve the parts of self that exist pre-colonially."

"How do they do that?"

"Honestly, I don't feel like explaining it to you right now."

"Okay."

The prickling shame of whiteness descended. I missed Aiden. I wanted to process white transness with him so that Blithe could be left in peace. I wanted other things from him as well.

"Have you heard from Aiden?"

"Yah." Blithe sounded sheepish when he said that.

"Are you, like, hanging out with him?"

"I did see him the other day. Just for juice."

"Hmph."

I didn't care that much. I longed for my library crush in a way that I could never have longed for R and our transac-tional encounters.

Blithe and I went to a taco stand and ate tacos with kimchi, tempura avocado, white peaches, smoked trout, and seaweed compote. We were both still hungry and got veggie burritos.

As we wiped our hands, I was compelled to say, "Blithe, I don't want to make you teach me anything about your identity or mine. Just let me know if I can support you while you're going through this."

"Okay, Pen," he said, resigned.

The next Thursday morning, I passed through the mirrored doors of Elemental, walked by the barista who used to be an actor, went up in an elevator with a group of people who didn't seem to question their life choices with any rigor, and found a disinterested, possibly gender-nonconforming secretary who directed me to a waiting area. I sat down on a severe bench. A painting was hung above my head, and a mirror reflected back its depiction of the MGM lion, hungover, lounging by a pool with an empty champagne bottle. A rather melancholic choice.

The secretary summoned me to a board room with plush couches and lounging areas instead of a long, presumptuous table. A team of writers wore bright shirts with cacti and beer cans and satellites on them. They were mostly white cis dudes.

I was flustered by the array of seating options and sat down on the stool of a crushed blue chaise longue.

"Hey, man, I'm Honcho. So tell us why you want to be a Lines-crafter here," asked a man with a prodigious beard and a captain's hat.

"Well," I said, noticing my higher range of voice, how I

crossed my leg at the knee while the dudes splayed as if they were taking up space on a New York subway, "I really admire the inventiveness and the creative atmosphere here." *Fuck*, I was too nervous to say what I meant. "My friend Blithe was a Lines-crafter—until he got sick—and he was always telling me about the freedom he had to create whatever he wanted." Everything I said felt twisted and untrue.

"What do you think about art-for-art's-sake?" asked a young Indian woman wearing a cape.

Was this a trap? "I think that we should not have a scarcity mind-set around creation."

She nodded.

We moved on to the writing test. A whiteboard surface was wheeled over to me. I had to create conflict, choose the best Lines, resolve labyrinthine plots, and decide when a Line was ready to be sent to the betas. I wrote furiously, and all the joy was sucked out of the act. I did not want to entertain these men or temper my ideas so that they would become palatable.

When I was finished Honcho told me to wheel my surface over to him and pick up a tablet to take my diagnostic dialogue test.

"A scene from an Elemental Arrow-Line, only the Speech-Explosions muted. You must write in your own."

How did Blithe ever keep a straight face around here?

I watched two ripped men screaming back and forth on a pirate ship. Obviously, they were evil gay whalers who had been kidnapped by sea-creature-loving pirates.

"All right, man, we'll be in touch," Honcho told me when I'd finished.

"Do you want my portfolio?"

I'd bought a plastic sleeve with some of my *G+T* fan fiction. Honcho shrugged. "Leave it on the couch."

"Do you have my number and everything?" I hadn't turned in a formal résumé, thankfully.

"Naw, we use other ways."

I went back through the building in a deflated state. For all of my giddiness about "new ways," Elemental was a replica of the same old shit. It was remarkable that Blithe had lasted there as long as he did. I found Blithe's car in the lot and slumped down in the passenger seat with my head against the wheel.

The one TV show that could not disappoint me was *Goblins and Trolls*. I asked Blithe if he could hook me up with *G+T*'s studio, but he could not—a tight-knit group of Radical Faeries and activists circulated the writing jobs among themselves. At least I could tell Margot that I was trying to find a job. Jillian and I arranged an ongoing *G+T* screening every Sunday night, after my call with Margot. We watched as the goblins, trolls, faeries, elves, and wizards fought and made up, birthed queer spawn with diabolical proclivities, and ventured far from the Kingdom of Tolle to seek their destinies. The Technicolor wonderland of their fields and castles and thatched huts entranced us as the plot grew more and more unwieldy. Jillian and I texted back and forth:

Wow, I can't believe they just killed off the Folding Wizard!

Yah, but the Mage can bring most creatures back to life.

Tru.

Who is that purple spiky guy?

I think they're the spawn of that villainous druid and the soothsayer.

Ah okay.

I pictured her, on her stately couch in New York, painting her nails and sipping wine while I lay on the rug with some of Blithe's meditation pillows around me.

Still, the future did not seem foreboding in L.A., as it had in New York. I knew that the old me would have scoffed, *Oh, now you think everything is swell because the temperature never dips below sixty during the day,* but I'd simply adjusted my expectations. I could linger in moments without waiting for a crescendo, a climax.

As Blithe emerged from his cocoon state, he became fixated on food. He would go to the fancy French bakery at least once a week and procure three different pastries and then reverse-engineer the recipes and bake them himself. He occasionally asked me to sample the two versions and try to discern the difference. My vocabulary was crude: *buttery, sweet, flaky.* His was like a weapon: *cocoa-chalk, smegma-like, scales of crust-density.* He said that he'd gone through this phase before, when he was transitioning alone in his parents' house. Each night, he and his mom earmarked a different Julia Childs recipe to try. I wasn't sure if his return to French cuisine was a good sign.

I kept on with my library routine. Inside the walls, I was safe from cares about the immediate present. With a spillproof coffee mug and a detective novel, I could burrow away for hours, interrupted only by glancing over at my reader-crush.

Then came the day when she was later than usual. Mid-morning, she walked in, unhurried, with a leather tote over her shoulder.

"Can I sit here?" she asked in a medium-loud whisper.

"Of course." I looked around to see if other tables were full. They were not.

"What are you reading?" she whispered.

I showed the cover of a vintage Detective Faroux volume, *The Mystery of the Fallen Oak*.

"And you?"

She held up a stack of files and I thought I saw a flash of magenta. "I'm Stone," she said conspiratorially.

"I'm Pen."

The fact that talking was discouraged made me want to keep whispering to her, but I went back to solving the mystery of a dead raven and she dived into a pile of books, musty with old resonance.

So this is daytime romance, I thought. *Queer nightlife had us hooking up in the moldy corners of bathrooms, seeking touch against sensory-overloaded clubs, going for folks who were already mapped by status based on how often their outlines turned silver with hologram dust.*

I had met Rachel in a queer bar.

Every known revolution comes from unsexy, incremental steps.

At lunchtime, I asked Stone if she wanted to get a juice with me. Of course, I wanted our first date to take place on some cliffside overlooking the water, replete with sea kayaking and the identification of rare birds.

She put down her field journal, rubbed her eyes, and said yes.

We walked over to the bright pink building. Decades ago, the Juicery would have been frequented only by fad dieters and anxious athletes, but it was 20— and everyone wanted to be well.

Shit, do I pay or is that chivalrous? Yes, I'll pay because I initiated.

We stood in line shoulder to shoulder, and I noticed her scent and the tips of her hair as we talked about the undergrad children, those who were post-tech and those who walked around in VR-immersion scenes.

"Where would you reside if you could live in VR?" I asked.

"Carthage," she said, and did not elaborate.

We got to the cashier. I added flax, fish belly, and argan balls to my cucumber and clementine juice, and Stone got a ginger carrot, straight up.

"You Americans," she said when I was handed my juice. She let me pay and we sat outside on a bench, facing the quad.

In a softly accented voice, she told me about her life. Stone was born in Greece, grew up in Portugal, and lived briefly in Philadelphia. Her parents were semi-stable professors who split over her father's feminist leanings, which her mother found undisciplined and airy. Her younger half sister lived in Florence. She dated her first girlfriend at fourteen.

Stone unspooled her autobiography as if she had never questioned her origins or her desires or her right to pursue her interests, which happened to be studying points in time, "nodes," when people made inlets against the force of capitalism. Yes, she was the student of that brilliant thinker and witch-lover. No, she was not a pessimist.

"My parents were geologists and died in an avalanche . . ."

I let myself remain in the ellipses.

A few days later, she offered me a ride home. She put her backpack in the trunk and then opened the door to the back seat and climbed in. She crawled to the far side, turned around, and beckoned for me to join her. Stone's car was clean, aside from the dust motes swimming in the sunlight.

We made out in the back seat of her car, the most suburban act of my adulthood, and in the enclosed space, pressed against her, I floated through all the years of my life.

We stopped, grinning and dazed, and went to her place, a one-bedroom on a shady street near the U. It was messily well-kept, with plant vines trailing along windowsills. An entire wall of bookshelves made me yearn for a quiet afternoon indoors with her. A French press had been left out from earlier in the morning. I ran my eyes along her breakfast table. A sweater dried on the back of a chair.

The wall off the kitchen was covered in photos of fountains: a stern marble face with water pouring out of it, a lion spout, a small urn with water spilling off the top.

"Whenever I find a little fountain in a square, I let it become a home for me."

I thought of all the mall fountains of my youth.

We cooked dinner and I chopped an onion the way Aiden had taught me, added it to the pan with the chicken.

She rubbed the body in sumac, and we roasted everything. We had a glass of wine, and I didn't feel like getting wasted to blur the distance between us.

The next day, Stone had already woken up before me and gone on a run. I found her at the kitchen table in her workout clothes. She poured me coffee from the French press.

"Morning," she said, and touched my hand. "What are you up to today?"

I told her that Blithe was taking me to the fish market to buy fresh cod.

"I'm going to the concert hall with a friend to see this visual symphony, accompanied by that quirky harp player. Want oatmeal?"

We ate oatmeal with syrup and butter and cinnamon, and I didn't feel like slinking away, like I often did after first hookups.

Stone had to go meet someone before the concert. She dropped me off, we kissed, and I went into Blithe's and threw myself down on the meditation cushions.

I was afraid of this slippage: the way in queer time, a night of sleeping together can magically transform into a serious relationship. I reminded myself that I didn't have to go along with this if I didn't want to.

I took a nap, and when I woke up there was a text.

Do this again next week?

Yes.

I thought about adding an emoji or a *can't wait*, but the

yes was resolute. In fact, extra signification would have detracted from its solidity.

In the library on a warm August morning, I was watching Stone read as I pretended to scan my eyes down the rows of words. My phone's projector lifted up and a slim silver hologram envelope appeared before me. An *E* on the front told me who it was from. I touched the letter and the hologram unfolded into a sheet of paper.

Yo, Pen, wanted to let you know we don't need any more writers right now. We also found some of your ideas fanciful beyond proven audience interest. Stay good. E.

"So much for that," I whispered. Stone could see the hologram text, backward, from where she sat.

"I'm sorry, babe," she said as the hologram grew wings and flew away.

"It's probably good for me to take a break from adv-tech, which leads me further into despair."

"Are you going to call Sid about dog-walking here?"

"No," I said, and the certainty surprised me. Sid and I had only hung out once so far, on a walk across Venice Beach. I was avoiding him because he reminded me of my past persona and other residual miseries.

We packed up our books and went to her place to make a pea soup with mint and discuss if white people could ever partake in indigenous practices without it being fucked up. We agreed that at minimum, white people would have to attribute these indigenous practices to their specific peoples, not try to profit off these experiences, and send resources toward the indigenous groups. Stone added that we should try to connect to the heritage of our ancestors, learn about those mystical experiences as well. I pictured my Russian Jewish relatives, whirling around with red kabbalah bracelets on their wrists.

I had slipped back inside the pool of life, not by working out or getting a good job or becoming sponsored on the Gram, but by living in infinite and everyday time with Stone.

Don't h8 on my happiness and call me a queer Nicholas Sparks, thanks, I wanted to tell the inevitable chorus of salty queers who detested love.

Every time I returned to Blithe's, I'd light a candle, pet Alice, open the guest nook window, and sit, entranced, as old stirrings came back to me, layers of resonance that I'd cut off when I transitioned, and before.

I collected them, in a basket, in my mind.

Blithe would come home from wandering the open-air markets and make an elaborate stew. Sometimes I would help him, and he'd order me around. It was good for our friendship when I was his kitchen bottom. I could never chop the glass onions finely enough. After I cleaned up, we'd smoke a joint on his couch and the tautness of the world would relax.

"I want to be on another planet," he confided one night during our postdinner recline.

I replied, "It's normal to be in Extra-Terrestrial mode. Just know that there are beautiful planets away from Earth, like Venus, and Pluto, if it is still one."

He glared through the pot haze.

"I'm not trying to be annoying," I said. "I'm just saying that I'm here for you and that you won't be in this state forever. Even if that's a stock saying, it's true."

He tightened his hoodie until it covered his face (it looked like a butthole, I might add) and did not speak to me for the rest of the night.

In my sleep, I dreamed of my parents and I dreamed in color.

When I woke up, they stayed with me.

I wanted to call Sophie and scream, *You never told me that everything lost could return!*

Hadn't she?

Margot was still hounding me about getting a new job, but the fact that I wasn't completely fucked beyond all new attachment formations allowed me to relax into our guardian-ward relation. The more I relaxed, the more she could open up. She held a new blouse up to the adv-camera on her computer, which did not translate into a 3-D reconstruction because I refused to enable such features.

"What do you think?"

I thought nothing good about sequins and stripes mixing together, but I was happy she was moving outside of her usual territory.

"Very cute," I said.

I wanted to go further than her fashion choices.

"Margot, what are your thoughts on socialism? I mean, they've got to be different from mine because your generation has grown accustomed to individual comfort and being carried by warm currents of prosperity, while my gen has experienced recession after recession after recession, paired with the knowing that the world has enough for every single inhabitant to be taken care of, if resources were distributed properly . . . Even the billionaires wouldn't lose comfort, only their hoardings."

"I don't think democratic socialism is a bad idea. I just think the status quo in our political system makes it very difficult to think of alternatives."

I stared at her, with her shining sequins. She was not always the enemy I had shaped her into.

When I got off the phone, I did not find myself cringing, curled up in a little ball, heart squished between the tensed shoulders, in unconscious trauma mode.

Occasionally, I was insecure about Stone's professional ambition and the surety of her academic path, even as she described the drying-up of higher-ed resources. I would catch myself comparing her to R and to the wrong future I could have had, with walled-off secrets and at least one pool. I was still the same old Pen, clenched tight like a fist one moment and exhaling with pleasure the next.

One Friday night, she invited some of her old grad school friends over. The first arrived in a periwinkle T-shirt and leather sandals.

"Here you are, my dear," he said, kissing Stone, "a perfect

red from a sandy, Mediterranean clime." He extended his hand to me. "And you are?"

"Pen," I said, lightly shaking his.

"Roland, charmed."

A couple, Su and Orhan, showed up. Su was pregnant, and somehow reminded me of all the alternate existences I could have had. And finally, Chris, a nonbinary professor who spent part of the year in Tunis, where his partner lived.

I served them seafood stew, mashed cauliflower, a salad with delicate herbs, and a thick, almost-savory chocolate torte.

As they spoke to each other about various repressive regimes, I was lost in a swirl of references I didn't understand. I admitted to them that I hadn't pursued higher education. When they spoke of the time they'd all sat in a yurt with their Italian philosopher idol, smoking hash-laced cigarettes in the Sierra Nevada, I almost stormed off. It seemed like nothing had changed since my first lover tried to seduce me with Lacan. Roland wanted to stay indefinitely and chat with Stone about time spent in an old dive bar near campus, but after I yawned loudly a few times, Stone said it was time for us to wind down.

I waited until they left to let my fragility show. "You know, you could have just not invited me instead of having me cook this huge meal and then not really involve me in the conversation."

"Pen, you *wanted* to cook. And this is my world, but they'd like to get to know you. I'll try harder to include you."

"Are you sure they would deign to speak to someone without a stream of academic credentials?"

"Orhan is not an academic. I told you he's a landscape architect."

"Oh, really?"

Every time we fought, I learned that we could survive it.

During a session when I was feeling particularly buoyant, I confided in Sophie that often my insecurities emerged after a blissful day, as a way to bring reality back into a closed and chaotic familiarity.

"You're learning, Pen," she said.

Yes, I was learning and also forgetting what I'd learned the moment an itchy feeling ran through me. Stone was leaving soon for a month-long string of conferences and site visits in the Southwest. One morning, I picked an argument with her because she wouldn't tell me anything about the conference.

"I don't understand why you won't tell me the name of the hotel where you're staying or even the name of the conference. What if something happens?"

"Pen, as I've told you before, there's a professional reason why I can't disclose this information."

"I thought you wanted to do away with professionalism?"

"I wish I could say more."

"Would you tell me if you were sleeping with someone else?"

"Are you kidding?"

"No."

She stood up and walked out of her apartment. After enough time had passed, I called Blithe to come get me.

•

I was sprawled out on the meditation cushions one morning when an Operatrix appeared in a hologram. She wore loose layers and looked to be in her sixties, with huge circular sunglasses. She held an herbal cigarette in her hand, but the smoke was not transmitted.

"They send me in when people are languishing, young man," she said.

Languishing?

"You are stuck in the Hinterlands."

"Excuse me?"

"When one passes through the Shadowlands, there are nuggets of wisdom that must be collected. If the nuggets are left untouched, transformation cannot occur, and one drifts into the Hinterlands. You're stagnating. And there are places that you need to go."

"Like where?"

"First, you must invert the hex that you cast. That is the holding bind. Start there."

And she was gone.

I did not disagree with the Operatrix's assessment of me. I was trying to change while staying in the same place, longing to evolve while still chasing chimeras of fame and surface-pleasure.

I knew that on the other coast, the Witch would have finished her morning incantations and headed off to a job or ritual. I decided to call her, figuring that she wouldn't answer.

"Yes, Pen," she said flatly.

"Hi, how are you?"

Silence.

"Okay, good, no small talk. I need your help. Do you know anything about the Hinterlands?"

"The Hinterlands is the place you end up when you don't learn anything from the Shadowlands."

I took a deep breath to stop myself from having a tantrum about the Difficulty of Life.

"Well, I'm stuck there. Do you know anyone out in L.A. who can help me invert the hex?"

She chuckled to herself. I could hear a vague drone of chanting in the background.

"The Coven of Ancilles has been known to help lost ones. They are known by their insignia. I suppose I can send you a ring. It does boost a witch's power to help those who have not yet evolved into their full potential. When you receive it, you must wear it on your right hand. They will come to you when they are ready."

"Thank you. Sorry about my abrupt exit. And general malaise."

"You cursed yourself, Penfield, ten times more than anyone else could ever curse you."

The ring appeared at dusk, taped to Blithe's condo door in an unmarked wax envelope. The coven insignia was a hand emitting sparks from the fingertips. I put it on and waited for a witch to find me.

The next day, I was sitting in the car while Blithe ran in to the culinary arts studio to retrieve a pan he'd left.

I jumped when I heard a knock on the car window. A

woman in a black linen tunic and head covering signaled for me to roll it down.

"You are looking for me," she said, clinking her rings against the top of the glass.

"Oh, yeah, you're the . . ." I could not say the word *witch* in L.A. in broad daylight.

She waited.

I unlocked the car door and she got in.

She reached into a leather satchel, took out a palo santo stick and lit it, blew the smoke through the car, and then arranged a group of stones on the dashboard.

"I need a lock of hair," she said, and held up a small knife with a golden hilt.

"Okay." I leaned toward her and she cut off a one-inch lock, lit the end on fire, blew it out.

"Yes, Hinterlands," she said, inhaling the singed air.

Why was I so unnatural, so immobile? All the old stories reappeared: my parents' deaths, my much-delayed adolescence, the immutability of my tentative nature, and then: *How could Stone be attracted to someone so cringey, so devolved?*

"Enough," this witch said, as if she could hear my thoughts.

"What do I need to do?"

"An inversion spell. The Shadowlands will invert, and then, in the natural order of things, there is a righting."

"Are you going to cast the spell?"

"Absolutely not. You must go to an energy exchange and find the one who will right you."

She took a yellow-green crystal from the dashboard and put it in a pouch before handing it to me, then packed up the rest, placed the lock of hair in a tiny jar, secured the jar in her bag. "Take this peridot and charge it in the light of the Sturgeon Moon and then leave it on La Cienega and W. Jefferson." Then she passed me an envelope stamped with the sign of the powerful hand and was off to commune with other mortals, other beings.

I opened all the windows, but when Blithe finally got in the car he looked at me.

"Some unfinished business from New York."

I opened the envelope as he drove. A slip of paper showed a simple drawing of an ominous moon, a date, a time, and an address. The energy exchange was in two days, on the arrival of the Sturgeon Moon.

"You want to come with me to an energy exchange?" I asked him.

"Sure, I'm bored with roasting chickens and I'd like to see what the witches will do to you."

That night, I wore my flax pants and a white T-shirt. Looking in the mirror, I felt like Aiden. Stone and I were only texting. She conceded that she could ask the conference organizers for permission to tell me where she was going. I conceded that assuming she was cheating on me was an uninspired, possessive, and heteronormative move. Before I left, I put the L.A. witch's crystal in the windowsill to catch the moonlight.

Blithe and I drove silently to Silver Lake. The note instructed us to find the congregation point by walking through a white gate illuminated by three candelabras, which we found positioned in a line on the walkway. I had to step around them to pass through a gate. A circle of people gathered around a large pool by candlelight. As we walked toward the circle, we were stopped at a folding table and asked for the invitation. I handed it over and in exchange received three brown dried stems.

"Put them on your tongue and swallow," a shadowed person told me.

Blithe pulled me by the elbow over to a spiky bush.

"Are you sure about this? I'm getting culty vibes here."

"You should go if you want. But I need to invert."

"No, I'll stay."

We swallowed the stems.

We joined the circle around the pool. A gong was struck, and we all bowed our heads. The gong was struck again, and the sound traveled through the water and into us, discordant and slightly unpleasant, like whale echoes in outer space. It wasn't until I stopped evaluating the enjoyability of the sound bath that I found myself floating in a warm liquid, sensing the vines moving from me through all the others in the circle and all through everyone I cared about and into the earth and back up again. I could have spent a year inside the note of jasmine in the air. All was gently fluffed in a quiet ecstasy. From this place, I could see the character of myself, neon with anxiety, misaligned, thinking my failure and my suffering were mine alone, reified by time, when a lazy society had manufactured so many of my thoughts and feelings and could not hold the mysteries that passed through me on that night.

I was at the edge.

The circle broke. Some people slipped into the water slowly, so as not to make more than a ripple.

A feather moved across my arm—the softness was its own room—and I was handed a small purple crystal. I somehow understood that I needed to hold it up to the moonlight. Blithe was handed something else and he moved away from me.

The gong was struck one more time.

When she approached, I could feel the potency of the crystal increase. I was not completely enchanted because I could logically think that I was glad Blithe was with me so I would never have to try to put into words an experience that was only discernible from the inside, held by ancient tendrils that caressed away human distortions.

She waited a few feet away from me, protecting my space. I could join her, or I could remain where I was. Small and petty Pen was comfortable in the Hinterlands, for all its discomfort. He wanted to stay, to remain childlike and dissatisfied. The crystal throbbed as I stepped toward her, hastening along my undoing.

She brought me to her house. Her outward form did not register, except her hands. She took off her rings one by one, leaving the ring of the coven. When I watched her uncoiling the rope, oiling the dildo, I could foresee all that she was about to do to right me.

She suspended me, naked, and I was never as free as in those confines. As I hung, my feet slightly higher than my head, my stomach facing the ground, I knew that all my strivings for agency, for poor approximations of power or might, for feeling, were nothing when they went against natural thrumming.

She hit me with various objects, to remind me where I was. She took me down and fucked me and it was energetic but not sexual. We were in the realm not of pleasure but of motion. She fucked me to remind me that none of us are tops, that we are all bottoming to something greater, and as she penetrated my butthole, the universe entered me.

By the time I collapsed on her bed, the mushrooms were fading. She brought me a tea, but I could only stare at the patterns on her duvet cover, wave-like lines traversing a mint-green sea.

"I saw Catalpa, Elemental, all of it, as these machines of whiteness. I was not in my own imagination. I thought I was tapping into this bright, universal well, and it was just the same old recycled images from other books and films with white people in them.

"I need to do something very, very different. I have been going far away from myself, and last night, I sat out on a dark lawn with other folks of color and we were our own magic. We were calling each other back. It wasn't like you getting fucked," Blithe said to me as we sat on his rug with Alice. I traced the patterns, the diamonds and the slightly irregular lines.

I shrugged off Blithe's derision and nodded.

"Did you know that shrooms could do all of this?" he asked.

"No. I mean, the word itself suggests trippy posters in dorm rooms and some white guy reading *On the Road* and wrapping himself in an Andean poncho."

"At Rita's, the Operatrix spoke of fungal goddexes, but I wasn't paying attention."

The puncture in my bliss was the fact that I would have to explain to Stone what had happened. She tolerated woo-woo healing modalities without seemingly ever needing to call upon them, but she was not one for bullshit and I knew that she would not appreciate a vague description of how I inverted during a coven's energy exchange by getting suspended, beaten, and penetrated by a strong-handed witch. All I could do was simply show her the change.

After lunch, I showered and then lay on my bed with Alice, listening to gentle flute sounds until it was time for my dinner reservation with Stone. We were seeing each other before her flight.

Unlike a hangover, which made me want to retreat further from the world, the mushrooms' aftermath was gentle. When I looked inside the bag that the witch had given me, it included more stems and instructions on how to micro-dose. I took a small piece. Then I pulled the peridot away from the window. I'd have to drop it off before dinner.

Stone was in a white jumpsuit, looking down at a menu. I prepared to lose her. That was just how my brain worked, spiritual fulfillment or not. I touched her hand and sat down. She smiled, and I paused in the moment before I further alienated her from me.

"I have to tell you about last night."

"Yeah, tell." She leaned her head to the side and combed through her hair with her hands. The light ran along the edge of her face.

"We have to start way earlier. There was a time when I would wake up every morning and the first thing I'd do was go to Aiden Chase's Gram to stew in his perfection and in my abjection. And I felt like my only option, the only thing I could do to make my life better, was to take him down. I convinced the Witch, my old roommate, to hex Aiden and send him into the Shadowlands. My other roomie, whom I call the Stoner-Hacker, hacked Aiden's Gram so I could post a photo of Alice. The problem was, the hex landed on Blithe instead."

Stone was trying very hard not to laugh at my foibles.

I told her about our "rescue" of Blithe, my hookups with Rachel, the end of the hex, Rachel's proposal to me, and then Aiden's acceptance, all the way to the L.A. witch getting into Blithe's car and then the energy exchange.

I wanted to make myself very small when I started describing the night, to say it was dumb and all drugs and L.A. bullshit, but I could not.

I was still full of immeasurable currents.

When I finished, her lips relaxed into a smile. "I trust you," she said. "And I wouldn't mind 'inverting' you now and again. And yes, psilocybin mushrooms, first used by indigenous Mexicans in their spiritual traditions, are often used to call the self back from the shadows—or the Hinterlands, as you call it—and into the world."

I was still gripping the smooth wood of the table. In all my worry, I had forgotten where we were, at a tiny Korean bibimbap restaurant that Blithe had recommended.

I could not believe that the future I had been looking for had arrived.

"When I watched her go up the escalator, it was like my mind jumped over the usual dread. She was leaving me, in real time—and she had not gotten permission to tell me about her destination—and I could withstand it. I didn't feel like my life was over."

"I'm so glad, Pen. You're building up a tolerance for secure relationships," Sophie said. We were speaking over simple video chat.

"I really do feel like I was inverted."

She nodded.

"Why didn't you suggest that I take mushrooms before? They're legal here for the purposes of healing and divination."

She laughed and light glinted off her new nose ring.

"You know the moment you described where you could step forward toward the witch with the matching crystal or remain with *small* Pen?"

"Yeah."

"As you well know, my job is not to tell you what to do. My job is to help you to have the courage to take whatever step is in alignment with what you truly desire."

I turned the camera so she could see Alice, thriving in the California light, closer to her origin.

Blithe was also preparing for a journey. He wanted to travel through north and west China. He was seeking a particular dish, a dish that was in his dreams, a dish that his ancestors had passed on and that could not be found in L.A. fusion kitchens.

"Maybe I could find it in some under-the-radar mom-and-pop restaurant, but honestly, I don't want my first taste to be side by side with white food adventurists in a strip-mall establishment," he said.

"Of course, travel in Asia always appeared to me as a jaunt that white kids take after college before settling down. I couldn't even conceive of the continent outside this gaze. I don't have a fantasy of somehow magically reconnecting with my bio fam, but I want to know more about my origins. On a core level, I need to be fed by Chinese hands, regardless if identity or borders or culture is all a construct."

"I feel you," I said. I was still floating in a new calm, opening myself to what he needed from me.

Blithe had asked the Rhiz to put him in touch with some Chinese queers who had repatriated. Pengkun and Yuanhao, a couple, now lived in Beijing. Yuanhao had traveled extensively through the north by bike and offered tips, including the name of a trans-inclusive bathhouse run by two lesbians. Blithe was often on adv-video calls with them. The two of them could be beamed into the room, and it looked like they were sitting across from him.

But the tech was only an approximation of closeness; Blithe would have to leave L.A. and go seeking.

I called Minna to tell her about my inversion.

"Do you know what the craziest part is?" I asked her.

"What?"

"I always thought that to change, I'd have to, like, become perfect or achieve something, but really I had to get over myself."

She laughed. "Yes, I feel that. And that's what all of our FBS studies basically conclude."

"But how do you get people to grasp this? It's really hard."

"Yeah, it goes against all sorts of programming. You can't force people to evolve. You can only model it and hope they get curious."

"Is that what you did with me?"

"LOL, you've always loved casting yourself as this cretin who doesn't understand anything. Hey, I'm definitely coming to L.A. in a few weeks."

"Amazing. Do you need a place to stay? I can ask Blithe."

"Yes. My sister and I always reach our threshold after a few days."

"What, do you have long arguments about FBS versus the Rhiz?"

"I mean, yes, we argue about philosophies of the

future—she thinks I'm a sellout for going to any sort of business school—but we also argue about everything: who pays for dinner, how to economically load the dishwasher, the least unethical ways of receiving electricity."

It sounded cozy, having a sibling to bicker with.

"I'll ask. Blithe is mostly out of his sleeping-bag phase now that he has a plan to go to China."

"K. I'm pretty low-maintenance as long as I can brew my adaptogenic coffee every morning."

"Got it."

"I'll see if we can visit the Rhiz's psilocybin dispensary. It's open to the public."

A slight shiver of misrecognition: I wasn't, like, the *general* public.

Even tho I was feeling pretty good about my life, I still tensed up when I had to call Jeff, my financial consultant, and ask for more funds to be transferred into my checking account. My expenses were not high (the Rhiz covered my health insurance, Blithe and I cooked at home most of the time, I didn't care to buy new clothes or go to bars very often), but I'd need to get a job soon. Margot was pressuring me to sign up for a service that matched creatives with emerging fields, like interior design for role-playing computer games and writing scripts for how to engage with problematic family members. When Sophie and I went back and forth about my future, she asked what I wanted to do, what I saw for myself.

"This job doesn't really exist, but I feel like a conductor, not a train conductor but a conductor of various energies. I want to move around and between spaces, like being a dog walker but without the dogs."

Her face was impassive. "That's pretty vague, but soon enough, you'll have to figure out something," she said.

Minna drove straight from the airport in a rented a silver convertible to pick me up. She was eating granola from a linen bag when I opened the car door. She appeared well rested after her red-eye, in a mildly psychedelic floral shirt-dress and big sunglasses. We hugged.

"Wow, Pen, you look great," she said.

"I think it's the mushrooms, I swear. I'm almost out, tho."

Minna had cycled through many balms, medicines, and clearing-poisons. It was hard to remember that she had worked to get to a place of calm and balance, that I didn't know too much of her shadows.

As she drove me to the psilocybin dispensary where one of her sister's friends worked, I asked her to tell me about New York, the smells, the angst, the adv-tech. She said that a rogue group was smearing Butt-meters in Tiger Balm so that they warmed without human contact, which was throwing off the official data. The newest liquid trend was a drink of black sesame that was supposed to increase vitality. That had already come and gone in L.A. From inside the convertible, I could comfortably miss the jostling, the collision of many universes, the inane hunger of my old city.

We pulled up to a strip mall. There, sandwiched between

a massage studio and an all-you-can-eat sushi restaurant, was a simple sign with a small toadstool mushroom. I saw the Rhiz symbol carved into the door.

The store had only a wooden table, some ergonomic rocking chairs, and an electric scale. Minna's sister's friend raised a hand in greeting, stepping out into the echoing room. Ellen was Black and extremely butch, in a red bomber jacket and worn-in work pants. I was surprised Minna used female pronouns with her, but I trusted that she got it right.

"Let's sit," Ellen said, and pulled three of the four rocking chairs to face one another.

"So, Pen, you're just now starting the fungal plunge."

"Yes. It's been everything. I mean, coupled with an encounter with an L.A. witch."

"Those two things often go hand in hand. We are all part of one great assemblage."

"Are you . . . with the Rhiz?"

Ellen gave me a knowing wink. "Are you?"

"I mean, they've helped me out."

Ellen shrugged and turned to Minna, as if turned off by my self-denigration.

They chatted about Minna's time on a wheat farm, where she bathed every night in milky oats and swore that all the inflammation of her life had been soothed out of existence. I was a long way from the Midwest of my youth, where you either looked for the easiest balms or you shoved your problems all the way down into unsuspecting organs.

The doorbell rang and a young person in a sweatshirt and platforms walked in.

Ellen rose. "What can I do for you?"

"I need some *product*."

"I see. And do you have membership in our org?"

"Your org? Huh?"

Ellen waited, the rocking chair still moving from her ejection.

"I guess not. My friend told me to come here."

"I see. I will walk you through a few key points. We are not looking for new members, but we want you to know the context of this substance. Do you understand?"

"I guess so."

"Psilocybin mushrooms have been used by indigenous folks in the Oaxaca region for centuries. With full attribution to the indigenous origins of the psilocybin mushroom, the Mazatec and Zapotec groups in particular, my group stands in awe of this fungus and the system it is a part of. We not only advocate for the integrative wonder of the psilocybin effect on a wide range of conditions—including PTSD, depression, anxiety, the enduring rage and exhaustion of being a Black person in this country, normative responses to capitalism, sundry disenchantment, et cetera—but also for the relational architecture of the fungal kingdom. Much of our society is structured around the arboreal: roots leading to a trunk and then to branches. Our systems of family, knowledge, and government are all organized in this way. Even radical folks who want to abolish these structures are often only thinking of tracing social ills down to the roots. But fungi live alongside the roots. They nourish the roots. They send messages. They negotiate. They thrive in paradox and complexity, and in the places where ruin meets renewal. We need to live more like them."

The customer's mouth was slightly open.

"All right, can you try to let that knowledge-drop saturate in you?" Ellen said.

"Um, yeah."

"Cool, show me your ID and tell me the type of comfort you are in need of. The deal is that you can start with two weeks of micro-dosing capsules and one macro-dose if you share at least three visions, okay?"

Ellen seemed to know exactly what was needed.

She offered me a month's worth of micro-dosing capsules designed to open the intuition, and added in a macro-dose. I wanted her to trip with us, but she made it clear that she had other things to do.

When Minna and I got in the car, I said, "Holy shit."

"Right?"

"How did she get here?"

"She's an ethnobotanist. She lives at the Rhiz-Port certain months and runs the L.A. dispensary in other months."

Minna had also received a supply of mushrooms. The next morning, we drove up the Pacific Coast Highway and pulled off into a state park that overlooked the ocean. We spread out a camping blanket and put all of our snacks on top of it. Then we attributed our opening consciousness to indigenous elders, including Maria Sabina, the Mazatec shaman who had allowed an American banker to partake in the Velada ceremony and thus opened the door to Western consumption of psilocybin, and swallowed the macro-dose.

I closed my eyes. I saw visions—ancient patterns carved in stone and marble, vines wrapping through the center of the earth, distant planets turning in languorous rolls—but the visions were only the surface of the experience. Inside was the total melting of the small Pen into a world woven together by joy. When I opened my eyes, the colors of the dried grasses, the sky, and the distant water were beyond language; they called to me as I inverted further.

Minna and I said the usual phrases to each other:

"I can't believe this," while staring at our hands.

"Did you know, like, *really* know that everything is love?" while gazing at the sky.

"We are all tender filaments reaching out to the others," while twirling in the middle of the afternoon.

I was still in my pajamas, petting Alice, whispering to her about the mysteries that I had encountered and that she knew well, as a succulent, when my phone rang. I didn't usually answer it, but the day after the true meaning of existence revealed itself, I was unbothered by anyone's demands at the other end.

Even Aiden's.

"Hello?"

"Hey, man." He sounded sad, but I couldn't tell if he was sad, or if he just wasn't as elated as I was.

"What's going on?"

My reptilian brain was still calculating how much of a dick he was and how much he would gain from his new alliance.

The mushrooms whispered to me: *No resentment, no animosity, no jealousy, just soft tendrils caressing.*

"I miss you guys, you and Blithe. Do you want to come over next week?"

He sounded almost whiny. I watched the sun coming through the window, warming the side of my face and Alice's skin.

"I guess so."

"Is it cool if . . . Rachel's there?"

"I mean, there's probably some stuff we need to process together about you fake-marrying the person I was sleeping with, but yeah, it's cool if she's there."

"Thank you," he said, and hung up.

"Huh," I said to Alice, shaking my head.

Minna and I watched *G+T* with Jillian that evening. As the wacky plot unfolded, I thought about the tendrils reaching underneath all our frantic activities—from Troll Elsan's meltdown at the Beltane festivities, to gentle Fae Feelty's journey to find a fawn that she had hugged years ago—and I was at peace.

On her last night before heading to her sister's, Minna and I cooked dinner with all of Blithe's fancy kitchen tools. While Blithe was out getting fresh sage for a garnish, I asked how she dealt with her dual family identities.

"It's not like I've made some clinical decision. I grew up closer to the Japanese side and that's how I generally see myself. My Russian grandparents died a long time ago. How do you deal with your Jewishness and your whiteness?"

I had no articulate answer. "Um, huh. I guess I generally the hide Jewishness unless it's advantageous. I always wanted to get away from the fixedness of it, from those big-haired, big-breasted girls in my bat mitzvah prep class who were going to marry boys they met at Jewish summer camp and start the cycle all over again. My parents clearly were thinking the same thing when they named me Penfield."

What hung in the air was that I could turn to whiteness as a protection. My family members who had immigrated from Russia and Romania during the pogroms in 1918 had soon learned to assimilate, to drop the unseemly endings from their names, and buy into whiteness, in food, in dress. I chopped an onion and thought about how the category, Chinese, had formed in my mind. Chinese American restaurants in our suburb growing up, Chinese New Year celebrations at school with paper dragons, vague notions that China was somehow overpopulated and unclean and more repressive than the United States. When I started to transition, I had only sought out work by artists of color. I wanted to remind myself of all the ways that *others* could been read as complex and nuanced. I found the writer who described the abject yearnings of first-gen Chinese American characters, the bright ennui of adolescent hours and loneliness and the Bushwick apartment building where one family first landed, with a toilet that couldn't flush large poop. When I first read the book, all the frantic, bouncing-off-the-wall energy of youth reminded me of young Pen, stuck inside Margot's house all summer while she was at work, even though I could read outside by the pool. My relating to the book was both self-serving and expansive, fucked-up and restorative.

Blithe returned with the herbs, and we baked a polenta lasagna with vegan cheese and mushrooms that belonged to the Moosewood subculture of Ithaca, New York. As we ate, Blithe told Minna about his plan to reclaim the past.

"When I was a kid, I hated Japanese stuff, except Hello Kitty because the white girls in my class loved her," Minna said in reply. "I was in the quintessential first-gen disavowal stage, staying in the car whenever my mom went into the Asian grocer. It's cool that you get to do this now."

"True, I could have been a *banana* forever," Blithe said with spite.

"LOL. Well, as far as food metaphors go, I'm like a banana-mochi-syrniki," she said with her usual lightness.

For the first time, I would be entering one of Rachel's primary living spaces. Blithe and I drove through dust clouds in Runyon Canyon at dusk. Turning into a long driveway, I could see an earthen bungalow surrounded by trees and beyond the thirsty green the desert canyon, parched and yawning. The smell of burning wood mingled with my desire to see Aiden.

Rachel's PA, Marcy, opened the front door.

"Hey, good to see you again," I said to her, friendlier now that our NDA was void.

"Likewise," she replied with that professional courteousness that could mean anything.

We were led through a winding corridor. In each room, plants were set in perfect pots. Books lounged on tables; sheepskin slippers were waiting on a turquoise rug. I wished I were wearing a fringed vest to go along with the gentle western palette.

Was it money, psilocybin, or my own romantic entanglement that marked every surface with rest, rightness?

Marcy left us at the doors to the patio. At the back of the yard stood a small grove of fruit trees. The light was fading, and behind the darkening branches the canyon stretched out like the mouth of a cave.

In the shadows, I could see Rachel and Aiden sitting on a long sofa. A firepit had been lit and fragrant wood burned inside it.

We stepped outside and Agatha darted up to us. Getting up and following her, Rachel reached into her long skirt and pulled out some treats. She clacked, and Agatha turned and snapped up the treats.

"Welcome. I didn't want her to bite you," Rachel said, and gave me a one-armed hug.

Her hair was tied back in a short braid. She wore clogs. They were domesticating each other. I couldn't believe that even in my early-transition despondency, I had managed to sleep with this beautiful woman.

"Pen," Aiden said, walking straight up to me and looking seriously into my eyes. "We cool?"

There were about three thousand ways to answer that. "Yeah, man."

I cherished his scent, smoky and also faintly floral.

We ate fish and designer greens outside, near the fire, and drank white wine from ceramic bowls.

Rachel rested her hand on Aiden's leg. Every few minutes, she would reach up to tuck a strand of hair behind her ear or take her mug in both hands, and the firelight would hit her ring and her earrings, and she shimmered.

Aiden's hair was still short, but the fade was not precise to the millimeter. He must have abandoned his weekly cuts once he stopped documenting himself on a daily basis. He had grown a slight paunch, perceptible only to a learned eye. He was wearing a gold amulet with symbols carved into the center.

"Tell us about what's around your neck," I asked him, glad that he could still wear jewelry even if he was going stealth.

"It's a Tibetan protection amulet," he said. "Rachel and I visited Tibet for my birthday a few weeks ago."

I paused for a moment because I could feel the reaction coming: *Damn, if only I hadn't been true to myself, I could have traveled the mountains of Tibet, buying appropriative jewelry.*

Blithe made a choking noise and asked where the bathroom was. I knew exactly what he was thinking.

Agatha hummed to herself as she licked honey from inside a little ball.

Aiden and Rachel filled me in on their renovation plans. They were breaking through a wall and expanding to build Aiden a boxing studio and a sunroom.

When they spoke of boxing, I wanted to punch him, punch his face inside a circumscribed ring, get punched, punch back.

"All his little hobbies," Rachel said.

"I'm getting pretty good at boxing and at growing these greens we're eating. I think you're going to enjoy having a house husband."

"Yes, these ancient dandelion greens were quite crisp, and I do love when you come in sweaty and masc from the gym."

"We are aware that we live in a desert, so we're getting a hydroponic gardening system put in that uses rainwater, and we'll only use drought-resistant plants," Aiden said.

I told them I was seeing someone.

"What does she do?" Rachel asked.

"She's a historian."

"In what area?" Aiden asked.

"Of spaces and cultures that have resisted capitalism."

Silence. The insects of the canyon hummed into the night. Blithe came back to the table.

"Well, in a hundred years, we will not have made the cut," Rachel said, laughing, trying to lessen the weight of the c-word. She tossed her head back and the earrings shook.

"What's going on with you, Blithe? I heard you were thinking about leaving the country," Aiden said.

"It's time for me to find my lineage." He spoke with barely suppressed anger, and the conversation died again.

"How does it feel to be stealth?" I asked Aiden, with genuine curiosity.

Rachel and Aiden looked at each other. "Well, we consulted with the Rhiz to make sure they were aware of the situation. The Upholder told us that it was up to us whether we wanted to enter into this neoliberal institution. He would not interfere. He reminded us that, historically, most Rhiz members had been, in fact, closeted. In order to marry and remain in the Rhiz, we will give twenty-five percent of all investments and inheritance for reparations."

I nodded my approval, wishing that I had more money left over to give, or that I'd been wiser about how I'd used it.

All those Gram mornings evaporated into the smoky night in the bosom of a canyon. Aiden's existence on earth was still as electrifying to me as any other natural phenomenon, a mixture of beauty and impenetrability.

Aiden went to go clean up. The fire smoked, and Rachel and Blithe and I moved inside, to a sparse living room, with Agatha following us.

I sat at one end of a large couch, draped with Pendleton blankets, while Rachel sat on another. Blithe kneeled down by Agatha.

"Is she an indoor-outdoor goose?"

"Yep," Rachel said. "When she shits inside, we put it in a bucket and save it for the gardener."

"How thoughtful," I said, switching back to my Cape Cod dive-bar brattiness for a moment.

She pulled her legs up under her skirt and gave Blithe a treat to offer to Agatha. Blithe held it out to her, and she let out a disdainful grunt, then took the treat in her mouth and ran down the hallway. Blithe followed her. He did not seem up to dealing with humans.

On the coffee table, there were squares of paper spread out. I picked one up and ran my fingers over the soft, woven fibers. The edges were feathered. It was rare to find a tactile surface for writing.

"What's all this?"

"Paper samples. For our invitations. Our relationship, it's turned real," Rachel continued, leaning back with a contented sigh. "Still, I think Aiden is having a hard time. We have been reaching out to his parents, and it's bringing up a lot for him."

"Are they coming to the wedding?"

"We're working on it. I think it would be healing to have them there. And our wedding planner wants to do something special, something trans-affirming."

I wanted to punch Aiden and make sure his bio family attended his wedding. There was no contradiction.

"Are we going to be invited?"

"Do you want to come?"

"Are you kidding? I should give a long, inappropriate toast about how I set you two up."

"Don't. Really."

I kept my mouth shut. If she wanted to appease her relatives, I would not try to describe the wildflower field that lies beyond pleasantries.

"How're you doing?" I asked Blithe as we drove home.

"I feel like you and Aiden are all juicy with connections and nutrients and this Rhiz bullshit, and I'm like a struggling and severed transplant."

"I hope that you can leave soon, for your sake."

"Thanks. I want us all to be bros, I do, but I have to follow these other longings first."

I was over at Stone's one afternoon, watering her plants, lingering in her absence, when I looked over at her wall of bookshelves. Somehow, we'd never seemed to find an afternoon to read together, as I'd imagined it. My reading habits had devolved on the other coast, and I wanted to start again, and get subsumed in a story that was not about who killed the lady on the tenth floor of the Santorini hotel. I browsed through heavily footnoted tomes on exchange economies and sprawling nineteenth-century realist novels. Many books of poetry. I felt bored and twitchy from the seriousness of her collection.

There, in the bottom right corner, one of the books was emitting a purple prism into the air.

I knelt down on the rug and waved my hand near the shape. I leaned forward and took the book in my hands. A title appeared on a translucent pearly-silver cover.

The Modern History of the Rhiz, written in curling letters.

I wondered if I'd accidentally macro-dosed, but I'd had my last micro-dose two days ago. I took the book to the couch and opened it. I ran my hands over the slightly raised printed text: "All matters that precede the modern history of the Rhiz are closed to the pre-summons novice. The modern history of the Rhiz is an unstable document, constantly shifting according to unfolding research. We acknowledge that most queer histories exist outside of normative record-keeping."

The modern history of the Rhiz began in San Francisco during the signing of the United Nations charter. As statesmen were discussing peace against a backdrop of recent war horrors, their fifty-one wives were dining in the back room of The Arched Umbrella, passing sweet and heavy foods across the table. Their looks were also sweet and heavy: It is a well-known fact that the wives of political figures are often lesbians. Never before had so many come together in one place. Afterward, over brandy at The Lovely Goose, cards were passed, a few ending up in the hands of straight women who did not understand the innuendos about fish and clams and lilies opening.

Meanwhile, in the corridors of the San Francisco Opera, the secretaries and valets of all these "great" men waited with capes and cloaks and extra ink and flasks. At least twenty-five of these attendants were what was then called homosexual. By the third night of the General Assembly, the merry lesbian wives and the homosexual butlers began organizing with one another. They wanted to create a foil of the UN that could link them across the ever-shifting nation-state borders. One of the secretaries, Venceslas, had grown up moving across Mexico, with a father who believed it was his personal mission to reinstill Catholic fervor in indigenous territories. V, as he called himself, spent his childhood in the state of Oaxaca, which had seduced his father because of the prominence of witchcraft. Early on in their stay, V befriended a young girl, Manuela, who brought their family modest meals in the evening. Manuela told him about the mushrooms that her grandmother ate during ceremonies, and how they transported her to other places with ancient designs and otherworldly patterns. Her grandmother despised V's father for reviving Catholic fervor, but she let him come over to play. While resting from her work in the fields, she talked and talked and talked in Mazatec, and V had no idea what she was saying, but the look on her face was one of bliss. In all of his father's sermons about the Body and the Blood and the Transmutation, in the rapture of incense, in the supposed balm of redemption, V had never encountered the ease that flowed from Manuela's *abuelita*. He begged Manuela to translate.

She described the great lines under the earth, how they gave nutrients to the trees and wisdom to the people and revealed themselves to her *abuelita* when she partook of the Velada ceremony. Her grandmother spoke about how in parts of Mexico and other colonized places across the Americas, people had connected to the lines and to one another, passing along secrets and food-stores and magic that could not be stolen by the colonizers because they had no idea what was going on beneath them.

On his twelfth birthday, V's parents gave him a new Bible and told him that they had to move on.

The anticlerical movement was growing. They would have to move back toward the north, where Catholics still had power. Before he left, Manuela's *abuelita* gave him a small bag of mushrooms and told him to take them in a quiet place.

He waited until his parents were out on a visit and then went out to the hillside. He swallowed a pinch of the pungent flakes. First, the sky brightened, and a softness burrowed into his stomach. He sat down in the earth. He could feel the direct line from the plants to his own body, which was no longer clenched in repression. His sensed that his bloodstream was viscous, open.

When he closed his eyes, he saw a landscape of roots, all attached underground. He fell into a light reverie and awoke, exhausted, but convinced that the world could be joined together. The second time he took the mushrooms, he tried to replicate the same conditions. He went out to the hillside. He lay down in the grass. First came a softness in his stomach, and then it turned, and when he looked up to the heavens, he saw a great violent mass of hornets trying to sting one another, buzzing in a maddening cacophony. He tried to close his eyes and cover his ears, but they were inside him as well. Eyes closed, he stumbled away from the house, lest his parents think he was more possessed than they already feared. In the midst of the nightmare, he fell asleep. When he awoke, the hornets were gone, and he knew that the world would reach the edge of war. He threw the rest of the stems into the dirt.

He did not think of them again until the Opera House in 1945, when the assistants to the heads of state were all whispering about forming their own collective. He wondered what had become of the small town, and if the vision had been some sort of message about a new way of being. The Arched Umbrellas was formed that night, with a goal of creating a network of gays spread throughout all their home countries and beyond. The AUs reached out to other "deviants" and began pooling resources to pay for members' medical care, the assassination of spouses, travel to libidinous cities, respite from factory work. There were fierce battles, fierce romances, and fierce betrayals.

During the normative fifties, the AU went far underground. V had been on the fringes of AU activity, traveling to indigenous communities in Mexico, trying to understand more of their practices, taking mushrooms in ceremonies, imagining a bolder organizing system. Nalita and Fran, two queer activists of color, found one of V's pamphlets in a Bay Area bookstore and reached out to him. V used some of the AU's funding to bring Nalita, Fran, and a few other members of their lesbian reading group to his home in Mexico, where they spent days dreaming about how to transform the AU into a more horizontal, rhizomal structure. And, with the blessing of most of the AU original founders, they did.

For subsequent chapters on the early Rhiz, the AIDS crisis, the arrival of a billionaire's heir on the scene, as well as the protocols behind income redistribution and the council of Black trans Elders, the pre-summons novice must advance.

I kept turning and found only empty pages. I wondered if post-summons novices and other higher members could unlock the chapters. Was Stone part of the Rhiz? How much did she get to read? I looked out into her empty living room. Damn, she was probably off at the Rhiz-Port or beaming into another queer's home. Come to think of it, she'd never exactly explained her affiliation with the U; maybe there was none, or she used their archives for some other purpose. I pictured her in the library, sitting right next to me looking through old Rhiz files as I read my mystery novels. For a queasy moment, I wanted to break up with her to avoid the untenable sense that she'd kept all of this from unsophisticated Pen.

Admittedly, I hadn't thought the Rhiz would be interested in Stone, who was so low-key about her queerness. In other words, I was surprised that Stone could be admitted into the Rhiz without seeming to have suffered greatly for her queerness.

Was that messed up?

I set the book down on its side. The prism still shot out of the Rhiz symbol on its spine. I cupped my hands around it. It glowed and then flattened into a large, illustrated holographic map. *The Rhiz-Port.*

The map hovered before me, about as wide as a coffee

table. I moved my hand toward a drawing of crystal towers, the Palace of the Elders, and an oval outline appeared above it, with a larger, animated view of the gleaming structures and the series of interlocking courtyards that spread out around them.

"Black trans Elders, mostly women, reside in the Palace of the Elders," a crisp voice narrated. "They eat fruit, bathe, play music, send out messages to summon lovers, whatever brings their desire. Every month, they hold open counsel sessions in their gardens. The Elders sit out on large divans near cascading waterfalls, and certain problems are brought to their attention, and either fixed or laughed at."

A more casual voice continued, "When Omen, the queer heir, arrived at the Rhiz-Port, he spent three days with the Elders, who roasted him continuously. He'd already enlisted a white punk named Garlic to figuratively and actually flagellate him for inherited sins, so he had a high tolerance for rebuke."

A fountain gurgled. I saw bodies moving in the Pleasure Gardens.

On the southwest edge, the Cloaking Mountain shot off mists. Flowered vines climbed across the low entrance walls. A circular building with smoke rising from its roof somehow smelled of rose and vanilla. I passed vegetable fields with stone-laid paths connecting them. Watched the spinning spits inside the Maze of Eateries. Felt a vertiginous pull as I stared into the rolling waves of the Lake of Release.

I lingered at the blinding white Cave of Re-Learning.

"Here, the Scholars gather the materials that have been

discarded from official archives of nation and academy. The oral, the messy, the upending stories," the original narrator added.

So that was where Stone would go.

When three bells sounded, the towers lost their glow.

"This is the evening call. All members walk to the Palace of the Elders for the daily bow. The Elders may come out if they wish," the narrator continued.

"They do not need to do anything except exist in a realm of pleasure," said the second voice.

The whole world flattened and was pulled back into the prism, which receded into the spine of the book. When I picked up the volume again, it had gone blank.

All at once, a deep sadness descended. Why hadn't I known that such possibilities existed before? Why was my childhood a series of miseries and only in my most recent phase of adulthood did delight pop up?

Well, isn't queer adulthood, if one is lucky, having the impossible childhood of your desires?

Stone returned, wearing a new sun hat and a white dress that accentuated her tan. She squeezed me in a hug when she found me at the baggage claim. Telling her about the book was easier than telling her that I missed her.

"Finally," she said as bags started shooting out onto the belt. "It must be your time."

"My time? Who decides that?"

"Well, I'm a Scholar. To become an Operatrix, which is

better suited for your temperament, one of them has to no-tice some *potential* during a mission."

"Who could have possibly observed my potential? The one I called a nightlife monk?"

She laughed.

"Does that mean they are going to recruit me?"

"The Rhiz does not have HR policies, but it seems like they are showing a sign of interest, yes."

"Did you know that my time was coming?"

"I had some idea," she said mysteriously.

"What about the fact that you've lied to me for so long?" I asked.

"Pen, I wasn't gleefully obfuscating my relationship to the Rhiz. It's part of the contract. It's way beyond my per-sonal preferences."

Ugh, she was always so articulate.

"Still, Rhiz or not, you hurt me."

"I'm sorry."

"When was your time?"

"I was nineteen. Living in a lesbian collective in the Ger-man countryside, fighting with my comrades about gender essentialism. The Rhiz did not have such elaborate tech then. They sent a person. And a xeroxed manual."

"What happens now?"

"I don't know what your path will look like. For me, I took a trip to the old Rhiz-Port in the Catskills, got involved in a complicated triad, and worked out a plan to study an-thropology in the United States for the purposes of Rhiz enrichment."

"What is it like to go to the Rhiz-Port?"

"I wish I could go there for the first time again. When I saw the revered Elders in their courtyard, it was more than I had ever imagined for us all."

"Could we go there together? And swim in the Lake of Release?"

She laughed. "Are you sure you wouldn't regret not entering the Rhiz-Port as a single person and sleeping with a slew of Operatrixes?"

"OMG, no." My voice went higher. "I missed you."

There, I'd said it.

"I missed you, too, babe."

I put my arm around her, and as we waited for her bags to come out, I thought of my parents, trooping around the world together, sharing cargo pants and carbide-tipped chisels.

I looked forward to the evening, when we would close the door of her apartment and spend the rest of the night inside, cooking, having sex, dreaming, reading, talking.

Aiden invited Stone and me back to the bungalow. He included Blithe, but Blithe said that he didn't want to bring everyone down. I told him that we could handle whatever was going on with him. He said no.

I wanted to tell Aiden about the Rhiz and the Rhiz-Port, but I didn't know all the rules. Part of me wanted to keep the childlike splendor to myself and not share.

"I feel like I saw your image at a bus stop somewhere," Stone said to Rachel, and I cringed.

You weren't supposed to talk to famous people about how famous they were, right?

"Probably my Vines shoot. They gave me their entire collection of colored tees, but I only wear white."

"Is that a religious thing?"

"No, it just seemed easier."

I thought that we would be eating amid awkward pauses in conversation, but somehow Stone and Rachel were drawn to each other. After dinner, they went to the garden with a bottle of calvados and didn't return. Apparently, they were talking about the wedding, a subject I didn't think Stone had any interest in.

"Hah! You're so wrong, Pen. I love weddings. I love them anthropologically and viscerally. I love the ritual, symbolism, waste, hypocrisy, and dresses," she told me when we got in the car.

"And what is it about Rachel that appeals to you?"

She stared. "Pen, you're the one who hooked up with her for two years. You should be able to recognize the charm that she has, as a being who receives adoration and capital from all directions."

"True."

Rachel and Aiden started inviting us over more. The wedding was only a few months away, and Rachel was trying to plan something so that her relatives were subtly disgusted. Stone was happy to help. They had a venue, a charming-yet-haunted inn up the coast that Rachel's mom had just booked, but their wedding planner promised that all of her vendors could work on an expedited timeline.

"Our hope is that we will send out the invitations late enough that some of my family will not be able to make it," Rachel said.

Once Stone and Rachel retired to the living room to wedding-plan, Aiden and I would check out the construction and the garden or box each other in the yard by torchlight. When I punched him, I knew my arm and its connection to my core. I became real to myself in a corporeal way. I decided to start lifting—something I'd thought was the dumbest, most masc waste of time—so that I could punch harder, feel my own strength.

We fought each other, guarding our bodies, and yet the lack of pretense opened us. After we'd kicked each other's asses one night, we sat in the moonlight, drinking tea and feeling hot inside our bruises.

Coyotes wailed as we lounged on a high-backed wicker outdoor couch. Aiden told me about his decision to marry Rachel.

"She asked me not long after that construction guy cornered me in the bodega. He was right. I'd made a livelihood out of being known as a hot trans guy, but how long could that last? How long before my sponsors found a younger, hotter trans guy? I know you looked down on me for my fame-seeking, but how else would someone from my neighborhood, my family, with no college degree, gain access to anything?"

Ugh, I felt bad. I had thrown all this shade at Aiden when I was seeing him in the wrong light.

"I was a doofus. Projection, you know."

The coyotes' laments paused.

"Yeah. So now I care about Rachel—I love her—and this is all more than I could have imagined."

Over in the living room, Rachel would be regaling Stone with stories about her wedding planner, Alicia, who did not touch princess wedding fantasies involving cakes shaped like Cinderella's slipper or the requisite incestuous rituals of handing a daughter from the king to her new prince.

Alicia had planned a wedding with Rachel's friends in which they eloped *during* their Scandinavian ceremony and were taken straight to a taiga. While the guests waited in a chilled cathedral, the couple was loaded onto a sleigh pulled by white blurs that looked like wolves.

"I don't give a shit about vinyl tents, china, sauces, or how to explain to the B-listers that a setting has opened up for them," Alicia had said to Aiden and Rachel when they first came into her vine-draped atelier. "So amuse me."

She handed them a form and left. Aiden froze up around the planning because it had never entered his imagination that he was allowed a wedding, so Rachel filled it out herself.

Rachel and Aiden

Color scheme: Sand and navy. Basically, the least-
  sexy colors.

Food: The simplest, no bloated appetizers or heavy
  meats.

Venue: A restored inn where something unspeakable
  has happened.

Marriage ritual location: On the beach, with no
  folding chairs except for the older folks.
Reception/dinner location: A cloth tent with pillows
  on the floor.
Officiant: ???
Lighting: Candelabras.
Music: Small orchestra. No pop-DJ-cover-band-
  fuckery.
Decor: Grandmother insists on ice sculptures for
  the reception. The ice sculptures will depict
  pansexual orgies.
Floral arrangements: Hanging upside down. Blue.
Gifts: Only drought-resistant plants or trees that will
  grow in our canyon home.

Alicia returned, read their form, then pulled out champagne from a special resting place under her distressed table.
After she sent her assistant home, the three of them ordered
Thai and Alicia opened another bottle. In a moment of drunk
confessional delight, the couple told Alicia all about Rachel's
grandmother and Aiden's gender.

"Ohh, me likey. Me really likey," Alicia said, sucking on
every detail, so happy that she briefly regressed.

Hearing all this, I respected Rachel more, knowing that
she was not simply trying to reproduce her family ways.

One quiet morning post-smoothie, I was loading the dishwasher at Blithe's when the older Operatrix in circular

sunglasses beamed in, with an herbal cigarette moving in and out of the hologram.

"Good. You have the ring at least. Now I have something useful for you to do," she said. "We need a risk assessment of Aiden's parents. We would like them to be involved in the wedding but are concerned that might create an unmanageable situation. You will go and meet with them. Say that you're a friend of Aiden's and that you have some news about him. See how they react."

After everything, the Rhiz was sending me to the literalized Shadowlands of Aiden Chase.

"Fine," I said sulkily. I didn't appreciate this Operatrix insinuating that I wasn't doing enough. Hadn't the inversion countered the hex? Hadn't the Rhiz started courting me? She reminded me of Margot telling me to pick up my clothes off the floor.

"I'll send over a specialized Bio-meter and some data," she said, and was gone.

Blithe said I could borrow his car again if I promised to pick up dried daylilies for a special soup. I found a specialized Bio-meter in its sleeve by the front door, along with a manila envelope, stamped with a magenta seal. The orb was the same size as the regular ones but only measured anger and fear across the entire color spectrum. Inside the envelope:

Chase Family profile
Here we use absence as presence. We must measure
    the family affect through the son.

Mother: He may feed himself the choicest
strawberries, but they drop down into a hole.
Father: His greatest desire is to punch his father in
the face, not simply to harm him, but to make a
notch in the man's reality.
Twin: *Only the silence that comes before the sob.*

The cars crawled along the freeway. It soothed me that in spite of modern attempts to increase the speed of life, L.A. traffic did not comply.

Exiting onto a suburban street, I made a few turns and ended up in a lower-middle-class neighborhood, where houses still had peach carpets and rusty screen doors. The house was a split-level ranch with a hand-painted mailbox that read THE CHASES. A flowering orange tree grew out of the letters. How antiquated.

Blithe's battery-powered car might give me away as an outsider, I thought.

I tapped my fingers on the steering wheel. I wanted to get a cup of shitty coffee and spy on them, like a true detective, but I was supposed to knock on their door.

Eventually a woman came to the door, using a walker. She looked worn, in slippers and a sweatshirt from a long-past sports event. Could it be?

She let a Jack Russell terrier out on the front lawn. The dog barked in my general direction and I slouched down. I waited for him to go inside.

I pretended that I was not Pen but a fleshy extension of

the Rhiz simply carrying out a mission for the good of all. I walked up to the door, smelling a whiff of gasoline, a neighbor probably filling their lawn mower.

I really didn't want to go in.

The Rhiz would have to deal with my executive decision to drive away.

Inside the flower market, I paused at a rose stand, looking down into the twelve cells of a rose box, pulled into the spiral of the petals. *Hello, my friends,* I whispered to them. Micro-dosing was an excuse to be able to say what I wanted to the flowers and other entities.

When I got home with daylilies and a bouquet of carnations for Blithe, I sat in my room, rolling the Bio-meter around in my palm, watching it remain a neutral yellow. I didn't bother to summon the Operatrix. I simply left the file and the Bio-meter outside the door.

In Blithe's condo, I spritzed eucalyptus into the air and wiped down the bathroom sink. Blithe was leaving for China, and Aiden was coming over to say goodbye. I was relieved that Blithe had a decent excuse for missing the wedding. He was going to let me stay in the condo and pay whatever rent was comfortable for me.

The buzzer sounded. Aiden walked into the condo, carrying a woven tote. As he shut the door, I saw gardening gloves tucked into his back pocket.

His luster had dimmed a few shades.

"I think I'm losing it, guys," he said, hardly registering the suitcase or the two of us.

He threw himself down on the couch and picked up a pillow to hug.

Blithe stood between the kitchen and the living room. I wondered if Aiden's state would soothe him in some way, make him feel less disgusted at Aiden and his accumulations.

"Maybe we should make congee instead of ordering in," Blithe suggested when we stepped into the kitchen.

"True."

Here we were again, the three of us having breakfast for dinner, with one member about to break down. Blithe brewed him a special ginseng root tea and put it in his favorite coconut mug. We let the pot simmer for about an hour. Aiden's eyes were closed. Blithe went into his room, and I sat there, watching Aiden in repose, the slight rise and fall of his newly curved belly.

When the food was ready, we sat down to eat in the dining alcove. Blithe moved the vase of orange and yellow carnations off the table. Aiden sighed loudly and stared into his bowl.

"It's like I'm living in two realities. In one, I'm getting married to Rachel and I can garden and box and negotiate my newfound closetedness. And in the other, I'm Aideline. I'm still this sad punk person who makes terrible decisions."

Aiden was once punk?

"Well, if I've learned anything, it's that rituals can keep you rooted in the right present. I'm not a witch, obvs, but maybe there's something we can do to show that you're here, in this reality," I said, surprising myself.

I'd learned something!

Blithe nodded.

"What makes you feel like Aiden?" I asked.

"Hm. I mean, boxing."

"And what makes you feel like Aideline?"

"My parents. Even though I haven't seen them in fifteen years, I know they're out there. I know there's a chance they might come to the wedding, and I'm terrified that I will just revert into their version of me."

"Have you talked to Rachel about all of this?" I asked him.

"Yeah, but I don't want her to feel like she made a mistake in proposing to me. There's so much I haven't told her," Aiden said.

He began to tell us about the life he kept outside of the frame, his mysterious twin who could not forgive him for leaving her alone in her female bitternesses. Then there was his father, who'd monitored his internet usage in high school and had him committed to a psych ward, his mother who could never muster the strength to publicly disagree with his father, his coworkers from a queer café called the Hole, an older abusive girlfriend, a friend who convinced him to break up with her, and the warm gaze of the camera after all the wrong looks.

A less-evolved Pen would have beamed with turquoise curiosity to hear the story behind Aiden's façade, but the past appeared faded, pressed of all juice.

"It took me years to get my own place, and a phone that wasn't on my parents' plan (they still paid for my phone and insurance even though we didn't speak), rescue a goose, and convince myself that I belonged on the Gram. Once I started, the Gram was the strongest drug, showing myself to people who actually wanted to see me. Now that I'm getting off of it, everything that I've avoided is returning to me," Aiden said.

"Sometimes, there is a way to regain that which was lost," Blithe said, uncharacteristically optimistic.

"Maybe," Aiden said, doubtfully. "Let's talk about your trip."

"What do you have left to do to get ready, Blithe?" I said, tho I was still thinking about Aiden and his family.

"Just call my bank and figure out the phone situation. I don't think I need Chinese adv-tech. I'm going to go as lo-fi as is permitted."

"I'm jell," I said.

We all sat on Blithe's couch and he pulled out a paper map with his route marked. He showed us the path he would take from Beijing, into the striped mountains of Gansu Province, through the Tibetan Plateau in Qinghai, and down to Sichuan.

"My healer told me to chart my path intuitively, without guidebooks or a travel agent. He said that my body already knows where to find what it needs. But I did look up where the giant pandas live," he said.

As Blithe spoke, his voice took on a different note. It was strange what the Shadowlands could do: destroying us and then rebuilding something stronger.

The big day arrived. I waited for Stone in the lobby as the wedding planner, Alicia, ran around with an egg timer, screaming at her staff. She wanted them to change the water of the agapanthus, hydrangeas, and roses every hour.

"You know what? I'll be like that one lady and do it myself," she shouted, grabbing two empty crystal vases and running toward the kitchen, sandals clacking on the old wooden floors. She must have missed the Future Business School study on leading by leaving people alone and administering gentle nuggets of praise.

The French doors of the lobby remained open to the lawn. The day was exceptionally warm for December in California. The inn had no air conditioning. Window boxes would ruin the building façade, and the inn didn't have the right wiring for central air.

Hanging with Aiden and Rachel, I'd had to endure hearing about the most minute minutiae.

Outside, the grasses had been trimmed, and the crass yellow wildflowers were taken out of their beds. As Stone would often point out, basic labor was always narrated in the passive voice; no one needed to know about the person doing the work.

I spotted Agatha the goose wandering around in her enclosure, far from the rose bushes, eating honeyed insects that the Witch had sent her. They'd showed up one day on my pillow along with a letter from her.

Dear Pen,

I have heard about your inversion. Still, you must honor the dark nests.

I moved into my coven, and I do miss your
normative energy.

Here is a spell for the upcoming occasion:

Take two raw, speckled eggs.

Crush one in each hand while whispering,

> May the shell crack and the real
> come out.
> May the shell crack and the real
> come out.
> May the shell crack and the real
> come out.

Our former living partner is not so far
from you, walking in the desert.

In warmth and in coolness,

The Witch

Stone came down to the lobby right as a young man hur-
ried by in the required navy tunic and wide-legged navy pants.

"I'm doing the lions right now," he yelled, carrying a bottle of polish.

She wore a windbreaker, cuffed jeans, and her gray
suede tennis shoes. I still ached every time I saw her and

remembered that every night we could go to bed next to each other. I trusted that she wasn't waking up to wonder if I was hot or smart enough for her.

We drove to the center of the coastal California town because Rachel's mother's CBD oil had exploded in her luggage and Rachel needed her to ingest it. We bought the oil at a family-run pharmacy with a ringing bell on the door and dropped it off at the front desk of the inn. Stone had a hair appointment soon, but first we were driving to a coastal refuge to take a walk. I hadn't gotten any signs from the Rhiz since I returned their Bio-meter and their file on the Chases. Stone insisted that she didn't know much about how the Operatrixes went about initiating people.

"Operatrixes have their own strange rites," was all she'd say.

Still, I secretly thought of us as a potential Rhiz power couple, and that offset my anxiety about seeing Aiden wed to Rachel.

We parked in an almost empty lot and entered a path cut between waving dune grasses. She went first and we walked silently on the hard sand. I wanted to know the names of all the plants around us, the rugged flowering bushes, the squat gnarled trees, the spiky grasses that protected the eggs of endangered birds. I tried not to think about the reports of Black Rain starting to fall in deforested regions.

After a few minutes, we reached the beach. We went out to the water, instinctively, like animals. The waves crashed privately for us.

For a moment, the desert gave way to the sea.

I dropped Stone off at Kinky Clippers (which had a clipper ship on the sign) and went back to the inn to find Aiden. We had preparations on top of the usual wedding ones. Mine included retrieving two raw and speckled eggs from our room's mini-bar refrigerator. I also had to visit Aiden and make sure he wasn't going to bail on either the wedding or the match.

In the lobby, Alicia was walking Agatha around in her jeweled harness yelling, "T-minus two, T-minus two," to her staff, and older guests complained to the front desk about the heat.

I found Aiden in his room in a robe. He hugged me, and I savored his scent as if we were two homoerotic pals who would rarely see each other again post-marriage.

"Dude, you are not ready at all," he said, taking in my sandy toes and barely buttoned shirt.

"I'll be fine."

I rubbed his hair, which was back to Gram-level sculpting.

The room was quiet. He and Rachel were following the straight-person tradition where you're not supposed to interact with your fiancé before the wedding ceremony, allowing each person their last few hours of "freedom."

"How are you doing?"

"I don't know, Pen." His voice was shaky.

I took a deep breath and imagined everything beneath the façade of a beautiful wedding. "I should tell you something."

"Yes?" he said.

"The Rhiz asked me to go over and talk to your family about your wedding. But I couldn't. I was afraid they would hate me. After you came over the Blithe's, I had an idea. I did a little stalking and found your dad's gym. I talked to his coach, who was surprisingly nice for someone highly invested in normative masculinity. And we set up a match between you and your dad. Today."

"Today?" He pulled back.

"During the reception, out on a semi-hidden dune. With only select spectators."

"Holy shit."

"Is that okay?"

"Did I ask you to get involved with him?"

"No. But I know that it's important."

"He's really coming?"

"He's really coming."

"What about my mom? And Ava?"

"Alicia gave me invitations to leave for them, and I have not heard back."

He walked over to the window and turned around.

"He agreed to fight me?"

"Yes, three rounds. We had to go back and forth about the weight differential because he's a big guy."

"I don't know, Pen. I'm already freaking out enough as it is."

"Yes, it's a lot, but think how good it will feel to face him, to punch him, even."

"Hm. What about my gloves?"

"Alicia has them."

"I'm blaming you if this all falls apart."

"Please do."

•

The crowd was nearly silent. At the front of the wedding party, closest to the water, the older relatives sat on armchairs that had been carried all the way from the inn. From the second standing row, I could see Rachel's grandmother in a navy turban that blocked some folks' view. I felt a camaraderie with her. I was also trying to further my own agenda.

I laughed silently to myself, rolling the eggs in my pockets. Stone had her eyes closed and seemed to be enjoying the breeze, the pause. Her gown was slightly more neutral than gold. The hair stylist had blown out her hair and it felt soft and lustrous to my touch. Around her neck, a long necklace held a single sapphire. I was in a sand-colored suit, my first. Aiden had taken me to a trans tailor who wrapped measuring tape across the important junctures of my bod. In our inn room, I'd almost wept with pleasure, looking at myself, properly attired.

Solar stood at the center of the roll of jute that stretched across the sand in two directions, wearing a navy suit and white shirt and holding a white scepter. The poet-ceremonialist was Stone's idea. Aiden had told me he was nervous that a gender-nonconforming officiant would coat their ceremony in exactly the kind of queer miasma that they were trying to disavow.

I'd rolled my eyes at him, but surrounded by the guests, mostly Rachel's relatives, I understood.

They waited as Rachel walked down from the east, alone, a fuck-you both to patriarchy and her father as a particularly malfunctioning extension of it.

When she stopped, Rachel's young niece scampered across the sand as Agatha pulled her in a zigzag, honking, snapping her beak. The goose ran so fast that the child let go of the leash and burst into tears. Alicia could be heard screaming at her staff to go after the goose, who was running near the water's edge, unsure whether the waves would save or crush her. Some guests laughed and others shook their heads.

Finally, Aiden walked in from the west full of nerves and full of joy, and unaware of all our looking.

No music played. All one hundred (hopefully one hundred and one) guests listened to the ocean, as measured and wild as ever.

Alicia darted over to me and whispered that Mr. Chase hadn't shown up at the meeting place yet. I nodded, feeling important.

I scanned all the faces I could see from the second standing row. Nothing.

Stone side-eyed me when I kept tapping my foot with impatience.

Other guests, in mostly appropriate colors, fidgeted with phone withdrawal. We struggled to remember how to document an event without the use of advanced tools.

Solar did not begin by explaining how Rachel and Aiden "met." Supposedly, they eyed each other on the set of Catalpa after Blithe had invited Aiden to spend the day with him. Their origin story was chronologically impossible because Blithe was fired before he flew back to L.A., but no one had pressed too hard.

Instead, Solar spoke of the bond of intimacy as the

strongest metal, of dark currents, of the trends toward over-stimulation and disconnection, of loneliness, of the date in the Hebrew calendar, 5 Cheshvan 578-, and how the ancient Jewish texts foretell less than 250 years until a time of Messianic peace. A seated great-uncle began to doze. The sea co-operated. The sun was historically hot.

Solar poured the kiddush, a requirement of Rachel's mother's side, and before various deities and transmutations, dear friends, and television stars, Aiden and Rachel promised to be good.

Under my breath, I chanted, *"May the shell crack and the real come out. May the shell crack and the real come out. May the shell crack and the real come out,"* and crushed the raw eggs in sealed bags in each pocket.

Now I knew what magic was, how it could only adhere to what was ready for its power.

The couple kissed, showing with a few seconds of thirsty tongues that their bond was erotic. Rachel had her hair pulled back and her gown was the simplest white. Aiden wore a white tux and their styles didn't quite align. He was fancier.

I cried.

For all my saltiness, I never thought I would be allowed to participate in group rituals as a trans, or that the world would bend to include Aiden.

The orchestra played, and the air was amber, sweet and liquid and stuck.

After the ceremony, guests were free to walk in the sand or hide under the tent eating oysters. The couple stayed down by the water, posing with Rachel's family. Only certain factions spoke to one another because of inheritances lost and regained. I stood with Stone, watching the Remedios clan, with their parasols and luxury watches and children who fought over Agatha's leash and their desperate hold on wealth and their inability to wear their own desires. Meanwhile, Aiden's mother was surely back in their house, on her couch, with her coffee, hoping that her husband and her child would not kill each other. And his twin? I couldn't say.

I left Stone sitting on a pillow and went to procure her a glass cone of champagne, throw away the eggs, and find Aiden's coach. I was proud. Finally, he was moving back toward his shadow. How simple it would have been for him to cut off the unsavory family organ and hide the rest of his life among celebrities and plants, getting yearly bonuses from the Rhiz for his excellence.

One of the catering staff, Rob, had scouted out a spot on the other side of the cliff wall that jutted out toward the water. Rob was to dig four posts into the sand and wrap a long-ass ball of twine around them. When the orchestra paused for a thirty-minute drone cymbal set, Aiden would make his way over.

I walked toward the table and was stopped by a round-faced leather daddy in a possibly vegan leather vest and pants, with nothing underneath.

"Good afternoon, Penfield," the leather daddy said.

Surely an Operatrix.

I bowed to him and did not ask about my current status with the Rhiz.

He bowed back.

I grabbed a cone from a caterer and delivered it to Stone.

I told her to meet me at the spot in fifteen minutes. She was content on her pillow, watching the guests with anthropological curiosity. I found Alicia at her post by the northern corner of the tent, and she pointed out Aiden's coach to me. He stood alone by the one of the ice sculptures.

"Interesting, isn't it?" he said, drinking a seltzer.

The ice artiste had chiseled a cascade of dicks in holes and hands on boobs and mouths under butts and grabbed hair. In the heat, breasts melted, and chubby dicks slimmed.

The coach seemed kindhearted, not macho, the type to hold ice on a friend's bruise. He was white and young. He'd mastered the dress code by wearing a sand-colored button-down shirt that encased his muscles and loose navy slacks and sandals.

I wondered if he had a traumatic brain injury.

"Yeah. So, remember, when the droning cymbals start, you grab Aiden and his gear and meet us on the other side of the northern cliff face."

"On it."

"Give him some sort of pump-up speech, too."

The coach nodded. He didn't understand the entire scenario, but he knew enough.

"And if his dad doesn't show, there has to be a rematch."

I walked away from him. The staff was setting out baskets of flip-flops for dancing. They were all pink with cheetah print, clearly for "women" who needed to take off their high heels. I slipped some on and left my dress shoes at the edge of the sand.

I went stumbling off toward the cliffs.

He was there. Mr. Chase hopped about, warming up, sweating in his gray tracksuit. He'd brought a friend to referee, an older man who waved when he saw me coming. The spot was secluded, hidden in between two jutting cliff faces.

Aiden's head appeared, and then his coach's. They climbed over and headed toward the ring, and though the distance was perhaps fifty yards, we all knew that for Aiden to get there, on that day, time had curved, space had expanded.

I was awash in a peace that I'd thought could only come from orgasms. I always knew there was more to Aiden than flatness, and here it was, the meaty confrontation. As I stood, in heating flip-flops, my calves against the hard sand of the dune, I was enormous and potent, not like a big dick, but an immense being.

Soon a boxing bell would ring out from the ref's phone as father and son stepped out from their corners, arms curled in.

A black car waited outside. The driver wouldn't speak to me, not even when I asked about the car's sustainability measures. About two hours into our drive, I swear we passed by a glimmering oasis. Otherwise, the desert stretched apathetically around us. The driver would not stop for a bathroom break. I looked out the window and texted Blithe about the wedding.

The summons stated I should I wear a representative outfit, and I'd thought about all the glorious garments Operatrixes had donned in my presence. I'd emerged from my quirky stripes phase and was feeling good about my light linen pants, airy T-shirt, vintage sandals, and a bandana to either flag or wear around my neck. I hadn't decided yet.

After another few hours, we pulled up to a simple, dusty path and the driver held up his hand, waving to someone. All that I could see before us were mountains with frothy yellow bushes and, way up toward the peaks, some streaks of snow.

We kept driving. As we approached the base of a grand mountain, the air around us began to hum and crackle. A sucking noise filled the car and the mountain gave way to a village, built of precious gems and stones. In the distance, a soft purple crystal rose toward the sky: the Palace of the Elders. A striped tower shimmered in the distance. We were no longer in the desert; flowered vines climbed across the low walls.

We pulled up to a fountain. The door unlocked. I got out.

"It takes a lot of adv-tech to lead a simple life," said a young person sketching by the edge of the fountain.

"Where do I go? I've been summoned here."

My acquaintance nodded to a circular building with smoke coming out of the top.

I walked in and was told to remove my shoes. I stepped up to the oval table where at least thirty Operatrixes sat, ones I recognized and ones I hadn't met, a lush composite. Some chatted among themselves; some drank from clay jars; some reclined on the long benches. They were all as exuberant and casual and threadbare and formal as, I presumed, they wanted to be. I was offered a cup of tea. I tasted rose and vanilla.

"Hello, Penfield," said Mar'iah, who had once warned us against making a trans-masc cave. She now wore a denim dress and low boots. "Welcome to the Assembly of Opera-trixes. When we began tracking you, you had hexed Blithe Freeman and ranked quite low on our Evolutionary Scale. Then we gave you a mission, to assist Blithe through the Shadowlands. You largely succeeded in that endeavor, and eventually you understood the true mission: to evolve from your resentment. You were given a second mission. To gather data from Aiden Chase's parents and ensure the safety of Aiden and his guests on his wedding day."

"You rejected our parameters and made up your own," said the Operatrix in sunglasses, pointing her herbal ciga-rette at me.

"You listened to some inner spark, and not the chorus around you," said my first, gown-wearing Operatrix.

The scent of smoke and honey and earth was strong.

"We had to test you. To see how you related to your own conditioning. The Rhiz cannot endure without those who read the deeper signs," said the leather daddy. He seemed slightly disappointed that I had not failed. Maybe he wanted to discipline me.

"Now we inscribe," said the nightlife monk, my favorite, placing a slightly glowing leather volume before me on the table.

"Now we inscribe that you are here to help, to grow, to fight, to plant, to agitate, to assemble in the spirit of queer abundance now and forever," they all chanted.

The words curled around me in the timeless present of the Rhiz, where we were always stretching toward our ancestors and the old ways, and toward our future beings and the ways to come. This was the place that I had longed for, before I knew it could be real. I thought of Stone, and how we could soon enter the Rhiz-Port together, and swim in the lake, emerging loose and unbothered.

How improbable, how strong, these pathways toward collective good, I thought.

Mar'iah stood near me. She now wore a necklace with a sprig of lavender. She handed me a crystal stylus and pointed to a page of names.

She began, "To be an Operatrix—"

"—is to slip in and out of rooms, to pass one sheath of information to another, to wear one's finest style, to have one's missions set against all the missions that the habitual world might demand, to love the darkness as one loves the light," they all chanted.

I looked at their expectant faces, and my wrongness was finally revealed as right.

And I signed.

Acknowledgments

Finishing this book certainly upended any remaining fantasies about writing as a solitary pursuit.

With gratitude to friends and professors at Columbia. To Lucy, Kathleen, Matt, and Naima for being there in writing and in venting. To Paul, for your humor. To Ben, for your care with language.

To Matthew Sharpe and Lisa Cohen at Wesleyan, thank you for encouraging my weird, queer writing.

Thanks to everyone at Art Farm, the Watermill Center, Queens Council on the Arts, *Women & Performance*, and Insight Meditation Society. Much love to all who have been a part of Trans at Rest, especially Grey, Nhu̇, Ita, Lorelei, An, Charlie, and Eli Ryn.

To dear friends who've kept me going in the salty times and the sweet times: Jaffa, S.O., Wendy, Yarden, Carla, Janel, Ariele, Weston, Elissa, Riitta, Elisa, Tara, Nicole.

To my family, for growing with me. Mom, for sharing your love of reading. Al, for listening to all my ideas. Dad, for giving me the sense that it all connects together.

To Violet, my faithful companion.

To Ady, for being there and showing me new ways.

To all my sources of inspiration and nourishment: Nic

Fleming's BBC article about plants using fungi to talk to one another, Lil' Deb's Oasis, Blood Orange, psilocybin mushrooms, Janet Mock, Tourmaline, Thomas McBee, Dean Spade, Andrea Lawlor, Jordy Rosenberg, Tara Brach, and the list goes on.

To Emma, for your hopeful intervention and literary care.

To Sarah Lyn Rogers, Sarah Jean Grimm, Megan Fishmann, Rachel Fershleiser, Katie Boland, Wah-Ming Chang, Samm Saxby, Laura Gonzalez, Roma Panganiban, Michael Salu, and everyone else at Soft Skull/Catapult and Janklow and Nesbit who helped this book enter into the world.

To Chris, for continually saying yes. I could not have pushed the book into its truest, strangest form without your guidance. To Yuka, for helping me take this apart and put it back together. Your attention allowed for the book's deepest manifestation.

To my trans and queer community, for everything.

JOSS LAKE is a trans writer and educator based in New York whose work has been supported by Queens Council on the Arts, *Women & Performance*, the Watermill Center, and Columbia University. He runs a literary sauna series called Trans at Rest. This is his debut novel.